VANISHED

Mary McGarry Morris is married and the mother of five children. She lives in Massachusetts. She is the author of three novels: *Vanished*, which was nominated for the National Book Award and the PEN/Faulkner Award; *A Dangerous Woman*, which was made into a major motion picture; and *Songs in Ordinary Time*.

MARY McGARRY MORRIS

VANISHED

PENGUIN BOOKS

PENGUIN BOOKS
Published by the Penguin Group
Penguin Putnam Inc., 375 Hudson Street,
New York, New York 10014, U.S.A.
Penguin Books Ltd, 27 Wrights Lane, London W8 5TZ, England
Penguin Books Australia Ltd, Ringwood, Victoria, Australia
Penguin Books Canada Ltd, 10 Alcorn Avenue,
Toronto, Ontario, Canada M4V 3B2
Penguin Books (N.Z.) Ltd, 182–190 Wairau Road,
Auckland 10, New Zealand

Penguin Books Ltd, Registered Offices:
Harmondsworth, Middlesex, England

First published in the United States of America by Viking Penguin Inc. 1988
Published in Penguin Books 1997

1 3 5 7 9 10 8 6 4 2

PUBLISHER'S NOTE
This is a work of fiction. Names, characters, places, and incidents either are the
product of the author's imagination or are used fictitiously, and any resemblance
to actual persons, living or dead, events, or locales is entirely coincidental.

THE LIBRARY OF CONGRESS HAS CATALOGUED THE HARDCOVER AS FOLLOWS:
Morris, Mary McGarry.   Vanished.
I. Title.
PS3563.0874454V36   1988   813´.54   87–40435
ISBN 0-670-82216-7 (hc.)
ISBN 0 14 02.7210 0 (pbk.)

Printed in the United States of America
Set in Simoncini Garamond

To Margaret, my mother,
who heard the Voice in every soul

VANISHED

Prologue

This is the true story. It starts once upon a summer day in Vermont, on a narrow mountain road, a few miles up from the Flatts, not far from Atkinson. A crew of smudge-faced, oily-backed laborers for the county are smoothing off the newly poured hot top. It is boiling hot and the mood of the men is dark and mean. They have worked most of the morning in silence. Though he is not sure exactly what has happened, the little man in the brown shirt and brown pants knows how swiftly their edginess could turn on him. So he works by himself far from the rest of the crew.

After a while, the talk starts. They lean on their rakes and in low voices pass on what they have heard. It doesn't take long before their banter runs as black as their sweat. Soon, one of the younger men, Bud, makes some crack about the dead man, James E. Johnson, and how his pants were half-burned and the mound of spent matches the deputies found on his crotch. With this, T. Garth approaches the men. He is Johnson's first cousin and also his uncle by marriage. The pores in his face are silted with grime. His eyes smolder. "Cold-blooded murder," he snarls. "They oughta shoot her on sight," he says, then spits out a glob of phlegm that sputters up and down on the hot tar like a sizzling egg. Bud's fists are clenched at his sides. "Goddamn crazy little bitch," T. Garth says, then spits again, and this time, it lands on Bud's boot. Bud says something and suddenly T. Garth grabs the red bandanna at Bud's sweaty neck and yanks him chin to chin.

Hazlitt Kluggs steps up to the two men and shoves them apart. Kluggs is the foreman of this crew and the little man's father-in-law. With just a few words, he cools the men down and gets them back to work.

Down the road the little man continues to stamp his metal padded striker up and down, back and forth over the hot top. His steps are cautious and measured, because of the square metal plates that are strapped to the bottom of his boots. If he is not careful, he trips and falls. After all these years, he still forgets that they are on his feet. He is barely aware of the scuffle that has just taken place or the reason for it. It does not concern him. There is little that does.

The sun climbs higher and higher—and so do the men's voices as they push their rollers and drag their heavy metal rakes back and forth over the blazing hot roadbed. Hazlitt Kluggs looks up quickly. T. Garth and Bud have just had words again.

"Hey, T.," Hazlitt calls out to the pock-faced man. "What'd the loonie say to the organ-grinder's monkey?"

"How the hell'm I s'posed to know," Garth growls. "Ask your son-in-law."

"Hey, Wallace," Hazlitt calls out then. "What'd you say to the organ-grinder's monkey?"

Everyone laughs. In the distance Wallace smiles a fuzzy little smile. He did not hear what Kluggs said. He had been watching his shadow work. He likes his shadow. He likes the afternoon shadow best, the way it stretches long and lean with the sinking sun. Sometimes he imagines there are two parts to him—two Aubrey Wallaces: the one they are grinning at now and this quick, dark one with its sure silent step.

It is noontime. They lay aside their tar-crusted tools and take turns over the buckets of water, splashing it on their faces and lathering their arms with umber suds. Friday lunchtime is the best part of the whole week. This is the day they all pile into the biggest truck and head down the mountain for subs and beer at Ida's.

"You coming?" Hazlitt calls from the back of the truck to Wallace, who shakes his head no.

"Aw, c'mon!" Hazlitt calls with a jerk of his arm.

"Can't," Wallace says in a resolute voice that causes the men to grin down at him.

"And why the hell not?" Hazlitt calls, though he surely knows why.

"Cuz of Hyacinth," Wallace says uneasily. "She's temperate."

"And what the hell's that mean, temperate?" Hazlitt calls back. Wallace chews his lip and thinks a minute. "Means if she smelt it on me, her temper'd be riled," he says so earnestly that they can't contain it any longer. They all burst out laughing. And none laughs harder than Kluggs, who, if the truth be known, is secretly fond of this strange little man, whom he will never see again once this truck rounds the bend.

Aubrey Wallace settles himself down now on a can of sealant with his lunch box propped on his knees. He watches the truck start down the road. From a distance he might pass for a child. He is short and small-featured. His hands and arms are squat, but strong. He is a shy man with eyes that are soft and brown and wary. Even his hair is lank and as fine as baby hair.

At times his movements are so self-consciously awkward as to seem furtive. His wife, Hyacinth, is convinced of this. To her he is a monster of deceit. There is no other way she can rationalize marrying this simpleton. He tricked her, plain and simple. She did not know that his silence was because he had nothing to say. But like a child, he has no part of himself that is truly secret, beyond that puzzlement of things he does not know or cannot understand. He has never traveled further than this mountainside. It is not that he does not want to, but simply that it has never occurred to him to do so. Why should he, when everything he needs is here?

As soon as the truck is out of sight, he raises the lid on his lunch pail and takes out a cheese sandwich made with crusts and wrapped in the bread bag. "Sure is hot," he mutters to himself as he works the knot out of the bag. "I'll say. Damn hot." He looks around, then says a little louder, "Hot enough for ya?" Then he shakes his head and chuckles. "I'll say. Hot as hell. Hot as Gorcey's unnerpants." And then he looks down guiltily. He's not sure who Gorcey is, but all the other guys say that. To each other, of course. Never to him.

People rarely talk to him. But that's fine with him. Conversations make him nervous. What happens is that he works so hard trying to come up with something to say when it's his turn that he usually ends up forgetting the whole gist of things or else the conversation will have taken a turn he hasn't noticed and he'll still be on Carson's goat and how bad it smells when everybody else is talking about Reverend Brassey's ailing mother.

Hyacinth hardly ever talks to him and he's noticed how it's the same with his two young boys, Arnold and Answan. Lately, when he tries to tell them important things, things his father told him, they look at him funny. Like their mother does, cold and filmy-eyed. The other night he tried to tell Arnold how if he'd just sleep with his two feet out of the covers, he'd never wet the bed. Arnold gave him that look and then Wallace said, "Well it's true. That's how I finally stopped. That and your mother beating on me every morning the bed was wet."

He chews in careful nibbles on his front teeth and stares up the heat-waved road. His eyes, beady bright, are fixed like a squirrel's, straight ahead on nothing in particular. He has to do something tonight—something for the wife. But damn it, he can't think what it is. He squints and tries hard to remember. It was something to do with dying. Get straight home from work, she said. There's been a death.

He tried not to listen.

found the body . . . deep in where she dragged it . . . musta dragged it all night and half the next day to get it that far. . . .

4

His sons listened in eager horror. Their cereal thickened to mush as they pestered her with questions.

But why her own daddy? Was he bad? What'd he do?

"God only knows," she muttered, her lips fanged shut with a mouthful of straight pins. She was doing up the hem on a black dress somebody from the church had sent over for the newly widowed Mrs. Johnson.

"Some daddies're bad," she said. "But you don't go bashing their head in, acourse. You just stay outta their way and make it a point to grow up better'n him. . . ."

That's when he got confused and lost track of what she had said before. Who was she talking about? Him or the man that died? He couldn't be sure.

His eyes slit to creases now, and he stops chewing. In the distance, down through the rise where the pine tops steeple the road in shadows, a girl in white skims toward him. As she comes closer, the light catches on her like a shimmer through a dark dream. She is barefoot and half-dressed in a man's large white shirt and nothing on under (he can tell from here) but panties.

For a long curious moment, she stands over him and says nothing. She watches his gulp and then the quick dry swallow that waters his eyes, which flit nervously between her and his father-in-law's pale-blue pickup truck. His first impulse is to run inside the truck and lock the doors. When she finally speaks her dry, gritty voice drags over him like rake prongs over concrete.

"A guy name Bud here?"

"Nope."

"Know where he went?"

"Downt' Ida's."

"Shit!"

"They went for subs."

"I'm sick, mister."

"Acourse beer too." He blinks uneasily. "And them subs."

"I ain't eaten in three days, mister. I feel so weak."

"Ida's ain't far. Five or six miles, mebbe. Got real good subs."

"Can I have a bite of your sandwich, mister? Please?"

He hands up the rest of his limp sandwich, which she snatches away. She moves off a few feet from him and with her back half-turned, wolfs down the sandwich. He gives her his apple, and his two brownie bars, and the rest of his coffee. All of this, she consumes without a word. Not even a thank you. Next, she asks for water for her feet, which are not only filthy, but raw with scratches and burns. Her hands are scabbed and dirty and her long reddish hair is wild and matted.

The water buckets have already been emptied so he points toward the woods on the other side of the road. A ways in, there's the river, he tells her and blinks, a little surprised to hear his own voice so clear and steady. Just follow the path, he tells her. She says she's afraid of getting lost again. Her voice is soft now. Like a little girl's. Would he mind showing her where.

He leads her a short distance through the woods to a wide flat rock that juts out over the river. She sits down and dangles her feet in the water. He stands behind her, thinking how familiar she looks. She slides off the rock and wades downstream with her arms out at her sides. The water is up to her chest now. A little further on, she turns, and all of a sudden in the sparkle of sunlight and the clear running water that breaks at her chin like a glass ruffle, he knows what she looks like. Like a picture in a story book. A picture of a fairy. A chill shivers through him. Sometimes at night when the wife reads to the boys, he listens from the hallway, as breathless and as spellbound as they are.

Sometimes if Hyacinth is mad at the boys, she makes up her own bad endings. All the princesses die and the frogs stay frogs forever and only the wicked stepmother lives happily ever after. The boys never protest, never say a word back; they don't dare. The dark silence from their bedroom always terrifies him. It presses over him until he feels smaller and smaller. All night long he lays next to his wife and waits for the right moment to sneak into their room and wake them up and change it all around the right way; the way stories should turn out. But he never does, never leaves the bed. The dark is not his time.

In the morning when he comes into the kitchen, they don't even look up from their cereal bowls. They always seem different to him after those nights; pinched and puckered. It is as if they wake up from those bad endings with some new part of their mother in them; not looking like her, he thinks, but being like her. It is as if in the night, in the telling of the story, she had pressed her sharp thumb to their soft flesh and reworked a bone here, tucked in the same hard, thin creases as hers, so that even their eyes, though once as brown as his, have begun to ridge up from their sockets like hers, as dull and as worn as the little gray stones under the drain spout.

The girl is swimming back now. She tries to climb onto the rock, but keeps slipping back into the water. He scrubs the seat of his pants with his knuckles. He can see right through her wet shirt. For such a slight girl, she has an awful big chest.

"Hey, mister!" she keeps hollering. "Help me out!"

He squats on the rock and extends his tarry hand to pull her out when suddenly, with a strange howl, she falls back and yanks him into the river.

She is up on the rock watching him. But he doesn't know that. He thinks he is drowning. Then he thinks he is dreaming. His arms stop flailing and his legs turn to stone as he sinks deadweight to the rocky river bed with the metal plates still on his boots.

A few minutes later, she has dragged him limp and gasping onto the rock. Part of him feels dead. His brain sloshes in his skull. His ears ring. Like a morning bird, her voice filters down through the trees and the streaming light, not making a bit of sense, but soft as glistening dew. He watches her unstrap the metal plates from his boots. He isn't used to soft and gentle things. As they come through the woods, she apologizes.

"It ain't your fault I can't swim," he says.

7

"Yah," she says, "but I shouldn'ta pulled you in."

"Well," he says, "that's one way a looking at it."

When they get to the road, he is relieved to see that the crew isn't back yet. He sits down on the can of sealant and the girl climbs up into his father-in-law's truck.

"Hey mister," she calls down to him. "Let's go for a ride."

"C'mon now," he wants to say. "C'mon and get down now." But she is starting up the truck and steering it past him. He springs off the can and chases after her. She laughs as he runs alongside, begging her to stop. He almost cries. She slows down, just enough for him to catch up; then she speeds up, laughing over her shoulder as he races after her.

"How far you gonna run?" she hollers out the window and then roars out of sight around the curve. He is out of breath. His heart pounds in his chest, but he keeps on running in his heavy, sodden boots. Without that truck, he keeps thinking, I'm a dead man. A dead man. He huffs and puffs down the winding road. And there, just around the bend, there she is, parked on the soft shoulder waiting for him. She won't open her door, but she reaches over and opens the other side to let him in. And then when he does climb in, she roars off while he's still gasping for breath, trying to explain how the last thing he needs is trouble with Hazlitt or any of them Kluggses, but she keeps on driving.

She keeps on going and going. He's pressed against the door trying to come up with a good enough story for Hyacinth and his bull-necked father-in-law. But who's ever going to believe a grown man could be stolen away by a fourteen- or fifteen- or sixteen-year-old; she has given him three different ages in the last hour and as many names. Finally she settles on Dotty.

He closes his eyes and keeps assuring himself that any minute now he'll figure a way out of this mess. Soon as they get to a phone, he'll call. Soon as they stop for her to go to the bathroom, he'll drive off and leave her. But he doesn't. Damn it. Half of it is, he just can't stand the thought of her coming out in the middle of nowhere and finding herself stranded. And the other half is, she always takes the keys with her.

That first night, they sleep in the back of the truck. She spreads her arms and legs under the starry night and tells him to help himself. It's the least she can do, she says. No thanks, he says, his face burning with shame. He wants to tell her how he's not that kind; how he's married and way into his forties, with two boys and the wife, but sweet damn Jesus, that girl's tongue is lapping up the words and sucking the breath right out of his toes. The things she does. . . .

All night long, he lies awake next to her. Strands of her coppery hair drift across his face like a veil. She smells salty and sweet, like his littlest boy in the middle of the night. He never felt like this before. He feels almost holy. For the first time in his life, the dark seems a wonderful place to be.

The next day, she lets him drive. He is lost, hopelessly lost. He's not even sure what state they're in. A while back it was New Hampshire. But now all the cars have Massachusetts plates. The tailpipe is rattling loose and he is starving. They pass through town after town. He has lost track of time.

Finally in one of these towns he pulls off the main road onto a side street and tells her they have to head back. Soon as he gets that tailpipe wired up. No ifs, ands, or buts, and he's sorry about last night, he says. But sometimes things just happen, right out of the blue, so fast you don't have a chance to think what's right or wrong, which is just how he'll explain it to Hyacinth and all them Kluggses.

With that, she grabs the keys out of the ignition and jumps out and runs down the street and disappears around the corner. All he can do is sit there and wait. Pretty soon, she comes tearing around the corner and into the truck with a loaf of bread, a blue mason jar filled with dimes, and a little baby girl with a pale pink ribbon in her yellow-white hair. The minute the baby girl lays eyes on him, she starts to wail.

"Who's that?" he keeps asking.

First she says it's her sister. Then she says some lady gave it to her. Then she says she found it. He is so scared, he almost wets his pants. Every time he looks at her, the baby screams. He stares straight over the wheel. The girl is hollering at him to go. Go, she says, or they'll both end up in jail.

Go! Just Go!

So now, he's got two stories to come up with. One about himself and the other about the baby girl. But he can't think straight. Dotty gets him too scared. It's easier to just go where she says, turn when she says turn, and do what she wants.

I

Five years had passed. And maybe a million miles. He was caught and he knew it, caught in a dream or a nightmare or one of Hyacinth's stories, and there seemed no way out of anything anymore, certainly no way of his own choosing. Even though he had come to love the little girl they called Canny, he continued to miss his sons. But when he tried to think about his dilemma, he would be seized with a helplessness so vast and so paralyzing that the only voice in his head would be hers, Hyacinth's, ending it her way. *Nothing anyone can do. Not after all this time. No way to make things right. He dug his hole too deep.*

Too deep, too deep, too deep, his heart kept beating, had been beating all night while he waited in these two unlighted rooms, waited with his eyes keen on the door and its unseen corridor and stairs, and outside, the long empty street. His head cocked now with the first sound of her, of her heels, of the click, click, click of her high heels, and then a man's harsh voice dissolving in the unmistakable caress of Dotty's laughter.

The minute she came in, he told her they had to go. It wasn't safe here. Not anymore.

Cursing, she grabbed her albums and he could hear her sliding them into a box he'd left by the table. One of the records fell to the floor with a flat, faint thud. He froze.

In the dark, Canny's eyes opened wide. He couldn't see her, but he knew by the catch in her breath that she was awake now and ready to go. She had been asleep on the couch. Except for her rubber sandals, which he had told her to pack in her toy bag, she was all dressed.

"Shit," Dotty muttered, picking up the record. She lurched toward him with the box.

"I can't put nothing else in," Wallace whispered. "The trunk's full."

"Put 'em in the back seat then," Dotty whispered back.

"There's just room for Canny!" he said.

"These records're going!" she warned.

The little girl sat up now and swung her legs over the side of the couch.

"The box is too big," he said. "Get a littler box."

"And where the hell'm I gonna find a littler box at four in the morning?"

"Down cellar," he whispered, knowing she wouldn't go.

"I ain't going down there!" she said, her voice rising thick and heedlessly. "You go down and get one."

"Shh! They'll hear ya," he said nervously.

"Let 'em! Let 'em fuckin' hear me!"

"Shh. . . ."

"I just wanna go to bed," she groaned. "I'm so smashed. . . ."

"Shh! You can sleep it off in the. . . ."

"Don't shh me, you little creep. You probably made the whole thing up anyways."

"No, I didn't. Honest, Dot."

"Jesus Christ," she moaned. "Every time I start having too good a time, it's the same old thing. We gotta go cuzza her."

"It's true," he whispered. "She was here. Ask Canny." His voice shivered and thinned. "We was eating supper and she knocked on the door and I said, 'Who's that?' And she said, 'Truant officer,' and then I said, 'What do you want?' and she said, 'You gotta little girl that's school age and I gotta find out how come she ain't in school.' "

"I hope you told her to go f . . ."

"I tole her, 'No, ma'am, we ain't got no little girl.' And she said, 'Well, that ain't what we been tole, Mr. Wallace.' She knew my name and everything! She said, 'We been tole you and your wife don't send yer little girl to school and that's against the law,' she said, so then I didn't say nothing else and after a while, she left and I started packing."

"Jesus Christ," she groaned. "I'm so sick of this. Here," she said. He groaned and staggered a little under the weight of the box she shoved at him. "But there's just the one little spot for Canny!" he protested weakly.

"Okay," she whispered fiercely. "Then the records go and Canny doesn't! That what you want?"

At that, the little girl's feet scurried across the floor. "Momma?" she whispered, groping through the darkness. "Momma!"

"She's right here," Wallace whispered. "By the door."

Dotty laughed uneasily. She reached down and swung the girl up onto her hip. "Had you going there for a minute, huh?" she said with her mouth at Canny's ear.

Canny's thin arms knotted tightly around Dotty's neck as they tiptoed down the creaking stairs past the landlady's apartment. Wallace held his breath. If they could just make it out of here without the landlady stopping them, they'd have the rent money to live on until they found a new place.

They left the front door ajar, then hurried along the sidewalk to the corner, where, earlier in the evening, he had left the car parked at the top of the hill. Dotty bent low and set Canny on the back seat atop a nest of blankets and pillows. Wallace pushed the box of records next to her and gently, ever so gently, pushed the door so that it barely clicked. Then he and Dotty slid into the front seat and held their doors closed. With one hand on the shift and the other on the emergency brake, he put the old car into gear and snapped down the brake. Then waiting, still not breathing, he looked neither right nor left, but straight ahead. Suddenly, through the dark musky heat, came a tomcat's howl. Dotty turned toward the sound. She seemed to strain forward. He imagined her hand closing over the door handle and her foot easing to the curb. Closing his eyes, he jerked his head back and forth as though to pump the car into motion. Just then the weighted-down tires began to turn. Slowly. Heavily. Ever so slowly. She was still looking back. And then they were rolling, picking up speed, turning, rolling faster, until all at once, at the bottom of the hill, the car came alive. The door banged shut and the motor roared and the headlamps burned and the tires spun and Aubrey Wallace gave a nervous little snort. He looked over at Dotty, who stared glumly out the side window. She reeked of beer and sweet perfume. She belched softly into the back of her hand, then looked back at Canny. "Look at her, sound asleep," she sighed. "What the hell does she care how shitty my life is." She rolled down the window and trailed her arm through the rushing night. Her hair caught in the wind and blew back across her face. When she did not lift it away, he knew she was probably crying. After a few miles, she'd be all right. Once they got going, she'd get into the spirit of things. She always did.

When she finally spoke her voice sounded flat and numb. "You know how many different places we been in the last year?"

"Nope."

She looked at him. "Eight," she said.

He nodded. Somehow it hadn't seemed like that many.

"Coulda been eighty for all you care," she said, still looking at him.

He hunched over the wheel and peered into the bug-shimmered silvery light of the headlamps. She lit a cigarette and the smell stung his nostrils. His nose began to run.

"Year before was five." She sucked in so deep on her cigarette that in the light of a passing car, her face appeared hollow and as high-boned as a skull. "And the year before that was four," she said in an exhale of smoke.

He glanced at her with an uneasy grin, then wiped his nose on the back of his hand. She was getting him mixed up.

"Pretty soon, at the rate we're going," she said, "we won't even have to unload the car." She glanced over her shoulder at Canny, who moaned in her sleep. "She looks hot."

"She don't feel good," he said, glancing into the mirror. "She said her head hurt."

"Where we goin'?"

"Don't matter," he said. "Figured we'd just go till we come on a market."

She laid her head back on the seat. "Tonight, I was coming home and I saw the way you had the car ready to go, and I had this crazy feeling inside like I should keep on going. Just keep on walking and let you go without me."

"I wouldn'ta done that."

"Yah," she said wearily. "That's what I figured." She leaned forward and turned on the radio full volume. The sudden blast startled the girl. She sat up and rubbed her eyes. She winced painfully with the thunderous beat of the music. "Momma," she said gently, but Dotty did not hear. Her head rocked and her shoulders shimmied as she clicked her long, painted fingers in time to the music. She sang the words she knew in a loud, husky voice.

> "Hey, lonesome lady,
> There's gonna be hearts to break.
> And gonna be love to make,
> You lonesome lady, lady there. . . ."

Wallace's hands tightened on the wheel. His eyes darted to the rearview mirror, where a blue light spun in the distance. His first thought was the landlady. She'd set the troopers on them for the back rent.

"Dammit," he muttered as the blue light grew in the mirror.

"Little, lonesome lady come on home," Dotty sang. She reached back and patted Canny's cheek.

"Dammit," he muttered again.

"What the hell's wrong with you?" she snapped.

"Cops."

"Jesus Christ!" She turned to look. "How the hell damn fast were you going?" she screamed, as the blue light loomed around them. A siren began to whine.

"Fifty," he said, wiping the sweat from his eyes.

"You asshole!" she screamed, as the cruiser broke loose. "This is it! It's all over now!" she shrieked when the cruiser was alongside. She cringed down in the seat with her hands over her face. "This is what you been wanting! Here it is! Here it comes! They're gonna shoot us! They're gonna shoot us dead, you stupid bastard!"

"Momma! Momma!" Canny screamed in terror. "Don't let them shoot us, Momma!"

"I hope they do! Oh God, I hope they do and then it'll be over!"

"Momma!"

"Shut up, goddammit," he groaned. "The two of you both!" he called over the throb of the radio and their screams. Like a quick, bright fish into the deep, the cruiser flashed ahead, then vanished. "They's gone! They's gone!" he cried, pulling into the breakdown lane. Dotty was crying. He turned off the radio and tugged at her arm. His hands still trembled. "It wasn't us! They's gone," he told her over and over again.

She continued to sob with her face buried in her hands.

"Don't, Dotty," he pleaded.

"Goddamn cops!" Canny gasped, her bony chest heaving up and down. "Goddamn, sonofabitchen cops. . . ."

He grabbed her wrist. "You watch your mouth!" he warned.

"I wish I was dead," Dotty was moaning. "I wish I was dead."

"It's okay, Momma," Canny said, wiping her eyes. She took a deep breath. "Nobody's here but me and Poppy. Look, Momma. It's just us."

"I can't take this anymore," Dotty sobbed. "Always scared. Always running. . . ."

"C'mon, Momma, it's gonna be all right," Canny said, running her fingers through Dotty's long hair.

"No, it won't. Nothing ever goes right for me. Never did, never will. . . ."

"Yes it will, Momma!" Canny kissed the back of Dotty's head.

"All I ever wanted was a little fun," Dotty wept. "That's all, just some fun for once. . . ."

Wallace closed his eyes. He was tired.

"We'll have fun, Momma," the little girl insisted. "We'll have Poppy look for a circus or a park and we'll go on all the rides. We'll have fun! You'll see!"

Dotty sat up. "You mean that? About the rides?"

Canny nodded.

"You won't chicken out like last time?" Dotty laughed and sobbed all at once. " 'member? You said you were gonna throw up?"

"I won't," Canny said.

"Even the roller coaster?" Dotty asked, wiping her eyes with the hem of her skirt.

Canny nodded solemnly, then sank back into her boxed crevice.

As Wallace pulled onto the highway, his eyes met Canny's in the mirror. Tired as she was, she smiled. All of a sudden, the strangest urge came over him. He wanted to tell her something. Something wonderful. Something beautiful. He glanced back at her.

"Canny," he said softly.

"What, Poppy?" she murmured sleepily.

"Nothin'," he said fastening his eyes on the dark road ahead. It only took a few miles before he was dreaming—wide awake and dreaming, which was just how it used to happen when he was little. Only then they called it a spell. He liked these moments; never struggled to flee them. Here was a sun-curtained window through which filtered all the voices and all the faces he had ever known. It was here at the center of things he had learned to exist; here, where there was quiet—a quiet so still it

17

had substance and color and sound. Here were all the things he did not know or understand and here they did not matter. This was the place where he kept Hyacinth and Answan and Arnold and the little white house with its bottle-blue door and a crazy girl with blood cuts on her arms who held a baby girl nobody wanted, or so she said.

"Where we gonna go now?"

"Just drive, dammit. I'll think of something."

"Drive where?"

"There! Turn there, and down that road. . . ."

"Now what?"

"Just keep going, dammit!"

Just keep on going. Turn when she says turn. After a while he barely knows the states through which they pass. The baby is getting so pretty and so big. She calls him Poppy.

"And who'm I?" Dotty giggles.

"Momma," the little girl says. "Momma." Says it like a song that runs through his thoughts day and night. "Momma," she says, closing her eyes.

Some nights he wakes up in a cold sweat and there she is. The other one in her skinny brown dress and her raw red hands on her ridged hips. In the doorway. So bright, he can't really see her face too good anymore.

"Where you been?" she keeps wanting to know. "We been waiting all this time. Where you been?"

Funny thing is, he doesn't know. And in here it doesn't matter. Because he's been here all the time, but acourse, try and tell *her* that.

2

The Blue Caboose had no menus, just hand-lettered signs taped on the walls, the register, the milk machine. HOME FRIES—85¢ . . . GRITS WITH ANY TWO EGGS—$1.45 . . . ONE EGG AND BACON—$1.55 . . . THE FOOD'S GREAT. IT'S THE COOKING THAT'S NOT SO HOT . . . FOR SALE—GUARD DOG. ATTACKS ON COMMAND—$65 OR BEST OFFER. ENQUIRE NEXT DOOR.

Taped to this sign was a curled snapshot of a German shepherd, its fangs bared, its eyes ringed with hate. Wallace tried not to look at it. Dogs scared him. All dogs, even the mutt Hyacinth used to have. When she was put out with him, she'd let the dog up on the bed—on his side. Those nights he slept on the couch. After a while, a crazy thing happened. He grew as jealous of the dog as if it were a man, stretched full out on the covers with his head on Wallace's pillow and his hind paws on Hyacinth's backside. Even his boys seemed to prefer talking to that dog over their own father.

Dotty sat between Wallace and Canny at the long stainless steel counter. She had been sound asleep when they stopped. All Dotty ever had this early in the morning was coffee. It was Canny who always had to eat the minute her eyes opened.

There were no waitresses here; just a tall, gray-haired man

with a towel pulled around his pointed belly. He was bent over the far end of the counter, reading a newspaper. "Be right there," he muttered, then turned the page, and muttered again.

Canny began to turn idly on the squeaky stool. Dotty winced at the high, grating pitch as Canny spun faster and faster. Finally Dotty grabbed her shoulder and yanked her to a halt. Wallace's eyes lifted warily between Canny's whimper of protest and the man who was folding up his paper now. Last month Dotty had slapped Canny so hard she blackened her eye and made her nose bleed. A week after that, she pushed her off a chair. The fall caused Canny to bite her tongue. Both times, Dotty cried her eyes out and wouldn't let Canny go. Sometimes it seemed Dotty was made up of great love and great anger, with as little in between as a candle blazing at both ends.

Her face was puffy and bloodless under the thin fluorescent tubes that hung from the stamped tin ceiling. Her hand trembled as she shaded her eyes from the light and the counterman's stare. He stood over her, waiting for her order. He rolled a dead cigar stub over his tongue and winked at Canny, who glanced up at Dotty. She was making him wait, the way he had made her wait. Canny nudged her.

"Coffee," Dotty finally yawned. "Black."

"That it?" the counterman asked.

She didn't answer, just dismissed him with a flip of her fingers.

"Make that two," Wallace said, eager to get things moving. "And juice here for her." He nodded down at Canny, who was picking sleep from her eyes. "And cornflakes," he said, reaching past Dotty to pluck Canny's hands from her face. She was always getting infections. Especially around her eyes, which he could see were getting pink and sore looking again.

The counterman had moved off a few feet. He was pouring coffee from a filmy glass pot.

"Dry!" Wallace called out suddenly.

The counterman set down the cup. "Dry what?" he said over his shoulder.

Dotty chuckled.

"Cornflakes . . . she don't like milk in 'em," he added sheepishly.

"They got doughnuts," Canny said hopefully, pointing to the pyramid of doughnuts under a scratched and yellowed plastic cover.

Wallace shook his head.

Canny leaned forward over the counter. "We could split one," she whispered past Dotty.

Again, he shook his head.

"Please, Poppy," she teased.

"Give her a doughnut," Dotty groaned, pinching the bridge of her nose, her eyes still closed.

"I ain't got enough," Wallace hissed out of the side of his mouth.

The counterman stood nearby, rattling through a shoebox of silverware until he found three spoons, which he placed in front of them.

"Please, Poppy!" Canny said, her voice rising. "I gotta dime!"

"That ain't enough," he said through clenched teeth. "And 'sides, last time, you threw up all over the back seat."

"Oh shit!" Dotty groaned, and buried her face in her hands. The counterman smiled.

"I won't get sick, Poppy, I promise! Please! Please, Poppy!"

"No, dammit!" he hissed, staring straight ahead. "Now stop teasing!"

"Jesus Christ," Dotty growled, opening her red purse. "Here!" She pulled out a twenty-dollar bill and slapped it down next to the coffee the counterman had just set down. "Give her a friggin' doughnut, will ya?"

"Jelly, sugar, or plain?" the counterman asked Canny with a grin. Wallace could tell he was enjoying seeing him squirm. People usually did. It was something in his eyes, something in the way they gleamed, as quick and furtive as the frantic nightward scratching of a rodent's claws behind the walls.

"No thanks," Canny said, her eyes downcast and miserable.

Wallace was staring at the twenty-dollar bill. Dotty snatched

21

it back into her purse. "I found it," she said. "Will you stop looking at me like that," she growled, before spinning off the stool and flouncing into the ladies' room. Canny gestured for Wallace to lean close. "It wasn't a guy," she whispered with her hand at his ear. "It was just some pills. I saw her sell some."

He nodded and sat up. Dotty always seemed to have money. He didn't know which was worse—men paying her to go out with them or the pills. Some of them made her real happy and some made her sleep. And there were some that made her crazy-mean, like those times lately with Canny.

The counterman brought Canny's orange juice and a little box of cornflakes. Wallace grinned watching her tear back the top and leave it hinged. He had forgotten how she loved those little boxes. Once he had bought her a whole pack of them, each a different cereal. She had stretched them out a whole two weeks, eating just a little every morning.

Dotty came out of the ladies' room. She had combed her hair and put on lipstick and eyeliner. She sat down and picked her tee shirt away from her wet armpits, which she'd just washed. Halfway through her coffee, she perked up. "Hey! Where's that?" she called, pointing up at the cardboard sign taped to the milk dispenser.

"Where's what?" the counterman asked, looking up from his paper.

"Hortonville," Dotty said. "The Hortonville Fair," she read, peering at the sign.

"North about two hundred, two hundred fifty miles," he told her.

"What's it, like a county fair or something?"

The counterman shrugged. "It's a fair—rides and shows, I guess. I never been. My wife goes. She likes the flea markets. Always bringing home crap and what-nots."

Dotty looked at Wallace and smiled. "That's what we do," she told the counterman. "Flea markets. We probably sell the same kinda crap your wife brings home," she said proudly.

"Oh yah?" The counterman eased down the counter toward

them. He rubbed his belly and shifted it into place. "You mean I got you to blame for all them little statues and empty perfume bottles she says're gonna be worth a fortune some day." He laughed.

"Don't laugh. I heard of that happening before," Dotty said. She tossed her head to get her hair off her shoulders. "You never know what you're gonna pick up."

"Ain't that the truth?" the counterman said, leaning back with his elbows behind him in such a way that his belly thrust obscenely upward.

"Once this girl I knew bought a ring. She only paid a coupla bucks for it, so even though it was pretty, she didn't think much of it," Dotty was saying. Her face flushed as she spoke. Her eyes brightened and her voice ran breathless and wet and her hands fluttered like little white flags and every now and again, she patted back her hair and flicked her tongue over her lips. "And then one night, this guy says, 'Hey, I'll give you twenty bucks for that hunk of glass.' And she says, 'Sure, why not,' which was more than she paid for it, the twenty, that is. And so the guy goes off with the ring and we're drinking Mai Tais, me and her, with the guy's twenty bucks and all night we're laughing and feeling guilty how she ripped him off and all. Then next thing we know, the guy's back with a roll could choke a horse and he says, 'Hey . . .' "

Wallace stared into the sludge at the bottom of his cup. He'd heard this story hundreds of times. Sometimes it was a diamond ring. Sometimes a solid gold bracelet. Sometimes the guy with the roll felt guilty and gave them fifty or sixty more. Other times the girl started to bawl when she realized she'd let something so valuable just slip through her fingers like that and then Dotty would take it upon herself to set things straight.

In any event, he and Canny could both relax now that Dotty was her old self again; full of chatter and that strange rush of laughter that always seemed to hang in the air a long time into silence, so that hours later, days later, it would still be with him like the after-cry of some distant wounded creature.

She and the counterman were both laughing. He shook his finger at her. "Yah!" he said, nodding and shaking his finger. "You know when you came in, I thought you were familiar." Hefting his belly into place, he leaned over the counter and studied her face. He snapped his fingers. "Raquel Welch, right?"

"Right!" she squealed.

"That's who you remind me of," the counterman said. " 'Cept for the red hair."

She laughed happily. People told her that all the time. She lit a cigarette. "Okay," she grinned and gestured at Wallace. "Now him—who's he remind you of?"

Under the counterman's scrutiny, Wallace's eyes scrambled from sign to sign. Dotty knew he hated this.

"Well, I can tell you who he don't remind me of," the counterman chuckled. "Robert Redford, Cary Grant, John Wayne, Burt Reynolds . . ."

"No, really!" Dotty giggled, squirming on the stool. "Look close."

The counterman leaned even closer and studied Wallace's narrow, stubbly face. Wallace blinked. Like Dotty's, the counterman's breath smelled of stale booze.

"I dunno," the counterman said. He shook his head and looked at Dotty.

"Willie Nelson!" she cried. "Without the pigtails of course."

The counterman narrowed his eyes and angled his head. Wallace sighed and looked down at Canny. With her fingers, she was eating her cereal flake by flake.

"You know, you're right!" the counterman said. "He does. It's the short hair throws ya off."

"And them mean little eyes," Dotty said.

"Momma!" Canny chided, and the counterman laughed.

Wallace wanted to go, but Dotty had ordered another coffee. She lit another cigarette and stretched back lazily. The counterman set down the coffee and started to scrub the countertop in front of her. "I think Raquel's taller'n you," he said with a thoughtful frown as if it mattered, as if it were the least bit important.

"Nope!" Dotty said, delighted to be back on the subject again. "We're the 'zact same. Five-nine."

The counterman folded his arms and looked her over. "How 'bout the eyes? Hers are brown, right?"

"Same as me," Dotty said, blowing on the hot coffee. "Green."

The counterman's gaze sank to the front of her tee shirt, which said HANDS OFF in glittery red letters.

"Same," Dotty laughed.

The counterman's face reddened. "How 'bout you," he said to Canny. "Who do you look like?"

Canny shrugged.

"You sure don't look like Raquel or Willie here," he said, leaning down and tweaking her nose. "Not with them big blue eyes and that blondie hair."

"How much I owe you?" Wallace growled, getting off the stool.

"Two bucks," the counterman said, a little startled by this sudden shift in mood.

Dotty swiveled off her stool and went outside. Canny grabbed her cereal box and chased after her.

The counterman stood in the window, scratching his belly. He watched them get into their beat-up Chevy. The rear window and the trunk were plastered with decals and bumper stickers and the roof was lashed with boxes. As they backed around, then turned in front of the diner, Dotty blew him a kiss with her middle finger.

"Take your pick," she said, opening her purse.

"Momma!" Canny squealed, hanging over the seat. "I didn't see you buy any of these," she said, choosing a furry white sugar doughnut.

"Neither did that asshole," Dotty laughed. Before Wallace could say anything, she held her fingers to his mouth for him to lick off the sugar.

———

At four o'clock they had only traveled twenty miles farther than the diner. First, the fan belt had snapped and Wallace had to walk four miles into the nearest town and four miles back with the new one. After he got the fan belt on, he had driven just a few more miles when the engine overheated and the radiator boiled dry.

He came along the edge of the roadbed now with a bucket of water and a can of coolant. He was exhausted. His shoulders ached and his eyes were red-rimmed and bloodshot under the fiery sun. The heat of the highway stung through the thin soles of his old black sneakers. His right foot dragged more than it usually did. Cars blurred past, spitting back bits of gravel like birdshot against his legs. He groaned when he saw the steep rise ahead. As he began to climb, his leg trembled and every step stabbed pain up his shinbone.

When he was just a boy and new to the Home, a doctor had come along the rows of beds early one morning and flashed a light in Aubrey's face. The doctor checked his clipboard and then he pulled down the bed covers and told the boy to straighten out his right leg. It only took him a few minutes to fit the cold metal brace to the boy's leg and flap the back piece under his heel. He fastened the straps and tightened the screws and went on his way so quickly that Aubrey fell asleep, certain that it had been a dream, until the bell rang and he needed help out of bed.

"What's he need it for?" his father had asked on his last visit. The duty counselor wasn't sure. Sunday counselors never knew much. So his father asked him. "I dunno," Aubrey said. "You got to know," his father said. "You don't jest lay there and let them strap a thing like that to you and never ask why . . . 'less you're a retard."

A few years later, another doctor came by all in a sweat and undid the contraption, which should have been put on Barney Hobbs. But by then, Barney Hobbs was long gone and Aubrey's withered and hairless leg was forever fused in its wide-angled step. Without his brace, he had a terrible time. Not only did he have to learn a whole new way to walk, but his new weight-lessness frightened him. Some days it felt as if no part of him was real or solid enough to keep him from drifting off the face of the earth.

Now as he came to the top of the hill, he staggered a moment under the weight of the pail. Looking down, he saw no car, just the beginning of another hill, this one even higher than the one he had just climbed. He set down the pail and took off his baseball cap, wiping sweat from his eyes with the back of his hand. Coming down the opposite hill, then climbing this one, was a liver-colored van with gold curtains on the windows. The driver sat high over the wheel. Wallace's eyes widened painfully on the young, bare-armed woman next to him. Her long, dusky hair streamed out the window as the van whizzed past. "Dotty," he tried to say, but his throat was dry and tight as his gut. Tears stood in his eyes that swam like milky lenses. He began again to climb this misshapen, wobbly hill, with the water sloshing against the sides of the bucket and running down his leg, and he knew, was absolutely certain that when he got to the top the forlorn and faded car nose down in the dusty weeds below would be empty. Of course it would be.

This was the moment he had always dreaded, this abandon-ment, which of all the mysteries and all the things he didn't know about her, was the one certainty, that one fixed point to which he had returned again and again, so that the loss of her had come to be as much of a throb in him as his jawful of stained teeth, splintered and rotten with the phantom pain that threatened to devour him with every bite, hot and cold, sweet and sour, and every breath, in and out. He was panting now as he ran toward the car, the empty car. Of course it would be empty, empty like that quiet center of his being, that strange and simple silence. Everything beyond was fairy tale, words from a story, just as a voice on the phone was no more than that— a voice on the phone. For some reason, he used to call late at night. Maybe it was the two boys. Maybe he was afraid if he heard their voices, the horror of what he had done would all come true. He never spoke, just listened; for what was there to say? How could he explain what he had never gotten straight in his own head; except to think, *It just happened. That was all. Some things just happen and there's nothing anyone can do. . . .*

"I know who this is," she'd say. "You don't fool me. Don't bother us anymore." Then one night, she whispered in the cackly witch voice she always used in the stories, "They're all gone. Her and the two boys. Moved away and gone forever, so stop calling here." So he did. Stopped calling and started guarding against the day of Dotty's leaving and Canny's; Canny, who wasn't his, but in a way was, he had tried once to explain to Dotty, was his, because she was all he had, like he was all she had in the whole world. "That's not true, she's got me," Dotty flared back, and though he knew that wasn't true, he took those words and put them in that quiet place, along with the old phone number, Piedmont 8-6705 and *she's got me,* because there, somehow, they were all connected and real.

"Where the fuck've you been?" she called out the window.

He looked inside, relieved to see Canny asleep with her head in Dotty's lap. Beads of sweat frothed her temples. Her lips were white and flaky. He stuck his hand through the window and felt Canny's forehead.

"She's hot," he said.

"Course she's hot," Dotty said, batting away his hand. "Baking in this shitbox all day long, you'd be hot too."

He filled the radiator with water and added the coolant, then closed the hood as gently as possible so as not to wake Canny. Dotty stared at him through the smutty windshield. When he got into the car, she continued to stare straight ahead.

"Think she's sick?" he asked.

"No, I don't think she's sick!" she said disgustedly.

"She looks sick," he said, turning the key with a hopeful wince until the engine caught. He smiled. "Mebbe we oughta find a place for the night," he called over the racing motor. "Get a good night's sleep."

"We're going to Hortonville," she said. "You promised."

He pulled onto the highway. All last night's driving and today's walking had exhausted him. But they were on their way to Hortonville, wherever the hell that was, and that was that. Just like always, wherever she wanted to go, he always took her. Up one highway and down the next, so that after a while they all looked the same to him now; maybe even were in a sense, the very same road, in and out of the same towns that were all alike, though they bore different names like Moundsville and Hayestown, with the same tired people drifting over the same tired streets and crumbled curbstones, home to the same tired shacks and bunks and rooms they could let a night or a season or until she was ready to move on for whatever the reason or whim: too hot, too cold, the landlady's too nosy, or the guy looked at me funny like he knew me from someplace, she'd gasp as she ran around filling up the boxes and bags they never discarded, but lived out of. Even Canny was expert at it now, always keeping her teddy bear and her coloring books and crayons in a good strong bag, ready to pack at a moment's notice.

"Where we going?" Canny would ask.

"Ask your Momma," he'd say.

Where are we? Ask your Momma. When we gonna get there? Ask your Momma.

"Don't you know anything, Poppy?" she'd say in that same faint, sorrowing, watchful tone of his boys.

Soon, they were seeing signs for Hortonville. On telephone poles and the sides of barns and even now on the radio. "The Hortonville Fair," the announcer drawled in a high nasal tone.

"Sounds like you, Aubie," Dotty laughed, pointing at the radio.

"The world's biggest twenty-four-hour flea market and rides and bingo and sideshows! Shop and relax while your kids Shoot the Bullet and hubby enjoys sparkling refreshment in the genuine, authentic Munich Beer Garden. Admission is absolutely free, and for all you entrepreneurs out there, selling space is still available."

Dotty was pawing through the glove compartment. She shook out a map and brought it close to her face. "Jesus, I can't hardly see the route numbers," she said.

"Mebbe you need glasses," he said, glancing through the mirror at Canny, who was asleep again. At the last rest stop, he had taken the records out of the box and stacked them on the floor, with blankets over them. Canny had more room to stretch out now. She had been complaining of a sick stomach and her head felt sweaty and hotter than before.

"Ya, four eyes. That'll be the day!" Dotty scoffed, running her finger down the map.

"You'd look nice in glasses," he said, more to himself than her. He'd like that. Glasses would make her look . . . He couldn't think of the right word. Neat? No, that wasn't it. Like she was all put together. Something like that.

She pointed suddenly ahead. "Take that exit!"

As he turned sharply onto the ramp, Canny moaned. She began to cough.

"No, left," Dotty said.

"She don't sound so good," he said, glancing back over his shoulder at Canny. He turned right.

"Jesus Christ!" Dotty howled. "I say left and you take a right!"

Just then Canny sat up, her cheeks red and her eyes heavy on him through the mirror. Without a word, she dropped back onto the seat. Certain she had fainted, he reached back, but couldn't feel her. Down the road was a shopping center. He raced ahead and pulled into the parking lot.

"She's burning up," he said, touching Canny's forehead. He took a dollar from his pocket and shook it at Dotty. "Go get her some aspirin and a soda," he said.

She laid her head back on the seat and closed her eyes. "You get it," she sighed. "I'm beat."

"Here!" he said, fumbling for another dollar. "Get yourself a soda too."

"I'm tired," she said.

"She's sick!" he said helplessly, looking from the outstretched money to Dotty, then back again.

"She's sick," Dotty repeated, her eyes still shut, her voice faint and whispery. "She's cold. Her pants're wet. Her ass is sore. Her nose is running. Jesus Christ," she groaned, opening the door. "I'm so tired of this."

"It ain't her fault," he said softly when she was out of earshot. He watched her move through the dusty haze of the parking lot, her red straw purse dangling from her shoulder, her small round hips tight and high on her long thin legs and the skinny strap heels that glittered like sparks with every step. A young man in a black tee shirt came toward her and every part of her seemed to come alive; her head cocked and her shoulders trembled and her buttocks seemed to flesh out and soften under the thin cloth of her skirt.

"Get ice in hers," Wallace called suddenly out the window. "And don't get grape! She hates grape."

A half hour later, she came back with two cups of soda.

"Where's the aspirin?" he hollered out the window.

"Shut up!" she hissed, rolling her eyes in the direction of the stout man in a silvery suit, who had followed her out of the store.

"Jesus, you're a mouth," she groaned, getting into the car. She opened her purse and flipped two bottles of baby aspirin into his lap. Also being removed from the purse were two brand-new lipsticks, eyeliner, blush, mascara, nail polish, and gold eye shadow, all stolen. Wallace knelt on the seat and gave Canny four aspirins and the ginger ale, which she gulped down; then, with a weak, grateful smile, she fell back to sleep.

"What took you so long?" he asked when they were back on the highway.

"I couldn't find the aspirin," she said, blotting her plum-colored lips on the road map.

"You pay for all that stuff?" he asked.

She turned from her compact mirror and smiled. "How do I look?" He grinned. She had braided her hair. She looked better than any movie star he'd ever seen. She blinked and the setting sun caught the flecks of glitter on her eyelids and he thought how she was even prettier than that first day they met; how she'd grown into a beautiful woman.

"I look like shit," she said, snapping the compact shut. She turned down the visor and closed her eyes. On the flip side of the visor was a picture she had found in an old National Geographic that had been left over from one of the flea markets. It showed the astronaut's first webby looking footsteps in the moon's dust. Canny thought the picture was scary and Wallace didn't like it either. Things like planets and moon walks fascinated Dotty. Once they drove twenty-four straight hours to watch a rocket being launched. Dotty said it was the most beautiful sight she'd ever seen. As they watched the fiery tail dissolving in the clouds, she told Canny that was just the way the spirit leaves a dead person's body. Just like a rocket. Canny wanted to know where the spirit went. "Into the black hole," Dotty answered. "And what's in there?" "Nobody knows," Dotty said. For weeks and weeks afterward, Canny had bad dreams. It scared Wallace too. He didn't even like the word *spirit*. A spirit was a ghost and many's the night his dreams were chock full of them.

"Hortonville's another eighty miles," Dotty said, putting the map back into the glove compartment. "Provided you don't get lost again."

"I won't," he said sheepishly. After they left the shopping center, Dotty had fallen asleep and he had taken a wrong turn, driving some sixty miles back the way they'd come.

"You still got no sense of direction whatever," Dotty was saying. "You'd think after all this time and all this moving around, you'd get to have some anyways."

He laughed. His getting lost all the time was an old joke with them.

"I'm serious," she said, and he squirmed on the hard edge of her voice. "How the hell'dya get around all those years before you met me?' She looked at him. "Well?"

He shrugged. "Just kept to the same roads, I guess," he muttered. She was on to something. It was there in her voice, in her words that darted like bright minnows below a calm, dark surface.

"I'll bet you never even left Atkinson till you met me." He didn't answer. Canny sat up and yawned. "Where's Atkinson?" she asked, leaning forward between them on the back of the seat.

"Not even Atkinson," Dotty laughed scornfully. "But the Flatts. That's where your old Poppy's from," she said with a peck at Canny's cheek. "You're all cooled off!" she said, and held out her arms for the little girl to climb into.

"Where's the Flatts?" Canny asked, snuggling into Dotty's lap.

"It's way up in the cold, snowy mountains, where the Kluggs and the Mooneys and the Wallaces all live and have babies with their sisters and their mothers," Dotty laughed and rested her chin on Canny's moist head.

"But where's that?" Canny persisted. "What's the state?"

"The Flatts is a state of mind," Dotty said, lighting a cigarette over Canny's head.

"I mean the fifty states," Canny said, with a little whine. She waved away the smoke.

Wallace stared over the wheel. Any minute now, she'd have Dotty screaming at her.

"Like all the states we been," Canny was saying. "In Florida, and New Mexico, and Tennessee . . . you know what I mean. Which one's Poppy's state?"

"How the hell should I know?" Dotty said, dragging deeply on her cigarette.

"You know!" Canny insisted.

"Don't start that whining!" Dotty warned, and she dumped Canny off her lap onto the seat between them.

"I'm not whining," Canny pouted. "Tell me the state."

"Vermont," Dotty said, and Wallace's mouth fell open. She looked at him and shrugged. "What the hell," she said, and shrugged again.

"That where you're from too, Momma?"

"No," Dotty laughed, rubbing her knuckles into Canny's scalp until she squealed. "I'm a creature from outer space. I came in one of those UFOs. We'd been circling around and around the whole country tryna find the handsomest, smartest man on earth. And then one day I got so sick of being in orbit all my life and I said to the driver—well, the pilot, really—I said, 'Set this sucker down, Zeebor. I'm picking the first pair of pants comes along.'" Dotty laughed and jabbed Wallace's shoulder. "And here he is!"

Canny and Dotty giggled. Wallace shivered. A chill crept up his spine as he thought of that day and how she *had* just appeared out of nowhere. His eyes widened. Barefoot over the blazing hot tar, she had come. Like she was floating. Like a creature from space would float. Coming toward him, her eyes had locked on his like a cat's on a bird.

"What's snow like when you walk on it, Poppy?" Canny was asking.

The car behind him blared its horn as he suddenly changed lanes and swerved into the breakdown lane. "I'll be right back," he said. He jumped out of the car and ran down the gully, unzipping his fly as he went. Afterward, he hobbled back. Lately, it burned so bad he wanted to cry each time he urinated. He was too embarrassed to tell Dotty and the last time he'd been to a doctor was in the Home.

Dotty was changing her clothes. She took off her bra and flipped it into the back seat. Canny was ripping open two bandages for her. Wallace picked grime from the crevices on the steering wheel and tried not to look at Dotty's naked chest. That is, he didn't want Canny to think he ever looked at Dotty when she was naked—not that it mattered to Canny or Dotty if he saw her like that. But it mattered to him. It mattered what Canny thought of him.

Dotty pressed a bandage strip over each pink nipple. "Don't they hurt when they come off?" Canny asked, watching closely.

"Depends on who's taking them off," Dotty laughed, as she slid her arms up through a white jersey dress with a big red parrot on the skirt. She raised her elbow. A price tag dangled from her underarm. "Can you get it?" she asked Canny, who caught the plastic strip between her teeth and bit it in two.

"Thirty dollars!" Canny said, looking at the tag.

"Well, that was just the asking price," Dotty laughed and threw the tag out the window.

"Momma!" Canny giggled. "You didn't pinch it, did you?"

"Course she didn't!" Wallace said sternly. "You know your Momma wouldn't do nothing like that." He started the car.

"Course not!" Dotty said, trying to keep a straight face. Even Canny was trying hard not to laugh.

3

Dotty said Hortonville wasn't too far from Washington, D.C. This was the farthest north Wallace had been in five years. Every few miles cruisers crept up on them, then sped past. Dotty said it was his imagination, but he was sure he'd never seen so many cops on one stretch of road. He slowed down to forty-five and slouched low behind the wheel with the visor of the baseball cap almost meeting his nose.

As the night wore on, Dotty grew more and more excited. She sang along with the radio and snapped her fingers and tapped her feet, and as one song ended, she would switch quickly to another station so there couldn't be even a moment of silence. Dotty hated quiet. She said when it got too quiet you could hear the planets pinging off one another's sound waves and the fizzy static of all the dead souls trying to make contact with someone on earth.

Even with the windows open, the crowded car was hot. The rushing night air seemed to crackle with Dotty's feverish energy. For the last half hour she had been either talking or singing. Rock music blared from the radio, its drumbeat pulsing in Wallace's temples. She could barely sit still. Like a child, she squirmed and stretched, then crossed her legs, then drew them up on the seat under her, then folded her arms and laid her head back on the seat, then sat up suddenly and, with a sigh, trailed her arm out the window through the humid, inky night.

Her laughter came like a bright, thin shatter of glass and he knew without looking that her cheeks flared with color. Next to her he felt small and drained, and all at once he was conscious of just how tired he was, how achy, and unshaven, and fuzzy-mouthed. His eyes felt dry and gritty and his throat burned when he swallowed. There seemed to be no air to breathe; Dotty consumed it all.

In the back seat, Canny tossed and turned and groaned uncomfortably. "Poppy," she murmured through her sleep. He turned down the radio, expecting Dotty to angrily turn it full blast. But she was busy brushing her hair. From the corner of his eye he could see the rapid flick of her moist white arms snapping the brush through her hair. Sparks seemed to trail the brush. A flutter rose in her breath like quick little wings. "Do I look nice? How's my hair? Oh jeez, I need more gloss. . . . We didn't pass it, did we? Close the window—my hair's getting mussed. . . . Canny! Wake up! Wake up, we're almost there. . . ." She knelt on the seat and reached back and nudged Canny. Sitting back down now, she peered closely out the side window at the passing lights and now at a sign that said HOR-TONVILLE, 3 MILES. With a frantic gasp, she began to brush her hair again. She lifted each arm over her head and rolled on more deodorant. From her purse, she took a slender glass atomizer and doused her throat with the smell of sun-drenched roses. Nervously, she snapped the purse clasp open and shut, then, leaning forward, began to tap her sharp glittery nails over the dashboard. Like the canary bird his boys used to have, he thought, its feathers puffed and trembling, just waiting for the wire gate in the little cage to lift open.

Dotty strained forward. Ahead, the dark sky was rent with bars of light. "We're here!" she cried, reaching back to shake Canny. "There it is! Look!"

The fairgrounds was a sea of rippling lights and pulsating

music and human voices that seemed to swell and crest, then fall, then swell again with the tumult of crashing waves.

Canny sat up sleepily. The fluorescent parking lights made her small face look bony and gray. She winced and rubbed her eyes. The flea market was part of the fair. Dotted among the sideshows and rides were hundreds of vendor tables and trunk setups. Wallace usually sold out of the trunk of the car. That way, if there were any questions about where he got his things, all he had to do was slam the trunk shut and be on his way. Sometimes, though not very often, cops came around the flea markets checking for stolen goods. It had only happened once to him, but fortunately Dotty had been there. Nervous as she was, she flirted and fooled around so with the cop, he ended up buying one of Wallace's plastic ice scrapers in the ninety degree heat a few miles south of Tampa.

As they drove along the outskirts of the fairgrounds, the barkers' voices flapped past the windows like tattered streamers.

". . . do you want to go faster? . . . she walks, she talks, she crawls on her belly . . . five packs of Camels on the red square . . . than the speed of light . . . at the stroke of midnight all rides will . . . march that little gal right up here—yessir, that one! The one with the monkey doll . . . five-gotta-five-gotta-five-gotta. . . ."

"The Magical Mystery Flight!" Dotty squealed, naming the rides they passed. "The Reptile! The Starlight Skewer! Jesus Christ, that thing's so high I can't see the top. . . . The Wonder Whirl! Look, Canny, the Black Hole. . . ."

Canny's eyes were heavy on his through the mirror. "I feel sick," she whispered at his ear. For fear of what Dotty would say, he pretended not to have heard. "My stomach hurts," Canny groaned.

Dotty whipped around. "You shut up! I'm so damn sick of you spoiling everything all the time!"

"She'll be okay," Wallace said quickly. "Won't you, Canny?" She closed her eyes and nodded.

"She better be," Dotty muttered, her attention back on the

swirling crowds and the spinning, whirling commotion of rides. "I never seen so many different ones," she gasped.

"I ain't got but a few things left to sell," Wallace reminded her.

"Look at all those people," Dotty said, smiling out the window at the young men in colored shirts and string ties and their broad-bottomed, pasty white women, all dressed up and drifting between the stands and flea market tables, nibbling cotton candy with their eyes dreamy and trancelike, looking to buy something cheap and pretty and not too chipped and worn.

"Buncha lookers, is all," Wallace growled, driving slowly until he found a parking spot that was far enough away from other cars to discourage conversation with other sellers. Dotty flew out of the car before he had even turned off the motor. She stood by the door, smoothing her dress over her hips. Canny climbed out and sagged against her. Before they left, Wallace made Dotty promise she wouldn't let Canny eat a lot of junk.

"She'll get sick if you do," he called after them. " 'Specially fried dough. . . ."

He watched them head toward the midway, where the Ferris wheel spun like fiery spokes in the starless night. Next to Dotty, Canny looked like a little hobo. She had on rubber sandals, a grubby pink windbreaker with the hood half torn off, and bright orange shorts, so big they flapped like a skirt around her skinny knees. Everything she wore, he had scrounged from Salvation Army and GoodWill bins. He took off his hat and scratched his head. Just then, Canny looked back and waved and before he could lift his hand, they had disappeared.

He lugged two boxes from the trunk and set their contents out for display on the warm dusty hood. Most of it was junk, some plaster figurines ready for painting, a few eight-track tapes of Christmas music, a half dozen green plastic pots for plants, a rusty tackle box, and a dozen wooden coat hangers. His big item tonight would be the eight cans of HiGrade motor oil he'd clipped at their last gas stop. He took out his white stickers and labeled each can a dollar. The other items already had prices on them from previous flea markets. Some had been marked down so many times, they bore four or five stickers.

It was long past midnight, and Wallace's only sale had been the eight cans of oil two hours ago. Since then no one had even stopped to browse.

In the distance, the midway had paled and the night drew closer and thickened. The rides seemed to turn and spin slower and slower and even the barkers' cries sounded thin and plaintive with fatigue. Close by the side of the car stood Wallace, his quick, furtive eyes scanning the rows of parked cars that flanked the wide descent to the midway. Everywhere he looked, he thought he saw Hyacinth, whose apparition lurked always on the cloudy peripheries of his vision and now, in easy step with his guilt and his dread, had assumed the gaits and distant images of policemen and prowling dogs and drug-swaggering thugs and even an old man, drunk and muttering curses as he staggered past.

The hair on the back of his neck bristled. It was always this way when he had been alone too long. Without Dotty and Canny he felt weak and afraid. He felt his knees grow stiff and bloodless as the aloneness and suspicion and dread began to clash in his head like shrill discordant songs that left no room for his own thoughts. Rooted here, he could not move. Dotty inhabited his brain, and the child, his heart, and if they did not return, he knew he might stand here forever.

On either side of him, the two sleepy-eyed vendors were folding up their display tables and returning their unsold goods to their cars.

"Slow tonight," one called to the other.

"Dead's more like it," snorted the man on Wallace's left. Up to now he had ignored their chatter. Their words came into his aloneness as strange and alien sounds to which he could affix no images.

Earlier, the two vendors had seen the big-breasted young woman alight from the rust-savaged car, her soft hips churning eagerly against her clinging dress, and after her, the stuporous, sleep-dredged ghost of a child with strawy matted hair and dirty limbs. They must have noticed the way the little man stared after them, his gaze both ardent and fearful, the whisker-smudged hollows of his face darkening as the woman and the child drew farther away. And then at the moment of their eclipse in the distant crowds, both men must have witnessed the quick, violent, yet strangely motionless seizure that had clutched him, pressing him against the car, where he stood now, still and depthless as a shadow.

They glanced at him and then with shrugs that came almost in unison, they gathered up the last of their merchandise—peacock fans and velvet paintings of Elvis Presley and Jesus Christ and John F. Kennedy. The man on Wallace's left slammed his trunk shut and, turning, called out to Wallace, "Hey, you been all them places?" He gestured toward the bumper stickers and decals.

In one quick, fluid motion, Wallace had darted around the car, had dropped to his knees, and then, on his back, had slithered headfirst under the car. With only his feet protruding, he banged loudly on the tailpipe with a rock. If the man said more, Wallace heard nothing, so frantic was his commotion of pretended repair.

Just then, he felt something grab his ankle. His eyes jerked the length of the car's pitted underbelly to the pale little face peering back at him.

"Poppy!" Canny gasped.

He slid out from under the car, relieved that the two men had already left. Canny's eyes were raw and her nose was running.

"Where you been, dammit?" he grumbled, turning his stiff and clotted handkerchief until he found a clean spot for her. "Where's your Momma?" he asked, looking toward the midway while Canny blew her nose.

"I couldn't find the car, Poppy," she said, taking a deep, sniffling breath. "I was in the wrong lot."

He stood on his tiptoes and peered over the top of the car. "Which way she coming? I don't see her."

"She said to tell you she'll be here in a while," Canny blurted, wincing up at him. "She said to just wait."

"But it's almost two-thirty!" he groaned.

"It's not my fault," Canny protested, her face puckered with tears. "She wouldn't come."

"Well you shoulda stayed with her then! What if she takes off?" he cried, shifting his weight from foot to foot as if trying to propel himself toward the midway.

"She wouldn't let me!" Canny said. "She made me go!"

"Well you shouldn'ta listened to her, dammit! You know that!" he said, his feet shifting frantically.

"But the man . . ." Canny stammered. "He kept . . ." She hung her head and clasped her arms over her thin chest and shrugged miserably. Wallace stood perfectly still now. He looked at Canny, but with his head half-turned and his eyes heavy and tired. His hands hung at his sides. A dusty little breeze whipped up and snapped his baggy trousers back and forth against his legs.

"We had slush and fried dough," Canny was saying. "And then we went on the Wonder Whip and then after, we went on the Leaping Lizard. It kinda wiggled fast like this," she illustrated with her hand. "Then it went, woop! Like this," she said, snapping her hand up in the air, "then down. And that's when I threw up. On one of the downs. So I told Momma I was too sick to go on any more rides and she felt real bad. 'Specially 'cause of the Black Hole. It has shooting stars and space music so we watched for a while and Momma kept teasing me to try it. She said it's built special, the way they do space ships for astronauts, and she said how they never get space sick now, do they—so acourse, I wouldn't get sick. . . ." She shrugged again, only this time it was more like a shiver. Her voice grew shrill. "Then these two guys in cowboy hats came up the ramp. And Momma was starting to get mad at me. She kept saying how I promised her all day I'd go on the rides and how I was always breaking promises and it wasn't fair. Then one of the guys laughed and he said Momma sounded like the little girl and I sounded like the mother." Canny laughed uneasily. "And Momma said, 'Well, that's kinda how it goes.' And then one of the guys said he'd do the Black Hole with Momma and I could stand and wait with his friend on the ramp. So I did and then when they came out, the guy with me went in with Momma and the first guy stayed. He put me up on the railing and he put his hand someplace, Poppy. . . ." She looked at him, but he didn't understand.

Dotty wasn't at the Black Hole or on the Ferris wheel or, as far as Wallace could see, on any of the rides. Canny was tired of walking and being jostled by the crowds. "Let's just wait in the car," she begged. "I wanna sleep, Poppy, please." As they came down the midway a second time, she staggered against him and moaned. Her cheeks and her eyes were fiery red and her fore-head burned against his hand. A woman passing by frowned and shook her head disgustedly.

"I'm so tired," Canny said weakly, sagging against him as he peered into the Munich Beer Garden, which was a raised con-crete pavilion over the midway. From here, all Wallace could see were tables and chairs and a bramble of sprawled legs and tapping feet. Country music twanged from the loudspeakers.

Canny followed him up the stairs and they made their way through the smoky haze and the jangle of drunken voices to the farthest corner, where Dotty sat between two men, both wearing cowboy hats. One of the men had his arm around her, his thick hand clamped like a hairy paw over her soft belly. The second man had the clay-colored, blunt features of an Indian. He stared blankly into his beer mug as Dotty drew his friend's chin close and brushed her pouty lips over his.

" 'Scuse me . . . 'scuse me . . . ," Wallace muttered past each table with Canny close at his heels. When he got to the table, his head hung and his voice could barely be heard. "We gotta go. . . ."

Dotty smiled and her smudged eyes closed heavily as she laid her head back on the man's shoulder.

Wallace cleared his throat and swallowed hard. "Canny's sick," he said, trying to say it just to her.

"Leave me alone," Dotty groaned. The man's hand lifted from her middle and she pushed it back and patted it.

The Indian grinned. His dark, flat eyes moved eagerly between his friend and Wallace.

"C'mon, Dotty," Wallace said softly.

"Can we go now, Momma?" Canny whined, rubbing her eyes.

"C'mere, kid," the Indian said, holding out his arms. Canny pressed in close to Wallace.

"For chrissakes, get her outta here," Dotty said through clenched teeth. The couples at the next table had turned to watch.

"Who's that?" asked the man with Dotty. He nuzzled his face in her hair and she giggled and whispered something in his ear that made him laugh.

"We gotta go now," Wallace said, snatching Dotty's purse from the table. Her hands flew for it and so did those of the man next to her.

"Drop it," the man snarled, pointing his finger like a gun. Dotty laughed nervously. The Indian laughed too. The man with Dotty stood up then and grabbed across the rickety table for Wallace's arm. The Indian tittered as the man yanked Wallace, half dragging him over the table.

"Leave him alone!" Canny screeched. All around them, heads turned, and for a second the only sound was Canny's voice. "You fat bastard—leave him alone! Let goa him!" She picked up a mug and cracked it across the man's temple. Moaning, he released Wallace and sagged into the chair. Blood soaked through the fuzzy white rim of his hat and his chin bobbed on his chest. "Momma!" Canny screamed in terror as the man tried to stand, then toppled across the table, splitting it in two. The glass pitcher and mugs exploded on the cement floor. Women screamed and jumped up as the Indian squatted over his groaning friend.

———

For the first hour, Dotty and Canny both wept while he drove blindly. The road signs meant nothing. All he cared about was a lot of distance between them and the Hortonville police. Dotty huddled by the door with her face buried in her hands.

"Is he dead?" Canny sobbed from the back seat.

"Probably!" Dotty gasped.

"What's gonna happen?" Canny cried. "What'll the cops do?"

"Shoot you!" Dotty screamed.

"Drive fast!" Canny screeched, throwing her arms around Wallace's neck.

When they had gone about a hundred miles, Wallace stopped at an all-night gas station and bought a bag of ice, which he wrapped in a towel and set against Canny's feverish head. She was exhausted. All she could drink of the Coke he bought were a few sips with her aspirin.

"Here," he coaxed, nudging the can at her. "Have some more." She didn't answer. Her sleeping face glistened with sweat.

Dotty leaned forward and pulled her dress over her head. "You know the guy she hit?" she said, slowly peeling the bandage strips from each nipple. "He was gonna get me a screen test. He said he knew somebody." She threw the bandages out the window and sighed. "The thing I been dreaming of all my life and that brat splits his head open."

"Here," he said, holding out a blanket to her. She ignored it and started crying all over again. "Nothing goes right for me, Aubie. Nothing. . . ."

Two cars pulled off the highway and up to the gas pumps.

"Cover up!" he said, turning the key with his foot on the gas, wincing as he drove onto the highway with Dotty's raging voice streaming out the window like a scarf.

"She's a noose around my neck! A goddamn fuckin' noose and it's not fair! I'm so sick of this, so goddamn, sonofamotherfuckin' sick of this! I gotta have some fun, Aubie, or I'm gonna go crazy! You hear me?" she screamed, pummeling the dashboard with both fists. "I gotta have some fun, goddammit! I can't take this anymore. I can't! I can't! I can't. . . ."

"Stop it!" he begged. "You stop it now!"

"I'll stop it!" she screeched, lunging for the wheel and turning it so that the car lurched into the next lane. "I'll stop the whole goddamn thing . . . this whole goddamn miserable life. . . ."

He pushed her hand away and a strangled cry caught in his throat. It made him dizzy to think that if a car had been coming, that would have been the end. He glanced back at Canny. She was still sleeping.

Dotty sat staring straight ahead in a cold-eyed silence with her arms folded over her bare chest. Over the years he had gotten used to her tantrums. It was her hateful, icy silences that frightened him most of all. In these, she was most like Hyacinth, who had once gone seven weeks and six days without one single word to him, or even about him, she later admitted quite proudly.

Dotty had begun to speak now in a soft, wistful tone that brushed his flesh with shivers. Just like that, she could go from crazy to calm, from hateful to sweet, from trying to kill them to snuggling so close her breast slung over his arm.

"It'd be easy, Aubie," she was saying, whispering, her mouth fluttering at his ear like a moth.

His brain felt jumbled and bruised. She was talking about it again; the same thing she always talked about lately.

" 'Member the day we got her and you put a note on her in the gas station?" She nudged him. " 'Member?"

He nodded stiffly.

"Well, we could still do that. Only I was thinking . . . we could leave her at a church. A church'd be . . ."

"Shh!"

"She's sleeping." Dotty continued. "A church'd be perfect. We could leave her with a note telling about her and then we could head for Hollywood, Aubie!" She hugged his arm between her breasts. "Think of it! Just you and me!" She sat forward and pointed to the sign ahead that marked the next exit as INTERSTATE 1, NORTH. "Take that one!"

A truck drew alongside and honked its horn.

"Put a shirt on!" Wallace called over the rumble of the truck, whose driver grinned down in disbelief.

"Turn and I will!" Dotty said, lacing her fingers behind her head and stretching back.

When he turned onto the ramp, she slipped her tee shirt over her head and then she threw her arms around his neck and squealed happily.

NEW YORK   NEW ENGLAND   ALL POINTS NORTH

Sweat dripped down his sides. He couldn't think straight. His foot barely touched the gas and yet the car flew along. Dotty snored softly against his shoulder. Her hair tickled his nose. Struggling against sleep, he held his eyes as wide as they would open. He sat up very straight behind the wheel and the queerest thought came to him. He thought, I could close my eyes right now and take my hands off the wheel and my foot off the gas and we'd still get there, no matter what.

4

Morning had slipped into his consciousness. The new sun spread in the gray sky, like a watery egg.

"How's it feel?" Dotty was asking.

"What's that?"

"To be so far up north?"

"I dunno. I ain't been thinking much," he said gruffly.

She laughed. "Well it feels good to me." She took a deep breath out the window. "Smells good too! Smells like clothes on the line, clean and stiff."

In the back seat, Canny stirred. "Momma?" she called in a far-off, panicky voice.

Dotty knelt on the seat and pulled the little girl over into her lap. "Poor kid, you're all wet," she sighed, peeling off Canny's soggy jacket.

"The ice melted," Canny said apologetically.

"Her fever's broke," Dotty said laying her cheek on Canny's matted head. Canny's hand went to the nape of Dotty's neck, to the soft little hairs she liked to stroke through her fingers.

"You're a good kid, you know that?" Dotty said hoarsely. Canny curled her grimy legs under her and nestled in the curve of Dotty's arms. "You were such a good baby," Dotty said with a sigh.

"Did I cry a lot?" Canny asked.

Dotty laughed. "Just when you looked at your Poppy." She laughed again.

"What did I look like?" Canny purred.

"You were the most beautiful baby I ever saw. You had big blue-blue eyes and one of them little button noses and your mouth was just like a juicy, little heart. And your hair was all soft and curly and so light in the summer it was almost white. Everywhere we went people'd say how you oughta be in TV commercials you were so pretty."

"Am I still pretty?" Canny asked hopefully, tilting her head back and looking up at Dotty.

Dotty studied her a minute. "Well I'd say you're a different kinda pretty now."

"Am I pretty as you?" Canny's voice shrank and she seemed to wince.

"Course you are!" said Dotty.

"Will I look like you when I grow up?" Canny asked.

"You'll look like you," Dotty laughed.

Canny frowned. "But I wanna look like you, Momma."

Wallace cleared his throat. Don't, he thought. Don't say nothin'. Don't tell her. . . .

"You don't wanna look like me, babe," Dotty sighed bitterly. "Jesus, I don't even look like me anymore."

He was surprised when Dotty said they were in New Jersey. She called out the different license plates. Besides all the New Jerseys and New Yorks, she had seen two Maines and a Connecticut.

"Look," she said, nudging him excitedly, "there's a Vermont!"

He stared straight ahead. What if it was *her*? What if he looked up and there *she* was, after all this time, right in the next lane, and no matter how fast he drove or where he turned, she kept right alongside him. His eyes blurred with the thought of her granite profile traveling in the next lane from state to state, from coast to coast. . . .

He veered sharply off the highway and onto a back road, not stopping until he came to a small grocery store. He gave Canny two dollars and told her to buy three doughnuts and two milks. A truck pulled in behind them. The driver followed Canny through the lot and held the door open for her.

"I'll be right back," Dotty said. "I feel like stretching my legs."

He grabbed her wrist before she could open the door. "We gotta talk, Dot, before Canny gets back."

"About what?"

" 'bout bringing her back."

"What about it?" she said, raising her eyes coolly to his. He looked away. He wasn't sure what he wanted to say. "Well?" she said.

He thought a minute. "What's the note gonna say?"

She shrugged. "Just that we'd like her brought back to her family, I guess."

"Who's gonna do that?"

"The people that find her!" She was getting exasperated.

"But I thought you forgot the town."

"Well if I say Massachusetts, people'll know. They can figure it out anyway." She looked at him. "Unless they're retards or something."

Canny ran up to the car then and handed Dotty her milk and the doughnuts. When she started to open the door, Wallace shook his head. "Your Momma and me're talking," he said. "It's private."

"I won't listen," Canny said.

"You wait out there," he said. "Go sit on the hill up there and have your doughnut."

"No! The grass is all wet! And it's cold, Poppy," she whined, balancing the milk carton under her chin so she could open the door.

He reached back and pulled it closed. She glared at him.

"Up there," he said, pointing to the grassy knoll over the road. He watched her scamper up the hill and sit down facing the car.

"Well?" Dotty asked, amused that he'd been so hard on Canny. "What else you wanna know?"

His eyes were on the solemn little girl, shivering as she bit into her doughnut. "What if the people that find her don't want to bring her all that way home?" He looked at Dotty. "What if they just keep her?" he asked, his voice thinning with alarm.

Dotty was opening her milk carton. She stuck in a straw. "Maybe they'll be real nice people," she said between sips. "A really nice family with kids and a dog and a nice house." She bit into the doughnut. A blister of crumbs grew in the corner of her mouth.

"But what if they ain't? What if they don't be nice and they get sick of her and jest drop her off sometime by the road and some other people find her and then it turns out they don't like her neither and she keeps getting dropped off and picked up. . . ." His eyes widened with fright. "And by that time, the note's all dirty, so nobody can read it, or mebbe it's even lost. . . ."

"How 'bout if I drop you off with her then, Aubie? Then every time the two of you get picked up and dropped off, you can hold the note." She tilted the carton and slurped out the last of the milk. "And I'll even print," she added scornfully. "Nice big letters so you can read it."

He thought this over, then shook his head. "That won't work," he said somberly. "Nobody'll want a growed man in their family."

Dotty coughed on the milk and choked so that her eyes teared and milky phlegm leaked from her nostrils.

"And what if the car broke down?" he went on. "What would you do then? How 'bout if we jest go to Hollywood, us three? I could mebbe do markets out there and we could get us a real nice place and then you could get in a movie and have diamonds and fur coats and mebbe out there, they don't need birth certificates to get in school and I'd get Canny one of them girlie lunch boxes she's been wanting and a thermos to match—like Cinnerella mebbe, and ever' morning I'd do her lunch up in them little baggy bags and cross her at the corner on them yellow cross lines. . . ."

He blinked. Dotty was running down the road. He hadn't even seen her leave the car. "Canny," he called, rolling along the breakdown lane with the door still open. "Get in! Quick!" Canny had already started down the hill. She scrambled inside and pulled the door shut. A few hundred feet ahead, Dotty trotted backward with her thumb out. "Motherfucker!" she screamed at every car that whizzed past.

Wallace pulled alongside, keeping a slow pace with her frantic backward gait.

"Get the hell outta here!" she screamed at them.

"Momma!" Canny called out to her. Suddenly she stood up on the seat with her torso out the window and clamped her arms around Dotty's neck.

"Little bastard!" Dotty screamed, trying to pull her off. "Lemme go—just lemme go . . . please. . . ."

Canny had to wait outside the car again. This time she stood close by Wallace's door holding on to the handle. The windows were closed and starting to steam with Dotty's tears. She had gotten him to promise they would drive straight on through to Massachusetts and drop Canny off at the first church they came to.

"Then what?" she sobbed.

"Then we turn around and head on out to Hollywood," he repeated softly. Canny was tapping on the window. "You said a minute," she reminded them.

"You promise?" Dotty asked with a teary gasp.

He nodded. Canny had begun to bang on the window. "Please, Poppy," she called with her face pressed to the glass.

"I promise," he said.

"You swear to it? You swear on your wife's life?"

"I swear."

"That's too easy," Dotty said, blowing her nose. "You didn't like her anyway, you said."

"She din' like me's what I said." He reached back and unlocked the door for Canny. "Here," he said, passing back a napkin. "You got doughnut sugar on your face."

Canny scrubbed her mouth and cheeks. She was burning mad, but didn't dare say a word. Whenever Dotty went off the deep end, Canny always knew her place.

"What was her name again?" Dotty was putting on lipstick, blotting it. "I forget."

He pulled into the traffic. "Hyacinth," he said after a minute.

Dotty knelt on the seat and grinned. "Say her last name. I love the way you say it."

"Kluggs," he said with a little wince and she giggled.

"What she look like?"

"Not too much, I guess."

"Tell me!" Dotty squirmed happily. Canny looked from one to the other.

"I dunno. Kinda short." He shrugged. In the mirror, his eyes met Canny's. He knew she was dying to ask who Hyacinth was, but didn't dare break the spell of Dotty's happiness.

"What about her teeth?"

"They was crooked and stuck out," he said softly.

"And how'd she walk? Tell me that."

"She walked pigeon toes. . . ." He looked at her guiltily. "I musta tole you a hunnert times, Dotty."

"Yah, but I like it when you tell me," she said, sitting back and hugging her legs. Her chin rested on her knees, and from this angle she looked like a little girl, younger certainly than the sharp-eyed child behind them. "It's like family I never met. Like she's my long-lost grandma or something and you keep having to tell me so I'll know who everybody is . . . you know what I mean?" Dotty said, dreamily.

"Nope."

5

By noon the pale sun had dissolved in a low gray sky. The windshield pimpled with drizzle and only the wiper on Wallace's side worked. After just a few miles, the car was damp and raw with the cold. The heater hadn't worked in two years.

"Jesus," Dotty said through a shiver. She reached back for a blanket. "I forgot how goddamn cold it gets. And here it is June." She threw the blanket onto the floor. It was wet from the melted ice. In the back seat Canny's teeth started to chatter. They were approaching the Star Bright Motel. Wallace looked questioningly at Dotty. She nodded and he pulled into the parking lot. The little motels were too hard. This one looked just big enough.

"Looks like nobody's checking out," Dotty said.

"Here comes one," Canny said, pointing at a tall, baggy-eyed man in a three-piece suit, coming out the front door.

"No suitcases," Wallace muttered. "Probably staying."

"All I can do's try," Dotty sighed, getting out of the car. She headed toward the man as he set his briefcase down and fumbled through his pockets for his keys.

"Good morning," Dotty called brightly. "Hope you had a good stay!"

"Very nice," the man muttered blearily.

"Well, I better get in there and get your room all fixed up nice for when you get back," she said with a little wave. The man opened the car door. "I checked out," he said.

"Aw, that's too bad," she said, hugging her arms in the chill. "What room'd ya have?"

"Two-twelve," the man said.

"Oh yah! You're Mr. Jones!" she called.

"Carleton," the man called back, then ducked into his car just as the drizzle turned into a downpour.

Wallace laid his head back on the seat and a little smile worked at his mouth. Dotty would tell the desk clerk that she was joining her husband, Mr. Carleton who had decided to keep room two-twelve another day. If all went well and it usually did, the clerk would give her the key, and as soon as she was in the room she'd take a shower. If the room had an outside entrance and no one was around, she'd clear out as much as she could—glasses and soap, the little bottles of shampoo, lotion, and mouthwash for herself and Canny; and to sell at their flea markets: towels, bathmats, blankets, sheets, pillows, bedspreads, and sometimes even the pictures off the walls, the shades off the lamps, and, once when the pills had made her most fearless, the curtains right out of the window. Wallace chuckled softly and closed his eyes.

"Poppy?" Canny said from the back seat. "You know that guy last night? The one I hit?"

"Yup," he murmured fuzzily, his arms and legs already weightless with sleep.

"Think he's dead?"

"Nope."

"You sure?" Her voice seemed distant and fading.

"Yup," he mumbled, his head bobbing forward with a snore.

"He touched a dirty place, Poppy."

Wallace's head shot up. "Mebbe he had to go to the bathroom," he said uncomfortably. Lately Canny was wanting to know about the birds and bees. But she never asked Dotty.

Always him. She was watching him through the mirror. Her mouth twitched and she looked away. "I mean my dirty place," she said miserably. He didn't know what to say. He leaned forward and scrubbed a hole through the steam on the window. He scratched his chest. He felt grubby all over. He lifted his arm and sniffed. His shirt stank of sweat. "Dammit," he muttered. "She's taking too long."

Canny leaned over the seat. She smelled too, rancid and stale. A necklace of grime circled her throat. Her hands were dirty, the chewed nails caked with brown.

"It wasn't my fault, Poppy. . . ."

"I know."

"It hurt!"

"Don't!" he choked.

"I hit his hand away."

"Don't," he warned. He shook his head and rubbed his stubbly jaw. His teeth ached, the few he had left. "It ain't nice to talk about," he said hoarsely. He was too ashamed to look at her. Except for the rain that drummed like hollow fingers on the roof, the car was quiet and cold as a tomb.

Sometimes he felt like a hundred-year-old man, instead of fifty-two or -three, whatever, he'd lost track. Sometimes he was scared so crazy of dying just the word could make him shiver all over. Then other times like now, this funny feeling swelled over him like a glassy bubble and everything that happened was really happening to someone else. And it was all right, perfectly all right. Nothing hurt. Nothing mattered. The boys used to wake up screaming in the night, clutching his waist and babbling on about ghosts. Dead men only die but one time, Hyacinth used to say from the dark of her bed, like a ghost herself, like something that was waiting to be joined in death.

"Somebody's coming," he said, tensing forward as the motel door opened onto a woman in black pants and a violet jacket, and then he realized it was Dotty wearing clothes he had never seen before. Her hair swung in wet braids as she ran through the parking lot, carrying a red plaid suitcase. She gestured angrily toward the car. In a motion, he turned the key and played the gas, inching toward her, his eyes keen on the motel door.

"Get the door!" he hollered to Canny, who slid into the front, opened the door, then slithered into the back again as Dotty pushed the suitcase onto the seat and scrambled in after it, laughing so hard it took twenty miles to tell the story.

After her shower in Mr. Carleton's room, she had heard voices in the hall. The husband and wife from two-ten were arguing about where they should leave their luggage while they went down to lunch. The wife wanted to put it in the car. The husband said she was a pain in the ass. Why should he get soaked bringing it out to the car when the desk would send someone up. So off they went, and Dotty opened the door and slipped the biggest bag into two-twelve. She emptied the suitcase, keeping only the outfit she had on. The rest of the clothes were shitbags, she said. Then she took the blankets off Mr. Carleton's bed, and some clean towels, and "this," she laughed, unzipping the suitcase. She held up a half-empty quart of Scotch. "Compliments of Mr. Carleton," she laughed, slipping the bottle under the seat. She passed a blanket back to Canny and spread one over her own legs.

Ten bucks easy, Wallace thought, eyeing the suitcase. Luggage went fast at flea markets.

"I always wanted a real nice suitcase," Dotty said. "Up there," she pointed suddenly ahead. "That's the exit we want."

"Where we going?" Canny asked as the old car groaned onto the ramp.

"Just going," Dotty sighed and closed her eyes.

"That's what you always say," Canny said.

"I know," Dotty sighed again.

"You love me, Momma?"

"Course I do," Dotty said sleepily.

The sign said WELCOME TO MASSACHUSETTS.

The rain had stopped and the sun burned its way through the racing clouds, but the air was still tight with cold. They got off the highway in Worcester and stopped at a drugstore, where Dotty bought a pad of paper and some envelopes. Their next stop was a gas station so they could get Canny cleaned up.

Wallace brought the ladies' room key back to the car.

"Get the men's," Dotty said, nibbling the end of the pen. "I gotta write this and I need quiet." She looked up. "What's the date?"

"June something," he said.

"Jesus, you're a big help."

The stink in the men's room was so bad he had to leave the door open. He plugged the sink with a wad of paper towels and made Canny soak her hands while he scrubbed her face and her neck with one of the motel towels. Then he held her over the sink so she could dangle her feet in the water, which was a puddle of black when they were done. As he rubbed her legs with the dry end of the towel, men's voices rose from the office. Canny was trying to tell him something. She kept tugging on his shirt. Two cars had pulled up to the pumps; their exhaust streamed past the door. Dotty was still writing the letter. He patted the towel carefully over the thick scab on Canny's knee. He peered closer; part of the scab was red and edged with pus. By tomorrow the whole knee would probably be infected.

"Poppy! Poppy!"

By tomorrow, she'd be somebody else's worry. Somebody else would have to tend to it.

She poked his shoulder. Don't, he almost said. Don't talk. Don't make me think. Can't think. Don't wanna hear nothin' or say nothin'. Just do what's gotta be done; what should've been done a long time before this, before his heart got so . . . so tied up in hers.

"How 'bout my hair?" she was saying.

"Sink's too little," he said hoarsely, taking his comb to the snarls in her hair. Some of them were as big as eggs.

"Ow!" she yelped, as he began to pry the biggest snarl apart with his fingers. Tears stood in her eyes. "Poppy," she said, as he bent closer to work out the next snarl. "I think I got bugs again."

He moved her into the light of the doorway and parted her hair to the crusty scalp. Holding her breath, she bowed her head.

"Don't see any," he muttered, parting strand after strand. She sighed with relief. "Any nits?"

"Nope." He combed her hair back into place, arranging the top layer as best he could to cover up the rest of the snarls. He balled up the towel and hurried back to the car. Dotty licked the envelope and laid it on the dashboard and winked at him. He sat behind the wheel, hesitating before he turned the key. He had that empty feeling he got whenever they moved out of a place—like he was forgetting something. Something vital. Some part of himself. The motor turned sluggishly. As he drove, the wheel vibrated under his white knuckles. His arms felt numb. Don't talk. Don't think. Their voices fluttered against his locked stare.

"Can I sit up front now that I'm washed?"

"In a while."

"I'm hungry."

"You just ate!"

"You made me eat too fast."

"Turn here—sit down, Canny."

"You mad at me, Momma?"

"Course not; try that left up there. Jesus, Canny! You're hanging all over me!"

"We looking for a place? 'Cause there's a sign! See!"

"Shut up, Canny!"

"I was just tryna help!"

"Well don't! Right there! Right! Jesus Christ, will you stop!" Dotty was screaming. The veins in her neck swelled like worms.

He jammed on the brake.

"It's a church!" Canny cried happily. She had been after them for a long time to bring her to church. She had never been before.

Dotty was explaining to her now that they couldn't go in with her. She had to do this alone. It was very important. Wallace stared straight ahead as the door opened. From the corner of his eye, he saw her get out of the car. She was so little. In the wind, her hair lifted stiffly like a lifeless wig. He knew if he looked close he'd see goose bumps on her legs. He pulled his cap close over his eyes.

"You just wait inside and pretty soon, somebody'll come, and you give him the letter," Dotty was explaining.

"But why?" asked Canny, poking her head in Wallace's window.

"So Poppy can get a job," Dotty said, her voice nettling impatiently.

He stiffened as they talked past him.

"But why can't Poppy do it?" Canny wanted to know.

"'Cause he's too damn bashful. You know that," Dotty said. Canny looked down at the envelope she held. "What's the job?"

"Cleaning the goddamn church, Canny! Now get on up there!"

"You gonna wait?"

Dotty rolled her eyes. "Course we're gonna wait. Now hurry up before somebody else gets the goddamn job!"

Canny leaned on the window well and whispered in Wallace's ear. "Can I help you do the cleaning, Poppy?"

He nodded and swallowed hard. Dotty squirmed on the seat. "Will you hurry up!"

They watched Canny run toward the wide granite steps that led up a steep little hill to the dark stone church. "Get ready," Dotty hissed. "Minute she's inside, go." Her leg stretched apprehensively.

"What's in the note?" he hissed back.

Dotty's eyes moved up the steps after Canny. She wet her lips nervously. "Just that it was a town in Massachusetts and it was five years ago and the house had a big round porch and how we're sorry and we don't want any trouble."

On the top step, Canny looked back and waved the envelope at them. She smiled.

Dotty waved back and drew in her breath. "Get set," she said, her face blank.

He had seen Canny step up to the wide oak door and now he closed his eyes and shuddered as a cry rumbled through his chest and into his throat, a wordless sob of such intensity, such terrible throbbing pain, that he thought he was dying, so certain was he that some vital pumping organ had just been torn from its cavity, bloodied, and shredded.

"Shit!" Dotty groaned, leaning over him with her elbow jabbing his crotch. "Pull harder," she called out the window.

"It's locked!" Canny shouted down to them.

"Dammit!" Dotty yelled. "Pull with both hands. Pull harder!" Her head jerked in a vicious nod. "Harder! You can do it!"

"I can't!" Canny called. "It won't open."

"Go!" Dotty said, easing over on her own side. She sat perfectly still. "Go!" At first he thought she was talking to Canny, until she dug her purple nails into his wrist. "Go! Now, dammit! Just go!"

He opened his eyes and looked at her. The sob was deep in his skull. He couldn't think. He wasn't even sure who this woman was, yelling at him, shaking his arm, her face long and wavy like a face in a fun-house mirror.

"Don't just sit there looking at me," she groaned. "Let's go! This is our chance!" She banged her fist down on the dashboard. "Start the fuckin' car!"

Canny had started hesitantly down the steps. She clung to the wrought-iron railing and kept looking back over her shoulder. Just then an elderly priest in a long black cassock and a soft black hat came around the corner of the church. With his hands clasped behind his back and his eyes downcast, his gait was measured and meditative. He had not yet seen the little girl.

"Hey mister!" Canny hollered, waving the envelope as she bounded back up the steps.

"Shit," Dotty murmured, as Canny crossed over the lawn toward the priest and handed him the envelope. Canny gestured anxiously toward the church and then down at the car. The priest bent low and smiled. His expression sobered as he glanced between the little girl and the battered car below. He stood up and turned over the envelope. Again, he looked down at them.

"Don't just sit there," Dotty begged. "Do something!" He smiled miserably. Tears ran down his cheeks. He held his hand to his mouth and sobbed.

"You're gonna pay for this, you stupid little chicken prick!" she spat. She jumped out of the car and hurried up the steps.

Wallace tilted his head curiously at her cool, easy strut and the way her hand met Canny's head, like it belonged there, like nothing on God's earth could possibly be wrong.

The priest nodded as she spoke; then he patted Canny's head and he laughed. Dotty was also laughing, laughing and waving goodbye with one arm on Canny's shoulder, steering her back to the car.

Dotty opened the door and threw the envelope onto the seat. "Thanks anyway," she called over the roof of the car. The priest waved. Canny got in and sat close behind Wallace. "You shouldn't have changed your mind, Poppy. He was all set to hire you." She laughed and tweaked his ear. "I told him how we were a disetvanaged family and that we'd do any kinda work to stay off the county." She winked at him in the mirror and he tried to smile. But all that came was a twitch.

"Start the car!" Dotty ordered as she shredded the envelope. "What else did you tell him?" she asked Canny in a wire-tight voice when they were a block past the church.

"He asked me where we came from and I said, 'All over,' and he said, 'Everybody comes from some one place,' and I said, 'Not us. We never stay any one place too long, and . . .' "

"You're getting an awful big mouth for such a little girl," Dotty growled. She grabbed Canny's tiny wrist and yanked it over the seat. Her face had drained of color and her lips were gray and thin. "You want to get us killed, dammit?"

"You said Poppy wanted a job!"

"You just keep your mouth shut from now on!" Dotty said, flipping her hand away in disgust.

"What'd I do wrong, Poppy? How come she's mad at me?" Canny lay on the seat and sobbed. "I was just tryna help. . . ."

NORTH, the sign said under thickening clouds.

"Where now?" he asked. She looked at him. "Keep on going," she said, her voice a sheet of ice so thin he dared not test it with even a sigh, much less a question.

Dotty wouldn't speak to him. They were eating pizza in the car. Behind the restaurant was a duck pond. Canny wrapped her pizza crusts in a napkin, then ran down to feed the ducks. "Save me yours," she called back to Dotty, who was still eating. The pizza had been Wallace's idea. That was Dotty's favorite, pepperoni pizza and beer. She was on her second cup now. She tilted her head back against the seat and drained the last of the beer. Without opening her eyes, she flipped the cup out the window, then shivered suddenly with a large fuzzy belch.

"Want some more?" he asked in a high voice.

She shook her head from side to side against the seat and belched again. She sniffled and rubbed her nose. Wallace looked to see if she was crying. She opened one eye, then sank against the door.

"I'm sorry," he said. "I got scared."

"Just drop it," she said in that dead tone that always panicked him. "Just forget the whole thing."

"But . . ."

"But nothin'." She sat up and started clearing the dashboard. She flipped the pizza crusts into the barrel, then glanced down at Canny with a little smirk.

"Whatcha wanna do now?" he asked.

With both hands she kneaded her waist. "I'll tell you what I don't want to do," she sighed, arching her back. "I don't want to have to sleep in this shitbox one more night."

"We could find a place," he said hopefully. "Mebbe just for a coupla nights till . . ."

"No, Aubie," she said firmly. "All I want's a motel and one good night's sleep." She looked toward the edge of the pond where Canny knelt in a swarm of quacking ducks. "And after that, you're on your own. You and her." She drew in her breath. "I'm splitting, Aubie."

He stared at her. His mouth fell open and he nodded as he tried to expel the words. "I . . . I . . ." He shook his head and grunted with frustration.

"Shit!" she groaned. "You make me feel so damn guilty, Aubie."

"I'm sorry," he said.

"You don't get it, do you? Do you?" she demanded.

He nodded. "You're mad at me," he said softly.

"Yah, but you think I'm just a little bullshit, don't you? You don't think I mean a damn word of this, do you?"

He nodded; then, thinking better of it, shook his head vigorously.

"What's that mean?" she asked disgustedly.

He shrugged. She had him all mixed up now. He couldn't tell if she was mad or not. She sounded like she was talking in her sleep.

"All you ever think about's right now," she was saying. "You're just like her down there, just a little kid. You leave everything up to me. Everything. And then when the time comes to do something, you freeze."

He had been fiddling with the button on his shirt. Suddenly he looked up and clenched his fist. "I'll figure something out!" he cried fiercely. "I promise!" His eyes creased to slits and his jaw clamped into the roof of his mouth.

"Aw shit, Aubie," she said, bursting into bitter, teary laughter. "You couldn't figure your way out of a fuckin' phone booth."

6

He'd show her. His plan was to head back south. Being so far north was giving Dotty the jitters. His shoulders hunched over the wheel. He was praying she wouldn't wake up and see how lost they were. As soon as she had fallen asleep, he had gotten off the highway and driven like a madman along what he thought was a southerly route. But all he'd done was snarl himself up in a hopeless circle. Ahead now was a little restaurant under a flashing neon sign that said PONDREST PIZZA. He held his breath as they drove past. No, he assured himself, it couldn't be the same one. Lots of pizza places probably had duck ponds. Hundreds probably.

"Poppy!" warned Canny, for she had seen it too, but the dry red bulge of his eyes through the mirror silenced her.

Dotty's hair fanned over the back of the seat and her eyes were still closed. Her breathing was raspy and troubled as if she might be having a nightmare. Or worse, not really asleep. Just pretending, he thought, glancing at her. Just waiting for another foul-up, so she could ditch them for good.

They were approaching a fork in the road. His mind raced with the engine and his own breathing quickened and his hands could barely turn the wheel they were so slick with sweat. Left or right. Left or right. Right . . . though no sooner had he turned than he had forgotten his way again.

The last strips of twilight sank like cold yellow blades behind the dark pine woods that loomed on both sides of the narrow road. They were passing a boxy little house, its doorway framed with a string of Christmas lights. A few miles after that, on the left, was a tinny, bullet-nosed trailer rooted to the hillside with propane tanks and the metal-runged milk carton that was its front step.

Canny pressed close behind. "We already been by here," she whispered.

Just then Dotty stirred and murmured something. She shifted down on the seat and drew up her knees against the dashboard. "Find one yet?" she yawned.

"Want the radio on?" he asked, turning it on before she could sit up. She reached over and snapped it off, then peered over the dashboard. "Where the hell're you going?"

"There's one!" said Canny, pointing ahead to a hand-lettered cardboard sign that dangled, curled and fading, from a lopsided fence post.

CABIN FOR RENT—BY THE HOUR—THE NIGHT—OR THE WEEK

He turned off the road and bumped along the dirt driveway that looped in front of a starkly weathered farmhouse. The roof sagged between two spiny pine trees like a sodden blanket heavy on a clothesline.

"You gotta be kidding," Dotty said, sitting up and looking around.

"Where's the cabins?" asked Canny.

A dog growled deep in the darkness and then a light came on over the squeaking screen door and a tall, wide-shouldered man stepped onto the porch. He came to the top step, where he stood with his hands on his hips and his head angled away from the glare of their headlights.

"What do you want?" he hollered, in more of a challenge than a question.

A big red dog crawled out from under the porch and began

frantically to circle the car. Strings of drool leaked from its jaw.

"I don't like it here," Canny whispered between them.

"You gonna answer?" the man hollered, coming down another step.

"Let's go," Wallace said, shifting into reverse.

"You got cabins to let?" Dotty yelled out her window.

"How the hell many you want?" he hollered back.

"Just one," she laughed nervously.

"It's yours," the man called back.

The cabin perched on cinder blocks on the other side of the driveway, opposite the house. The steps they climbed were also cinder blocks, mortarless and loose underfoot. As the man forced open the door a fetid sourness bellied past them into the night air.

"For five bucks you can't go wrong," said the man, hopefully. He switched on the dangling overhead bulb, which was the long room's only light, filmy and stark. Wallace squinted in the sudden glare. The room contained two narrow iron beds, their rust-webbed mattresses seeming to writhe beneath the swaying glare of the bulb. Between the beds was a wooden chair, its plank seat split and charred with cigarette burns.

The man pointed to a plastic turquoise curtain that hung in a doorway on the farthest wall. "In there's the can," he said, lifting the curtain. "Don't flush till you leave though. We're on septic."

Wallace nodded grimly, his hand clenched in his pocket. No way would Dotty stay here, he thought.

"When's checkout time?" Dotty said from the doorway. She took a long drag on her cigarette, then exhaled in a smoky sigh. The man turned and grinned at her. "Whenever you want."

"The fuckin' sign didn't say chicken coop, mister." She looked at him. "It said cabin!" She flicked her ashes disgustedly on the floor. The man faced her squarely now. "I'll tell you what," he said, his eyes icy blue, his grin just a twinge. "You make believe it's a real cabin and I'll make believe you're a real polite lady."

Her cigarette fell to the floor and she ground it out slowly, her eyes wide and deliberate on his. Wallace took a step toward the door.

"Give him his lousy five bucks," Dotty said hoarsely.

After the man left, Dotty flopped dejectedly onto the bed. She lay there staring up at the rafters while Wallace and Canny carried in the pillows and blankets and a bag of clothes. He made up the beds as fast as he could. Never had he wanted sleep so badly.

Canny and Dotty lay in the same bed, the springs creaking as Dotty shifted back and forth. Wallace's eyes closed heavily. He was asleep.

"I'll tickle your back," offered Canny through the darkness. Dotty didn't reply.

"You crying, Momma?"

"Go to sleep," Dotty said in a tight voice.

"I love you," Canny said softly.

Hours later, his eyes opened wide and raw in the darkness. Dotty stood in front of the screen door, her arms crossed, her hair loose on her shoulders. She was smoking. She looked toward the house, where a child was crying. The second-floor lights went on and the crying stopped. When the lights went out, Dotty climbed back into bed.

The next morning, the cabin shimmered white with the new sun flooding through the two small windows. Wallace sat up on one elbow and shaded his eyes. Dotty was gone. Only Canny was in the bed, with the blanket over her head. He stepped into his sneakers and hurried to the door, relieved to see the car still there. He shook Canny awake and told her to hurry. "We gotta find Momma before she gets too far!"

Canny dragged the blankets off both beds and staggered down the steps and into the car. Her eyes kept closing.

"Goddamn . . . goddamn," he muttered, starting the car and turning on the loop.

"Hey! Hey, where you going?" a voice called from the house.

"It's Momma!" Canny cried, pointing up at the porch where Dotty stood, waving them back.

The house was small inside, cluttered and airless. The kitchen was the largest room and the most cluttered. Toys lay everywhere; dolls and cut-out books and broken crayons. Next to the big white gas stove was a rusted red play stove, and next to that, a rusted play sink with a sharp dent in the front as if someone had once given it a vicious kick. A wooden rack with stiffly drying white socks stood on the other side of the stove. In the middle of the room was the metal-topped table and four metal chairs. A jar of grape jelly and a smeared knife were on the table, next to a child's blue sneaker. On the floor behind one of the chairs was a toaster, its frayed cord plugged into the kitchen's only outlet. A slice of toast had just popped up, acrid and smoking. A pair of flattened and soiled pink bedroom slippers lay next to the toaster.

From here, Wallace could see into the living room to the long brown couch shored up on tomato cans. A red lamp on a sagging metal TV tray and a large color television set were the only other furnishings. In the window over the couch, a white sheet had been safety-pinned to the shade roll.

"This is Alma Huller," Dotty said. Wallace nodded. The fat woman smiled, exposing two large gray teeth that cut into her lower lip. She wore red striped pajama bottoms and a man's dingy undershirt that strained against her pregnant belly. Wallace forced his eyes onto her face.

"And this here's Krystal," Dotty said. "With a K." The little girl didn't look up. She sat on the floor, eating fistsful of sugar cereal from the box. "She's four," Dotty said. "And over there's Kelly. Kelly's five." Kelly looked up sullenly. She had her mother's limp, thin hair and pasty-white, coarse features. "And this is Kyle," Dotty laughed, patting the woman's belly.

"Or maybe Kristen," Alma said. "With a 'K' acourse."

"I was just telling Alma about the Brandon family that was all Bs," Dotty said. "'Member them, Aubie? That time in the

Keys? Belle and Bobby Brandon? There was Barbie and Bobb-anne and Briget and Babette and Billy-Sue and the boys were Baxter and Brendon and Bart. . . ." Dotty shook her head. "God, they were a cute family. I said to Belle once—she was expecting again—I said, 'Belle, what're you gonna call this one?' and she says, 'Bastard.' And I said, 'Christ, Belle, that's a shitty name to pin on a kid.' And with a straight face, she says, 'I got to. It ain't Bobby's. And besides, that's what I call them all anyways!' "

Alma shook with laughter. The fat on her arms jiggled and her cheeks blotched redder and redder until tears streamed down her face. "You're too much!" she gasped.

"Ready to go?" Wallace asked, fingering the rim of his base-ball cap.

Canny peeked around him at the box of cereal.

"C'mere," Dotty said, holding out her hand to Canny. "C'mere and say hi to Kelly. I was just telling Kelly how lucky she is to have a little sister." Dotty hugged Canny. "I told her how you always wanted a little sister."

Wallace was cleaning out the car. It was noontime and Dotty was still talking to Alma. They sat on the porch steps watching the three little girls play school. Canny was the teacher. Kelly and Krystal sat on wooden boxes Canny had dragged out of the barn. She waved her stick to their singing cadence of the alphabet. When they were done, Canny pointed her stick at the older girl, Kelly. "What's A for?"

Kelly shrugged.

"You know," Canny coaxed. "A big red . . ."

"Apple!" Krystal shouted and Kelly pinched her.

"Very good!" Canny said, clapping her hands. "What's B for?"

"Boobs!" Kelly hollered before her younger sister could an-swer.

On the steps, Alma and Dotty giggled behind their hands.

Canny marched up to the girls. "Miss Kelly, you go sit in the hall now on accounta your dirty mouth!"

Kelly looked around. "There's no hall!"

Canny rolled her eyes. "Make believe there's one. Over there. The cabin steps'll be the hall."

Kelly marched off, momentarily proud to be the outcast. She perched on the cabin steps and threw stones while Canny and Krystal resumed the alphabet names.

"D!" Canny announced. Krystal thought hard. She bit her lip and closed her eyes. Next to the car, Wallace paused. "Dog," he whispered. He and Canny had learned a lot of words from "Sesame Street."

"Canny's smart," Alma said.

Dotty stretched back on the steps. "She's like me—she adjusts good."

"What's adjests?" Alma asked, narrowing her vacuous eyes on the gnat that fed on her arm. She squashed it and licked off the blood.

"Getting along with new people," Dotty explained. "Like how she is now with your girls, playing like they're old friends."

"Kelly don't have any friends," Alma said. "She's too damn mean like her father." Alma sighed. "One of them crazy mean tempers. . . ."

"What's K stand for?" Canny shouted happily. So far Krystal had gotten every letter right. The little girl shook her head. Her older sister snickered.

"That's easy," Canny laughed. She bent over Krystal and lifted her chin. "Same as you," she said kindly. "K stands for . . ."

"Cunt," Kelly shrieked from the steps. "Creepy cow cunt like Krystal!"

"Ma!" Krystal wailed, and Alma waddled off the porch and thumped Kelly's back.

"I hate you!" Kelly screamed and kicked out at her mother, grazing her chest.

"Little shit!" Alma roared with pain. "You son of a bitch,"

she cried, pummeling her fists on the child's bent head. Kelly screamed and swore back at her mother. The big red dog bounded out from the porch steps, barking and snapping at Wallace's heels. Upstairs, a window rattled open and a gunshot whizzed through the treetops. Wallace dropped to his knees and flattened his cheek against the car's hot fender.

"Now shut the hell up," Jiggy Huller warned. He leaned out the window, bare-chested, the gun dangling over the windowsill. Alma's fist slipped from Kelly's arm. Krystal hugged her scratched legs against the wooden box. Canny's face was white with shock. The dog slunk back into the dark hairy weeds under the porch. Wallace winced at the explosion of Dotty's sudden laughter, which beat at the dreadful silence like a blizzard of loosed birds.

The house was hot and sticky. For supper Alma had cooked spaghetti. The dirty dishes were stacked in the sink. Dotty had insisted on washing them, but it was ten o'clock and she and Alma and Jiggy were still sitting around the table. In the living room, Wallace sat on the couch, next to Canny. The two Huller girls had fallen asleep on the floor. The dog sprawled beside them, its muzzle carefully planted at Wallace's feet. Every time he moved, the dog looked up at him.

Wallace's eyes flickered between the television screen and the scene in the kitchen. It was like watching two shows at once; only in one, he knew the star. Her skin glowed with happiness. Talking was good medicine for Dotty, and being the center of attention was all she ever wanted.

"One more," Alma said, going to the refrigerator for a can of beer.

"Listen to her," Huller scoffed. "One more!" He leaned in confidence toward Dotty. But his voice was loud and good-humored. "You're not gonna believe this—but when I first met Alma she was skinnier than you and she couldn't even stand the smell of beer!"

"What'd you expect!" Alma laughed. "I was fifteen years

old!" She stood behind her husband's chair and kneaded the ropy muscles in his shoulders.

Jiggy tilted his head back against her sagging breasts. "Fifteen years old and just as dumb. She thought kissing made babies," he said, with a wink at Dotty.

"I did not!" Alma laid her chin on his head.

"Her father was so glad to get rid of her, he cried the whole wedding day," Jiggy laughed.

"Listen who's talking!" Alma said. "My poor father's heart was broke because of this crazy man I was getting mixed up with!"

"Crazy man?" Jiggy snarled and grabbed her wrist. "You wanna talk crazy man? How 'bout your brother Carl practicing to be a vampire, killing chickens and keeping their blood in the fridge."

Alma looked hurt. "He just did that once. At least he don't start shooting just 'cause his kids are acting up!"

Dotty looked from one to the other.

"I told you," Jiggy warned. "I ain't used to that screaming anymore. And you don't do anything to keep 'em quiet so I can sleep."

The dog's head lifted. The youngest girl cried out in her sleep and coiled closer to her sister on the flat, musty rug.

"Why the hell should I?" blurted Alma, her voice thin and rising and quavering with tears. "So you can sleep all day and chase all night?"

Jiggy reached for her arm and squeezed it close to his clenched jaw. "Fuck off," he growled, his eyes blazing up at her.

She pulled away and started to cry.

Wallace watched curiously as Dotty jumped up with a startled little cry and ran to Alma's side. She moved back and forth between Alma and her husband, bearing messages, whispering in Jiggy's ear, then returning to hug Alma. She led her back to the table.

"The trouble here is," Dotty was saying as she took her seat on the other side of Jiggy, "Alma's the type that speaks her mind and Jiggy's one of them sensitive types."

"Yah, real sensitive," Alma sniffed, popping open her beer.

"No, he is, really," Dotty said. "I can always tell by the hands." She reached for Huller's hand. She brought it close to her face and traced her finger down his palm.

"You read hands?" Alma asked eagerly.

"Palms," Dotty said softly, her head bent. "This here long one's the life line and here's the love line. . . ." Her eyes lifted to Huller's. "Jesus Christ, but it's the biggest one I ever seen!"

Huller grinned sheepishly, his face reddening.

Wallace stood over Dotty's bed. Beside her, Canny was sound asleep. Dotty lay with her arms folded and her eyes closed.

"I don't like them Hullers," he said.

"You don't like anybody," she murmured, turning her back to him.

"When're we going?"

"Shit, Aubie, leave me alone, will ya? I'm beat."

He lay down. He felt good inside. He could tell Dotty had other things on her mind than ditching him and Canny. He smiled. Tomorrow early he'd have the car all packed and ready to roll in case she woke up in the mood to go. If Dotty was happy, then Canny was happy, and if they were happy, then he was safe.

Wallace closed his eyes. He didn't like being the last one awake.

"Canny?" he whispered a few minutes later.

"Jesus Christ! Will you go to sleep?" Dotty groaned.

He began to breathe deeply, forcing himself into a quick, deep sleep.

The mid-morning sun was oven-hot. The car had been packed for hours. Wallace sat on the porch steps. Facing him on the dirt path below was the big red dog. His baleful eyes locked on Wallace's.

Wallace took off his baseball cap and scratched his head. The dog growled. Ever so slowly, he replaced the cap and inched his hand back onto his knee. The growling ceased. Wallace cleared his throat and the dog's flabby wet lips lifted, baring stained and pitted fangs. The little man's eyes widened. He sat perfectly still, frozen.

This morning they had been awakened by Jiggy and Alma Huller yelling at one another. Then the little girls had screamed and Alma screeched and then moaned with pain and the next thing they heard was Huller's pickup truck tearing out of the driveway. Dotty ran across the driveway to the house, wearing only her nightie.

She and Alma were still in the kitchen. There was an angry welt on Alma's cheek and her eyes were red and swollen. Dotty told Canny to keep the girls busy so she could tend to Alma. Canny got their breakfast and then she took them for a walk in the woods.

Wallace exhaled slowly against the burning in his groin. He had to go to the bathroom, but he didn't dare move. Dammit, he thought, if it weren't for the dog, he'd round up Canny and Dotty and take off before Huller got back looking for last night's five bucks.

"It's like we're two different people," Alma was saying from the kitchen.

"That can happen," Dotty said. "Two and a half years is a long time. I had a friend once, Thelma, that got sixty days. Just sixty days. Me and her were the best friends you'd ever want, but when she got out, she was like a whole new person too."

"All we do is fight!" Alma moaned, bursting into tears again. "All the time, over everything."

"Same with me and Thelma! One night she broke a bottle over my head. I saw stars like the real thing."

"It was wonderful his first night home," Alma blubbered. "That's when I got pregnant. But now he don't want anything to do with me."

"What was the fight about?" asked Dotty.

"I asked him who the slut was and he said there weren't none and then I said something real bad and that's when he hit me," Alma bawled.

"What'd you say?"

"I said . . . I said, 'Are you turned queer like them gay boys you told me about in jail?' "

"What was he in for?" Dotty asked.

"He'll get mad if I tell."

"I won't say anything. You know I won't," Dotty insisted.

There was a silence. The dog's tail flicked back and forth, snapping off the hard-packed earth.

"He killed a guy," Alma said, her voice rising warily. "But it was a fair-square fight, so they had to call it manslaughter."

Wallace's knees pinched tightly together and his heart began to pound with the sound of the approaching motor. Huller's truck swerved into the driveway in a storm of spitting stones and dust. The dog leaped to greet him. Huller slammed the truck door and shoved the dog out of his way. His eyes narrowed on Wallace as he stalked up the steps. Then, pausing, he looked back.

"You got that five on you?" he asked coldly.

"Here," Wallace said, thrusting it up to him.

Huller glanced toward the kitchen door and then he sat down next to Wallace. For a time, neither man spoke. Huller pleated and repleated the five-dollar bill. The dog lay up on the porch now, close at his master's back. He smelled like swamp gas, Wallace thought. Black and foul, like rot. Like death.

"Dotty said you move around a lot," Huller said, squinting up into the sun.

Wallace nodded.

"That must be the life," Huller sighed. "No bills. No hassles. Just go where the work is." He gestured bitterly over his shoulder. "And nobody bitching all the time. Just you and your kids." Huller cupped his hand over his mouth and whispered. "Course if it was me, I'da left 'em all behind with the old lady." Then, seeing the confusion on Wallace's face, Huller said quickly,

"Hey, I hope I didn't say anything wrong, Pops. I just thought.
. . . Your wife's not dead, is she?"

"Nope," Wallace said.

"Dotty says you're close to home." Huller looked at him.
"That where you're heading? Back to the wife?"

"'Scuse me," Wallace murmured. He stood and hurried off
the porch steps and into the cabin. He lifted the toilet seat. His
eyes blurred with pain as he stared at the sign tacked to the
wall stud, DON'T FLUSH. A lump rose in his throat. Hyacinth
had put up a sign once. It had been meant for him and the
boys. It said, PUT THE SEAT UP OR USE A TREE.

Wallace flipped the hamburgs. Alma and Jiggy hadn't spoken
a word all day. Dotty had that glassy-eyed look she got whenever
she was soaring toward one of her breakdowns. With her fraz-
zled hair and her trembly, nonstop voice, she reminded him of
a storm-battered bird. Wallace had seen Huller give her two
pills earlier on the porch when Alma was napping.

Barefoot and still in her nightgown, she was all over the
kitchen, opening a can of beer for Huller, running into the front
room to prop up Alma's feet on the hassock, wiping Krystal's
runny nose.

"How 'bout salad?" she called out to Huller as she rummaged
through the refrigerator. It's light glowed through her nightie.
Huller stared at her.

"Scratch the salad," she laughed. "No lettuce. Well, how
'bout some of this then?" she said, laying a saucer of fuzzy green
mold in front of Huller. "Name this mystery dish and it's yours,
mister! Absolutely free of charge!"

Huller shook his head disgustedly and pushed it away. "See
what I have to put up with!" he said gruffly.

"Aw, c'mon, Jig!" She mussed his hair. "It's a joke!"

"Some joke," he pouted.

She leaned over the table and brought her face close to his.
"You got yourself all worked up over nothing," she whispered,
with a glance toward the living room and Alma's lumped form.

"No," Huller said huskily, his eyes meeting her gaze. "Not over nothing."

Wallace turned back to the sputtering hamburgs, his mind made up. They were leaving tonight, no matter what.

After supper, Alma went upstairs to lay down with Krystal, who was complaining of a stomachache. Kelly had been sent up in the middle of supper as punishment for spitting in Krystal's milk. Alma told Dotty to be sure and wake her up if she fell asleep in Krystal's bed.

Wallace waited until Huller went into the bathroom and then he told Dotty that they were leaving tonight. She burst out laughing. "You gotta be kidding!"

"I ain't kidding. We're goin'," he said uneasily.

"Goin' where with eight lousy bucks to our name?" she hissed.

His jaw dropped. "But you got twenty!" He still hadn't told her that he had the unpaid rent money. The minute she found out she'd be pestering him for it.

"I only got eight now." She glanced anxiously toward the sound of flushing water beyond the door. "I had to pay for our meals, didn't I?"

The bathroom door opened and Huller came out, buckling his belt. His eyes were hard and bright. "Something wrong?"

Dotty shrugged. "Poppy's afraid we're overstaying our welcome." She laughed with a nervous glance at Wallace. "He says fish and company stinks after three days."

Huller frowned and put his arm around Wallace's shoulder, leading him to the table. "Fish stinks and this house stinks and right now, I stink—but not you," he said, poking the little man's ribs. He grinned. "Friends don't stink."

The dirty dishes were piled on the stove and in the sink. Alma was still upstairs. Canny had fallen asleep on the couch. Though no one was watching it, the television set was still on; Ed McMahon was introducing Johnny Carson. Wallace sat at the kitchen table, his eyes heavy with sleep.

"So anyways, Poppy's got it down to a real science," Dotty was telling Huller. "He gets a lot of it from dumps and those

GoodWill boxes, but his best stuff comes from garage sales. He waits until five or six on a Saturday night when all them sad sacks are all sunburnt and beat from standing out front of their houses all day and he drives up and tells them he'll be glad to haul off whatever's left they don't want. And nine times outta ten, they not only say yes, but they help him load the car. And the next morning, he's got it all tagged and selling at some flea market. Right, Poppy?''

Wallace didn't bother to nod; they weren't even looking at him. Dotty had just taken two more pills.

Huller shook his head. "I don't think I got the right way with people for that." He looked at Dotty. "I'm not too good at begging or even asking—if you know what I mean."

There was a pause. Under the table, the dog's tail snapped against Wallace's shinbone.

"Well," Dotty said, looking toward the front room and yawning. "I guess we better get Canny to bed."

Before she could change her mind, Wallace jumped up and had Canny's limp, sweaty body in his arms. "I'll be right over," she said over her shoulder. "I'll just clean up some, so Alma won't have to in the morning."

Wallace paused in the doorway, looking back at Dotty, at her wild hair glistening coppery red under the ceiling light. For a moment he felt dizzy and his arms weakened under Canny's weight and the air seemed to glow with the bright sweat that slicked down Huller's naked shoulders.

Once in the cabin, he put Canny in bed and drew a sheet to her chin. Her hand groped for his. "Where's Momma?" she asked sleepily.

"She'll be along," he said, looking across the way as the kitchen light died.

"My head's itchy, Poppy."

"Jest don't scratch," he said, laying down on his own bed with his hands clasped under his head.

An hour had passed before Dotty tiptoed into the cabin.

"Took you long enough," he said through the darkness.

"There was a lot of dishes." She yawned.

"You wash 'em all in the dark?"

"Yessir," she laughed. "Every damn one of 'em!"

"He thinks I'm your father, don't he?"

"Shit, Aubie. I don't know what the hell he thinks and I don't really care."

"You tell him we're heading back home?" His voice rose. "Back to . . ."

"I told him nothin'! He's just one of them guys you say one thing to and he hears another." She sank down onto the bed beside Canny. "Now leave me alone. I'm beat after listening to that dumb hog bawl her brains out all day long."

He lifted his head. "Then why'd ya do it? Why don't we jest go?"

"'Cause," she sighed. "I'm tryna figure a way out of this mess we're in, that's why."

"What mess?" And the minute he said it, he winced. She meant Canny.

"What mess!" she groaned. "Jesus Christ, you drive me up a wall!"

The next morning he tried to get Dotty alone so they could talk, but right after breakfast, she and Alma and Jiggy drove into town. They dropped Alma off at the welfare office. While Alma kept her appointment with her social worker, Dotty and Jiggy were supposed to be doing the food shopping.

Later in the afternoon when they came back Alma flounced into the house, slamming the door behind her while Dotty and Jiggy giggled drunkenly in the truck.

Soon after, Dotty apologized to Alma, who said it wasn't her fault, but Jiggy's. That night she and Jiggy went at it all through dinner. It finally erupted with Kelly's constant whining for milk. Alma told her to look at her daddy's beer belly if she wanted to know how come there wasn't any milk. At that, Jiggy threw his plate off the wall. Alma threw her fork at him. "Bastard!" Kelly screamed at her father. Huller hit Kelly, and Alma hit him, and in a flash, Dotty wedged herself between the two of them, then pushed and dragged Jiggy outside to his truck. Then she ran back inside, haggard and breathless, to tell Alma not to worry; Jiggy just needed to cool off, and she'd see to it he didn't get in any fights or go very far.

Alma looked at her. "Have him go too," she said, meaning Wallace.

They ended up at the Angle Iron Café, where the band, two skinny guitarists and a drummer, were pushing together the large overturned wooden crates that would be their stage. Wallace kept yawning. The haze of cigarette smoke and the flickering webbed light of the citronella candles on each table made his eyes water. He was sitting alone at a small rickety table near the pay phone on the back wall. Dotty had been in the ladies room for a long time, but he was used to that. Flying as high as she'd been all day, she might be doing any number of things in there—smoking a joint, or putting on fake fingernails, or even sleeping. Huller was still at the pay phone, with his back to Wallace. The person he kept calling either wasn't home or wouldn't come to the phone, and with each try he grew more sullen. Wallace sipped the warm, flat beer Huller had ordered for him an hour ago.

Dotty had just emerged from the ladies room, her drug-bright eyes forced wide. Stiffly, on high golden heels, she made her way through the crowded tables. Wallace noticed how each man stared as she passed by.

"She's still not back," Huller muttered, wheeling around to the table. He swung his leg over the back of the chair and sat down. "Hell with it," he muttered. He looked up and smiled at Dotty's approach. The band had just completed the final screechy adjustment of their sound equipment. As they began to play, Dotty sang along with them. It was a loud song with words too fast for Wallace to make out. Huller was laughing now. With her arms over her head, Dotty's hands flew in the air and her shoulders shimmied and she shook so in her chair that she soon had it jumping and dancing out from the table.

"Poor little girl," said a stocky man with big white ears, a large pitted nose, and slicked-back hair as he came toward her. "Poor thing wants to dance. C'mon, you poor little thing," he said, holding out his hand. As she got up, a slow, lazy ballad began to play. The man held her close, his mouth at her ear, and as they danced, her eyes closed and her face seemed to grow smaller and smaller.

"Shit," Huller muttered, watching them. "Of all people. . . ." He looked at Wallace. "She's got a magnet for trouble, doesn't she?"

When the song ended, Dotty turned away, but the man swung her back. She said something and the man glanced at Wallace and Huller.

"Holy shit," Huller muttered again. As they came toward the table, he took a pill from his pocket and washed it down with a slug of beer.

"Hey!" the man said, standing over them now, grinning, his hand out to Huller.

"Hey!" Huller nodded, kept nodding, as he shook hands.

"You're out!" the man said, belching softly into the fist he kept rubbing his nose with.

"I'm out!" Huller said, nodding. Sweat glistened on his upper lip.

"So what's up?"

"Not much," Huller said, the nodding now a kind of rhythmic rocking. "You know. Just getting the feel back."

"Well, I'd say you're on your way," the man said, putting his arm over Dotty's shoulder. She laughed and stumbled against him, then eased into her chair. She looked dizzy. Before the man returned to his table, where three swarthy men waited, he told Huller to be sure and keep in touch.

"That's Wipes Callahan," Jiggy said. "What the hell's he doing here?

"Who's Wipes Callahan?" Dotty asked. She kept looking back over her shoulder.

"He's big," Huller said. "I mean *big*!"

"He don't look so big to me," Dotty said, looking over at Callahan, who winked at her. "Just ugly as piss," she said, with a grin and a little wave back.

"Jesus Christ, turn around. A guy like that . . . you don't know . . . shit," Huller muttered as Callahan got up, his beer bottle dangling from two fingers as he came to their table.

"Hey," he said to Huller, "I just got thinking, uh, you need any, uh," he belched softly with a sour face, "you know, help or anything, just uh, you know." He shrugged modestly. "I'm around."

"You live around here?" Dotty asked, her eyes fixed now on the man's face.

"More or less," Callahan laughed. "Maybe next month, less." He rolled his eyes. "I got a hearing," he said in disgust, his hand raised as if in oath. "If I want!" he added. "I still ain't decided yet."

Wallace's narrowed eyes slid between the thick-featured man and the fevered sheen of Dotty's face and Huller's numb expression. They had lost him. He had so little idea of what they were talking about that they might as well have been speaking another language.

At the far end of the café, the door opened onto a young woman with waist-length dark hair and inky black eye makeup. She stepped inside and peered through the smoky shadows. The band was singing the sad tale of a wandering husband.

"You don't say," Dotty kept saying, as Callahan leaned over the table, sharing some confidence out of the corner of his mouth. His face twisted with that look of bitter inner juices rising in his gullet. The bartender had come around the bar to the young woman at the door. He was shaking his head. She craned her neck, trying to see past him.

Wallace sipped his beer. Actually, his favorite was root beer, sweet with a sting the way Hyacinth's mother made it up every summer in ribbed brown bottles she always sent over to Answan and Arnold.

"Place is loaded. Crawling with antiques," Huller was saying, suddenly very eager.

"Where's that?" Callahan asked.

"The old Bass place. Old lady Bass, she's dead," Huller said.

"Sure," Callahan was saying. "Whatever. Hey, I can give you names." He leaned inches from their faces. "I mean this is so specialized now, I got guys that only do periods. You know, like history? Like we're all gonna end up needing fucking degrees!" He shook his head. "It's come to that! Believe me or not! Really! I know these things! That's what I do!" He tapped his temple. "Know things."

Something had slipped from Dotty's face, the veil of flesh containing color and moistness and life. She questioned Callahan in a sharp probing tone.

"Shit!" Huller said, standing suddenly and gesturing toward the bartender, who was easing the young woman by her elbow to the door. "Ellie!" he called, then hurried to the door.

". . . from this real big house," Dotty was saying. "You ever heard of anything like that?"

Huller had returned with the young woman, who was obviously only a teenager. Arms folded, the bartender stared at them, waiting.

Callahan said, "Yah, something like that. Maybe five or six years ago, and the kid was one or two, and she disappeared from her own house. Just like," he snapped his fingers, "gone!"

"Yah! Yah!" Dotty said breathlessly. "Yah!"

"Yah, and I think the mother was right in the house even," Callahan mused. "Something like that."

"We gotta go," Huller said.

Still regarding Dotty, Callahan shook his head. "Big commotion! Lotsa people got called. Not me. I mean, they knew that shit wasn't my . . . my . . . you know, my thing."

"C'mon!" Huller said, jiggling the table for their attention. "Ellie's under age. She's not supposed to be in here."

The girl glanced nervously at him.

"So let her go," Dotty said, shooting Ellie a look of disdain.

"I can't. She's Alma's sister," Huller said, gesturing to the bartender that they'd be right along.

"You said to meet you," Ellie whined. "I saw the truck."

"But not here! I been calling you," Huller said, through clenched teeth. "C'mon!" he said to Dotty, who was again talking to Callahan. "Hey look, Pops," Huller said at Wallace's ear. "I'm leaving! Right now!"

"So you been what, following it? Or you know somebody or you heard something?" Callahan asked.

"C'mon!" Huller said, turning abruptly, with Ellie hobbling behind him on high heels, her tight black skirt binding her knees together.

Dotty jumped up and so did Wallace, both trailing him to the door. Callahan called after them: "I can find out! That's my business! I can make a call!"

With Ellie in the middle and Dotty on Wallace's lap, they drove around a while after they left the café. Dotty had her arm around Wallace's neck, fiddling absently with his earlobe while she made a point of telling Ellie how much she resembled her sister Alma. Same eyes. Same nose. Same skin. Same figure.

"No, I don't!" Ellie said finally.

Wallace shivered with goose bumps from Dotty's touch. Her soft breasts grazed his cheek.

"Take my word for it," Dotty said, looking Ellie up and down. "You sure do."

Ellie made a face and turned back to Huller. "I gotta tell you something," she whispered.

Huller glanced at her sharply and made some gesture with his head.

"I only got a half hour before Ma gets back," she whined.

At that, Huller turned abruptly, and in a few minutes they were in his driveway. Wallace and Dotty both climbed out, but then suddenly Dotty jumped back into the truck.

"I gotta bring her home," Huller said.

"I don't mind," Dotty said, with a sweet smile for Ellie. "I like kids."

They left, and Wallace went into the house to get Canny, but she was trying to play Barbie dolls with the two little girls. Kelly kept hiding her sister's doll. Alma was sprawled on the couch watching "Love Boat." She said she'd send Canny over after the show.

In the cabin he lay on the sagging bed. The raspy cry of crickets filled the night woods. He knew it was important to try and remember what Dotty had said to Callahan, but the harder he tried, the stranger were his memories; faces and names and places he hadn't thought about in years. He kept thinking of the two thumbs on Camelia Crebbs' right hand and the story of how one night her husband came home drunk and cut off one of the thumbs and threw it on the floor, where the dog found it and ate it, and how after that Camelia Crebbs couldn't turn her back on that dog for the hungry way it was always sniffing around her ankles.

His father had told him that story on the long snowy ride to Burlington, told it in a cold, toneless voice as if it were just a thought he was sounding aloud, so that when he turned down the gravelly drive and passed under the iron archway and pointed up at the big brick house on the hill and said in that identical voice, flat and colorless as an ice pond, "Up there's the Home, boy," Wallace hardly even lifted his head to look, much less to cry or protest in any way, so easily lulled had he been, and still was, by certain voices.

At first, his daddy came every Sunday. Then it narrowed down to every few months. Then Christmas—if the roads were good, which they usually weren't. And then his daddy died.

He jumped up and turned on the light. Remembering was too much like grave digging. Every stone-clang on the shovel struck cold and hard through his bones. You never knew what you might turn up. After just one day on the job, he had quit. Just like he'd quit remembering all these years. Too hard on the nerves. Too spooky.

For remembering he relied on Dotty, who always knew the right roads to take and which diner had the best prices and which grove paid their pickers minimum plus housing, and which crew boss not to sign on with. If he said, "Dotty, where were we May of '82?" she'd know—the city, the weather, the people, and who said what and to who. And if she wasn't sure, she'd rummage back as if she were turning the pages of a book in her head, murmuring, "March '82 was the cold snap and then April was Canny's scarlet fever and after she got better, we got that place near Tampa. . . ." It had been almost the same with Hyacinth. All he ever had to worry about was the present. If he could just take care of that, they kept track of the past and presided over the future.

He sat down on the edge of the bed. An owl hooted. Moths beat at the screen door. Hyacinth said moths were all the dead souls that were too bad even for hell. Taking care not to look at the moth-covered door, he got back up and turned off the light. He wished Canny would come over.

A few minutes later, he heard footsteps cross the driveway. Alma Huller's white face rose behind the screen. "Canny's asleep, Mr. Wallace."

"I'll come get her," he said quickly.

"That's okay," she sighed. "She can sleep with the girls to-night. Besides, she's gotta get used to us." She peered through the screen. "You're gonna miss her, huh? Well don't worry, she's gonna be treated just like one of my own. And every penny Dotty sends'll be spent on just her. And that's a promise! Course it's too bad the welfare thing didn't work out. But they're just so damn picky over birth certificates and whose kid's whose. Jeez, they don't even know Jig's here. They say, 'Where's your husband?' and I say, 'Who the hell knows!' "

She looked over her shoulder toward the road and her voice dropped. "I hope he don't mouth off someplace. That's how he got in the last trouble. I just hope he don't give Dotty a hard time."

She opened the door and came in. She sat down heavily on the wooden chair. A dreamy look floated across her face and she sighed. "You must be real proud. Not just of Dotty's looks acourse, but her being such a nice person." She clasped her hands and rocked forward a little. "Oh, I hope she passes that screen test. That'd really be something, having a real, honestaGod movie star for a friend." She bent forward, her belly ripening over her thighs. "You feeling all right, Mr. Wallace?" When he didn't answer, she got up and stood by the door. "You're just the quietest man I ever saw, you know that, Mr. Wallace?"

7

Dotty snored loudly, her mouth open, her nostrils flaring. Her makeup had run to black half-moons under each eye. The cabin reeked of sour booze and cigarettes. Wallace stood over her bed. Her dress was tangled around her thighs and as he nudged her awake, he saw the grapey love bite on her soft white throat. She opened one eye and swore at him.

"I gotta talk to you," he whispered.

"I'm sleeping!"

"Wake up, Dotty. It's about Canny."

"She's all set," Dotty murmured, turning on her side. "The Hullers are gonna keep her."

"Nossir!"

She turned and looked up at him through dull mucousy eyes. "Aubie!" she warned.

"I'll go get her," he said, opening the door.

"Aubie!" she called, scrambling out of bed. She chased him across the driveway and threw her arms around his neck and flicked her body against him as she spoke. "Please, Aubie—nothing's definite! We were just talking!"

He looked toward the sleeping house.

"Listen to me!" Dotty insisted, with her strong arms encircling his neck. She drew back her head and looked at him. "We're only ten miles from Stonefield, Aubie!" She smiled brightly and kind of shook him against herself. "Just ten miles!"

"What's that?"

"That's where she's from! From Stonefield!"

"How do you know?"

She looked at him. "The guy last night said it."

"Why'd you tell him?"

She squeezed his arms. "Look, Aubie, the important thing is, she's close to home and maybe in a year or two after we get settled someplace far away, we can send her a letter telling where she came from and that way, she can get back herself and there'll be no trace of us. Aubie? Listen to me. . . ."

He looked down at the ground.

"It'll be a whole new life." She laid her hand on his whiskery cheek and grinned. "Okay?" she asked softly.

He nodded.

She pinched his sideburns and sighed. "My scaredy cat little old man. Afraid of his own shadow and everybody else's." She blinked and the gold flecks in her eyes burst with light. "You're such a sweet guy, Aubie. What would I'da done without you all these years? Christ, I'd probably be dead somewhere by now. . . ."

He nodded dumbly.

"C'mon," she said, leading him by the hand back to the cabin.

When it was over, she was all business. She stood by the bed wiggling her jeans over her hips. "Jiggy's gonna ask you to give him a hand with something," she was saying, as she struggled to close the zipper. "And you be nice now; poor guy hasn't made a dime since he got outta jail."

He nodded dazedly up at her, his body spent and sore beneath the coarse woolly blanket that lay like sandpaper against his raw, wet groin. Her image was ringed with dazzling light. She looks like a fairy godmother, he thought. Just like the most beautiful fairy godmother he had ever seen. She was putting on her bra. She leaned forward and adjusted each breast in its cup.

"When're we going?" he asked in a small voice.

"In a coupla days," she said, slipping a gauzy red shirt over her head. "Soon as I get the details worked out."

He closed his eyes and turned his head to the wall.

A little while after Dotty left to go next door, Canny burst into the cabin. She closed the inside door and locked it.

"She wants me to get in the tub with her kids!" she cried indignantly. "She said I stink and I probably got cradle cap the way my head's so itchy. I hate her, the fat pig! Thinks she can boss me around all of a sudden!"

He took her into the bathroom and had her kneel on a chair in front of the sink so he could wet her hair, which he lathered with bar soap. He rubbed her scalp gently until her head was a fuzz of bubbles. Her slender back was gritty and flecked with grime. From her shoulder blades to her hairline ran a trail of scabby scratches.

"Bend lower," he said. The rinse water trickled brown into the sink. "You gotta have a bath, Canny," he said, turbaning her head in one of the motel towels.

"Not in the same tub as them two!"

"What's wrong with them?"

"I hate them!" she said, jerking her head so viciously that the turban hung lopsidedly.

"You been having fun with them!" he said, straightening the towel. "I seen you! You been like a big sister," he said anxiously.

"I don't wanna be a big sister. They're mean, Poppy. Not mean 'cause they're mad about something. But mean in their blood. 'Specially Kelly! Last night, she cut all the hair off Krystal's Barbie!" Her mouth trembled and her eyes brimmed with tears. She rubbed her nose and sniffed. "How come we have to stay here, Poppy? I hate it here."

He held out his arms and held her close.

"I can hear your heart beating," she said, with her ear to his chest. "It's so loud. . . . It's going ba-boom! Ba-boom! Ba-boom!" She laughed. "I never heard your heart before."

"How come?" His eyes were closed. He didn't dare open them.

"You never hugged me this tight before," she said in a muffled voice, then added, "You're hurting me, Poppy. I can't breathe."

He let her go and she drew back and watched him carefully, unblinking, her blue eyes clear and deep and solemn. She took a breath so deep that her ribs hooped out like barrel staves, strained and ready to burst. "Kelly said I'm not your real kid. She said Momma told her mother she got me from some gypsies."

He picked up Dotty's hairbrush from the back of the toilet and ran his fingers through the tangle of reddish hairs.

"Hey, Pops!" Jiggy Huller called from the driveway. "C'mere for a minute!"

"Here," Wallace said, holding out the brush. "Get all them snarls out."

Instead of the brush, she seized his wrist. "Poppy, did you get me from gypsies?"

"Hey, Pops!"

"Did you?" she insisted, her face pinched and as white as the toppling turban.

"C'mon, Aubie!" Dotty was calling.

"Tell me!"

"No, dammit!" he said, pulling away and hurrying outside.

Dust veiled the windshield. Huller's truck sagged and sprang with each rut in the dirt road. Beside Huller Wallace sat straight as a pole, his head jiggling on his rigid neck like a dashboard doll. He kept blinking.

Huller glanced at him over the wheel. "Dotty say any more about that guy last night? Callahan?"

"Nope," Wallace said.

"Jesus, you're quiet!" Huller said with a faint smile. "You remind me of this old guy in the cell next to mine. Never said more than one word at a time. 'Yup, nope, huh, sure.' And that was it. 'Cept for at night. He talked in his sleep—all night long. He'd have these whole, long conversations in all different voices. Some nights you'd swear there were ten people in there all talking at once. Kids' voices and broads' voices." Huller shivered. "A real weirdo. Buzzer was his name. He set fire to his house and wiped out his whole family." Now Huller laughed. "One night the bugger across the block got sick of the voices and he threw a lit rag in the cell and Buzzer woke up to find his bunk flaming under him and he just laid there staring up at the ceiling and never even stirred off the bunk or yelled or screamed or nothing. Just laid there while the clothes burned right off him. He died a coupla days after and they said he never said one word. Not one single word."

Huller glanced at Wallace. "You ever serve any time?"

Wallace's face was white. He was thinking of the man in the story and he was suddenly very scared. Huller repeated his question.

"Nope," Wallace said. He folded his arms over his chest and tried to look strong.

"Dotty says you two been together five years. At first I thought you were her old man."

"I ain't," Wallace said, knuckling the flesh of his upper arm so that it bulged like a muscle.

"And I thought Canny was her sister. . . ."

"Where we goin'?" Wallace said, leaning forward. He peered intently at the winding road ahead.

"Up to the old Bass house. Another coupla miles. Old lady Bass's funeral was last week." Huller looked out of the corner of his eyes at Wallace. "Dotty says you got a wife and kids."

Wallace looked out the side window. The trees blurred past in a stream of sparkling light. The sun felt hot on his face. Huller's voice tumbled over him. "She said you and her just met on a road once, and five minutes later you were driving off in some guy's truck together." Huller snorted. "Course, half what that girl says, I take with a grain of salt."

They had come to a fork in the road. Huller hesitated, then bore left as if it didn't matter which way he went. His voice lifted over the motor. "Like her being runner-up for Miss Florida and having to take a screen test in Hollywood . . . not that she's not good-looking enough, of course. Just that her stories get so mixed up, I noticed, and changed, depending on who she's talking to. Like last night . . . the things she told that guy Callahan. And then after, to me."

The truck had slowed to a crawl. Huller spoke quickly now. "This is big time, Pops. I need it straight. I can't be screwing around. This could be big dough or a lotta years . . . or worse. How'd you get the kid? And where'd you get her?"

"I dunno," Wallace said.

"What d'ya mean, you don't know?" A wormy blue vein slithered up Huller's temple. "What kind of answer's that?"

"I jest dunno," Wallace said numbly.

Huller's eyes narrowed. "Well she's not your kid then, or else you'd tell me. Right?"

Wallace stared ahead over the dashboard. He could smell Huller.

"So is she Dotty's kid?" Huller asked, laying his arm over the seat. His fist was inches from Wallace's face.

"Ask her," Wallace said.

"I'm asking you," Huller snarled.

Wallace's lips sucked back and forth over his teeth and he began to rock a little and his eyes batted frantically.

Huller leaned close. "Well?"

"Ask her," Wallace said again.

"I'm asking you!" Huller exploded.

"Well don't!" cried the little man miserably. "Jest don't."

Huller studied him for a moment. He tapped his fingers on the steering wheel; then he wet his lips and smiled. He backed

the truck down into a ditch, then shot forward back the way
they had come, with that smile, that knife-flick of a smile, never
once leaving his face.

Alma sat up on the porch, soaking her feet in a bucket of
sudsy water. Below her on the hard-packed dirt yard, Dotty
sprawled on a blanket. When the truck careened into the driveway, she sat up in a quick wiggle of fastening her skimpy halter
top.

"Where's all the stuff?" Alma hollered down to them.

"We got waylaid," Huller said. He climbed down from the
truck and clasped his hands behind his head and straddled back
in a long, powerful stretch.

"What the hell do you mean, waylaid?" Alma yelled back.
She lifted her soapy feet onto the porch floor and sat forward
with her hands on her knees.

"Me and Pops met these two broads and we got laid along
the way," Huller called back. At that, Dotty jumped up and
swatted him. He covered his head with both hands and ran up
on the porch past Alma, who reached out and whacked his
bottom. Dotty took the steps two at a time and went at his back
with a flurry of light jabs. "You're awful!" she squealed. "Just
awful, saying that about poor old Aubie. . . ."

Huller grabbed her wrists and backed her against the house.
Dotty's laughter rippled down from the porch. Wallace watched
from the truck as she squirmed and giggled and butted her head
against Huller's chest. "Help!" Dotty laughed. "Help me, Poppy!"

"Leave her alone!" Alma called shrilly. She rose from the
rocking chair and moved closer until she was behind her husband.

"I said leave her alone, Jig. You're hurting her. . . ."

"Ya, Jig," Dotty cried. "You're hurting me!"

"You crazy bastard! Let goa her!" Alma screamed as she
grabbed a fistful of Jiggy's hair. His head jerked back as, with
a wounded bellow, he spun around, his thick hard arm meeting
his wife's swollen belly like a club. First, she doubled over,

breathless and stunned; then she staggered back, her eyes rolling to whites, her arms poled out at her sides like sails as her bare feet skidded over the soapy puddles at the top of the stairs.

"Oh . . . oh . . . oh . . . oh . . . ," she moaned with the thud she made on each step.

Wallace was the first to reach her. "They was just foolin'!" he said, with a note of wonder. Streaming down her hairy white legs were bright red clots.

8

It was Alma's third day in the hospital. The aborted baby had been a boy. Since Monday, Dotty had been at the hospital day and night with Alma. But now her sympathies had begun to wane. Alma's whining was getting on her nerves, she complained now while Huller worked on his truck out in the front yard.

Wallace couldn't help but notice how happy Dotty looked. Her cheeks were flushed and her eyes glistened watery and bright as fever blisters. Her voice reminded him of churning water. The crazier life got, the better Dotty liked it. She thrived on turmoil and confusion. The thing about Dotty was, she could spin just as fast as the world could spin—outspin it, in fact, until, like the hummingbird's wings, she was just a motionless blur of energy.

"To listen to Alma, you'd think Jig didn't give a damn! That she was the only one hurt." Dotty lit another cigarette and sipped her coffee. Wallace was at the stove, frying her an egg. A few minutes ago, he had asked her if she wanted the yoke hard or soft. She still hadn't answered, so he slid the spatula under the egg and lifted it carefully from the pan's heat.

"She's so goddamn thick," Dotty said.

"Hard or soft?" he interjected quickly, the spatula still poised in midair. Dotty wouldn't eat it if the yoke broke.

"She doesn't understand how it is for a guy. 'Specially a guy like Jig that keeps everything all locked up inside!" she said.

Just then the truck started up. It rumbled close to the porch and the horn blew. Dotty jumped up from the table. "We'll be at the hospital most of the day," she said, pouring the rest of her coffee down the sink. She glanced toward the door. "In and out, that is," she added. "Jig's not very good at sitting still for a long stretch," she said with a slow warmth that made Wallace look up quickly. The egg splattered down into the hot grease. Huller tooted again. Dotty was still talking as she ran around the kitchen, gathering up her pocketbook and her high heels, and, from the hanger over the bathroom door, Jiggy's blue plaid shirt, which she had ironed late last night after Wallace had gone over to sleep in the cabin.

"It's her nerves more than anything else," Dotty said, bending to fasten her ankle strap. "The least little thing sets her off. Last night it was how she was gonna have her sister move in here to take care of the kids. I told her how good you are with kids. Probably better, I said, than a real mother. And next thing I know, she's mad at Jiggy, 'cause she thought he said something behind her back about being a bad mother. I told her you're doing just fine and for her not to worry." She looked up as the horn blared steadily.

"Jesus Christ!" she hollered through the door. "I'll be right out!" She turned back, hopping on one foot as she fastened the other strap. "So if she calls, you tell her that. How you and the girls are doing just fine."

Wallace froze. "She gonna call?" he gulped. Telephones scared him. He never said the right things on them. He either told too much or just went totally blank and couldn't hardly say two words into the receiver.

"I don't know," Dotty said, with a fixed look of warning. "But if she does, you better answer it, Aubie! If you don't, she'll think something's wrong and she'll send her little bitch of a sister over for sure then!"

Huller hollered and Dotty ran outside. Wallace peeked through the door and as soon as he saw her climb into the truck, he took the phone off the hook and buried it under a pillow. He sat at the table and ate Dotty's egg. Then he filled the dishpan with water and let the breakfast dishes soak while he picked up the girls' toys. Every now and again he cocked his head and listened. In the distance he could hear the girls' squabbling voices, high-pitched and wild as loons. After a while the telephone's insistent buzz cut through the pillow and droned in his ears like an electric saw. He took a cushion from the couch and pressed it over the pillowed receiver and continued his chores.

He hoped Alma didn't send her sister over. He liked being alone with the girls. He liked taking care of them and picking up and cleaning the house. And now with all the grown-ups gone, the girls seemed to like him better. They seemed more relaxed, happier; more like little kids. Even Kelly had calmed down some. Last night after supper, they had all played hide-and-seek. Canny showed him how. He was the seeker and the girls were the hiders. By the end of the game, the girls got so daring they weren't even bothering to hide, but would stand right behind him while he leaned against the side of the house with his face in his hands, counting, "97, 98, 99, 100. . . . Ready or not here . . ." And before he even got it all out, they'd swoop around his legs and tag home, screeching, "Allee, allee, umphrie!" Just thinking about it made him happy. "That was so much fun," he said under his breath. "I never had so much fun," he sniffed, and shrugged his shoulder against his runny nose. He put his hand to his chest, to the peculiar swelling that was his heart, and he pressed his fingers tight as if to contain it, to hold it in place, to keep it from getting too big.

It was eight-thirty at night and Jiggy and Dotty weren't back yet. The telephone was piled high with pillows. The little girls had been too tired after supper to play hide-and-seek. Wallace had been disappointed, but Canny promised they could play the next night.

He dried the last supper dish and put it away. On the table were four glasses and a plate of sugar cookies. He poured lemonade into each glass, then stood back to see if he had forgotten anything. Paper napkins! Finding none in the cupboard, he folded squares of toilet paper, which he set next to each glass.

The three little girls were in the living room. Kelly and Krystal sat on either side of Canny on the couch. They listened to her story as intently as Wallace listened from the kitchen.

"So then all the princes came back again to the castle on their big white horses," Canny said. "The king looked out the window and he said, 'Hey, you guys, I told you! The only way you can marry the princess is if you find her.' The head of the princes was on the biggest horse. He told the king how they . . ."

"Wait!" interrupted Krystal. "What do you mean, the head of the princess? Is the princess already dead? Who cut off her head?"

"Nobody cut off her head!" Canny laughed. "She's not dead. She's hiding someplace."

"Well how come her head's talking?" Kelly wanted to know.

"Not her head," Canny explained patiently. "The head of the princes means the boss of all the princes."

In the kitchen, Wallace nodded. "Oh," he said. "I get it." He eased himself into a chair at the table and listened carefully.

The princes had been riding through the countryside for twenty days looking for the hidden princess. They had encountered ferocious bears, crocodiles, man-eating flies, a crazy man named Herman who sliced off all the horses' tails, and now, a dog that had just sunk his bloody fangs deeply into a prince's arm.

Wallace sat on the edge of the chair, his eyes rapt on the shaggy hulking beast on the other side of the screen door, where Huller's dog lay, feigning sleep, his wet muzzle pulsing.

"All the other princes kicked the dog and one even smashed a rock on the dog's head. . . ."

Wallace hunched over the table, his jaw tight, his nails gripping his sweaty palms. The dog lifted its head and looked back at him.

"Just then, the head prince saw something really weird on the dog," Canny whispered. "He saw this big, long zipper up its back."

Wallace shaded his eyes and peered at the dog.

Canny's voice came in a rush. " 'Don't hit!' he told the other princes. But it was too damn late! They were all throwing rocks and sticks at the dog and one even took his sword out and stabbed it. And he unzipped the dog and sure enough . . . there was the princess."

Krystal gasped and Kelly laughed nervously. In the kitchen Wallace scratched his head.

"Her head was smashed and her arm was broke and she had a hole right through into her heart. . . ."

Wallace was confused. He tried to hear the rest, but Krystal and Kelly were arguing again. He called the girls into the kitchen for their dessert. When they were at the table, he asked Canny what happened to the princess.

"Nothing," she said, biting into her cookie. "She was dead."

His face fell. He bit into his cookie and thought a minute. "How come the dog was guarding the castle?" he asked. He looked puzzledly at Canny. "Didn't the king know the dog was the princess?"

"I don't know." Canny glanced at the two girls. "He just didn't."

"Well it don't make sense," he said.

Kelly smiled, enjoying Canny's discomfort.

"It was just a story, Poppy," Canny said. "You know, a fairy tale."

"Yah, but fairy tales end happy everafter," he said. "They're s'posed to, Canny!"

"Yah," Kelly said. "That was a stupid story."

"Yah," Krystal agreed. "And dogs don't have zippers."

Canny squirmed in the chair. She looked as if she were going to cry.

"Whyn't you tell us another one, Canny? A nice happy one," he said eagerly.

"No!" she pouted.

"C'mon, Canny," he teased. "Tell the one I like. The one about the old witch and the frog." He leaned forward and clasped his hands expectantly. "C'mon. . . ."

"You tell it," Canny said.

The three children watched him bite his lip and frown. He screwed up his mouth and his lips trembled on the edge of thought. "Once . . . once 'pon. . . ." His hand groped in the air, then fell. Dismally, he shook his head. "I can't," he said, blinking miserably. "I can't think of the words."

For a moment the three little girls just looked at him.

"Are you a retard?" Kelly asked him.

"Course he ain't!" Canny snapped.

"Dotty said he is!" Kelly shot back.

"She did not!" Canny said, her eyes blazing.

"Yes, she did!" Kelly insisted. She turned to her younger sister. "Didn't she?"

Krystal shrugged, and at that, Kelly snatched the little girl's last cookie. Krystal began to cry.

"Give it back," Wallace ordered.

A coldness like the father's blanked the child's eyes. She bit into the cookie, then took another bite, watching him deliberately as she chewed.

"You ain't a very nice girl," Wallace muttered. Sweat ran down his back and the hair on the back of his hands stood up. The girl unnerved him. He took three cookies from the box and gave two to Krystal and one to Canny. "And none for you," he said in a shaky voice. "Now if you'da asked, 'stead've grabbing, you'd've got one too."

"Old fart," Kelly said under her breath.

"You shut up!" Canny said.

"He ain't my father!" Kelly spat. "And I don't have to listen to his shit."

"Yes you do," Canny said. "You have to do what he says till your daddy comes home!"

"No, I don't," Kelly said. "And you don't have to, 'cause he ain't your father either!"

The littlest girl put down her lemonade. She wiped her mouth and looked at Wallace, who stood close by the stove. "Ain't you a father?"

He took off his apron and folded it into a small, tight square. Canny looked at him. "He's my father, so acourse he's a father!"

"No he's not," Kelly said, a note of triumph rising in her voice. "And I heard Dotty say so. She said they got you from gypsies and they're gonna give you back to the gypsies."

"You shut up," Canny warned.

"It's a secret," Kelly gloated. "But I know all about it. They're taking you back to the gypsies and the gypsies are gonna pay a thousand dollars and they're gonna sell you to a mean old lady. And she's gonna make you eat dog food and sleep down the cellar with the rats and the spiders!"

Wallace shivered.

"Poor Canny," Krystal shuddered.

"You're crazy, you know that?" Canny said, her voice quavering and small.

"I know another secret too," Kelly said, in a singsong voice. She smiled and her eyes glowed like hot coals. "They're taking off with all the money the gypsies give 'em and they're gonna move far, far away to Hollywood—just the two of them. . . ." Her voice trembled. "And me!" she added triumphantly.

After Krystal and Kelly had gone to bed, Wallace sat on the couch watching television with Canny. "I hate her!" Canny said, twisting her hand to her mouth so she could chew a strip of cuticle.

"Buncha lies is all," Wallace said. He pulled her hand away

and set it in her lap. Her fingernails had been gnawed to the quick.

"Why'd she say it then, if it wasn't true?" Canny asked. " 'Specially in front of you!" She started to raise her hand and he pushed it back down.

" 'Cause," he said, then thought a minute. " 'Cause she wants to be happy and she's jealous 'cause you're a happy girl. And being mean's the only way she knows to do it."

"To do what?" Canny had started braiding the threads hanging from the cuff of her shorts.

"To be happy."

She looked up. "That don't sound right, Poppy."

"I know," he had to admit. But somehow it was true. In order to explain it better, he would have had to tell her about Hyacinth, who was that way herself; always searching for happiness and hating whoever found it before she did.

Canny yawned. She lay down with her head in his lap. As soon as she was asleep, he eased out from under her and began to tidy up the kitchen. He piled the toys in a big box and laid the children's sneakers on the stairs. Then he scrubbed the stove top with ammonia and scoured the sink gritty clean. After that, he set the chairs upside down on the table so he could sweep and mop the kitchen floor. He needed to keep busy. It was the one way he knew to stave off fear and loneliness. Of course the girl was lying, he told himself. Everything she said she made up to hurt Canny. "That's all," he muttered, bearing down on the mop and scrubbing as hard as he could. "Just a buncha lies," he sighed.

He drew the mop across the floor and backed into the living room. He stood in the doorway watching the dry streaks widen in the cracked, dull linoleum. Outside, the darkness thickened with heat. It seemed that he could hear each cricket, each bullfrog and hissing leaf, separate and apart from every other sound. Even the muffled buzz of the telephone grew distinct and clear. It filled the house.

Before he sat down, he uncovered the telephone, and the

minute he replaced the receiver, the phone rang. He let it ring a long time before he finally picked it up.

"Hello? Hello?" demanded a woman's voice. "Can you hear me? Answer me, goddamn it. Where the hell've you been, you bastard!"

"I dunno," he said hoarsely. He thought it was Hyacinth. He closed his eyes and shook his head.

"What do you mean, you don't know?" the voice shrieked.

But it was true. For at that instant, he not only did not know where he had been for the last five years, but had no idea, not even the slightest sense, where he was right now.

"You know what it's like sitting here all this time waiting for you to come? I mean, who the hell do you think you are?"

He shrugged and did not answer. His head hung in shame. He felt something tighten, then swirl free, in his throat, like a sink suddenly unclogged.

"I been lost," he tried to say, but it came out sounding like a wheezy cough.

"Who's this? Is this Jiggy? Jiggy, this is Alma . . . you been drinking?"

He blinked and cleared his throat. "They ain't back yet," he said, and hung up.

He sat on the couch and lifted Canny's head back into his lap. In her sleep, she scratched violently at her head. He was remembering his boys, short like himself, with bowed, runty legs and cowlicks sprouting up like weeds from their slicked-down pates, so that all through Sunday service, Hyacinth would be licking her fingers and pressing the hair into place.

He tried to concentrate on the television show, but everything was reminding him of Hyacinth and the boys. The telephone had begun to ring again. He stared at the television. It was one of those preacher shows. "Reverend Maximilian Green," read the gold-leafed nameplate on the desk, where the preacher sat with his hands clasped on a bible. With the phone still ringing, Wallace couldn't hear a word the preacher said. His slicked-back hair and bushy mustache reminded him of Hyacinth's uncle, the Reverend Pomeroy Hind, a hell-raising, womanizing wife beater who, before he got the calling, used to make blood sausage in between insulating jobs. Hyacinth said Pomeroy had six visions, each one more "terrifrightning" than the one before. The sixth vision caught Pomeroy way up top Bald Peak in his truck, without a stitch on. The troopers called Aunt Berthie, who swore to her dying day that the young man the troopers saw leap from the truck and dart into the woods was the very same horned devil of the first five visions.

The phone stopped ringing.

On the front porch, the dog had begun to growl. Wallace reached for Canny's soft, sweaty hand and clutched it in his. The dog's sudden racking bark hit the night like a volley of gunfire. It began to pace back and forth on the porch, its bushy tail sweeping across the screens. Wallace tensed forward, hoping to hear Huller's truck. The sky rumbled with thunder and the whole house shimmied with the resounding crack of light that split the black night like a jagged seam. With a howl, the dog leaped at the screen door, its red eyes raw with fear. At the next clap of thunder, the dog began to whimper and paw miserably at the bulging screen. Wallace tiptoed over the drying floor and opened the door. With the dog cowering at his heels, he closed all the windows, he and the dog both flinching each time the panes flared with lightning.

When Dotty and Huller finally got home, Wallace was asleep, his head bobbing over Canny. Hunched close to him was the dog. Dotty's eyes were heavy and smudged as she bent to wake him up. Opening his eyes, he cringed back. In the flickering silvery light of the television, her face had the hollow boniness of a skull. Instinctively, he reached for Canny.

"In the kitchen," she was saying. "We have to talk. . . ."

Huller was setting the chairs on the floor. He had opened two cans of beer, one for himself and one for Dotty. His shirt was unbuttoned and he raked his nails across his chest, regarding Wallace's sleepy entrance with hard, glassy eyes.

Wallace sat down with his knees pressed close together. He

had to go to the bathroom, but would not with Dotty and Huller so close by the bathroom door.

Everything about Dotty seemed mussed and out of kilter. Her hair was damp and straggly. Her eyes flitted between the two men. She shifted in the chair and wet her lips nervously until Huller sat down. When he did, she leaned, strained toward him, as he took a piece of paper from his shirt pocket. He looked at her, then opened the paper carefully, and laid it on the table, running his finger along the crease in the black-and-white picture.

"Aubie!" Dotty said, reaching out to touch his arm. "I want you to . . ."

"You be quiet!" Huller ordered.

Like a child, she drew back her hand and sat staring anxiously at the paper, which Huller had pushed in front of Wallace. It was a picture of a small child.

"Recognize her?" Huller asked in a tight voice. Outside, sheets of rain billowed across the porch.

Wallace leaned forward, angling his head under the flickering light. In the picture, the little girl wore white overalls. Her hair was pale and short about her face like a thin wispy cap. She stood with her arms outstretched as if she were about to take her first step—or fall, Wallace thought. Her blurred features were lost in the grainy shadows.

"Well?" Huller said, tapping his fingers on the tabletop.

"Can't see her face too good," Wallace muttered. He leaned closer and squinted until his eyes were almost closed.

"Tell him!" Dotty said, breathlessly. At that, Wallace's head shot up and his eyes darted toward Canny still asleep in front of the television set. Her hand hung from the couch in a tight fist.

"He knows," Dotty was telling Huller. "He's just scared." She leaned over to Wallace. "Don't be scared, Aubie. It's okay." She tried to smile, but all her features seemed to quiver and jerk. Wallace's chin clamped into the roof of his mouth as he stared at her. She blinked and looked away.

"Where'd you get that picture?" he asked her.

Dotty looked at Huller. "See!" She grabbed his arm. "He knows!"

"I told you to shut up!" Huller said fiercely. He shook his arm free of her grasp. "I want to hear it from him!"

Her face twisted. "Tell him, Aubie!" she hissed. "You know it's her—just like when we got her!" She slammed her fist onto the table and moaned to see his eyes blank on hers.

"Where'd you get that picture?" he repeated dully.

Dotty looked to Huller, who just sat there, patient as a cat now between two gutted birds.

"The post office," she said slowly, her eyes rising to Wallace's.

"Aubie, there's a reward! Her family'll pay twenty-five thousand bucks to get her back! But Jiggy's gotta know for sure. He wants to hear it from you. . . ." Her voice pitched and caught like the twangy whine of a fiddle's high string. "Tell him, Aubie! Tell him who's in the picture. Tell him!"

Wallace looked down at the picture. He rubbed his knuckles over his palm. The room dimmed and seemed about to swallow itself in darkness. He shook his head. Huller chuckled and picked up the picture. Dotty grabbed it and thrust it under Wallace's face. "Look at it!" she warned. "And you better say who it is, goddamn you, or I'm walking out that door this minute, and by Jesus, this time I mean it!" She started to get up, but Huller pushed her down in the seat.

"Is it Canny?" Huller asked.

"I dunno," Wallace muttered.

"Bastard!" Dotty groaned, jumping out of the chair and flying at him. He looked up just as her open hand cracked across his cheek.

"My one chance! My one big break and you're gonna screw it all up?" she cried, slapping him again. "No sir! I'll do it myself. Like I always had to do everything. . . ." She picked up the paper and threw it at him. "I knew this would happen. You don't want to give her back, do you? You want to keep her and keep on running. Well you better start running now, 'cause I'm done running and I'm done with you and that brat in there. And I'm gonna tell you something else, you stupid little prick. When I'm gone, you've got nothing left and nowhere to go and you know it!" She ran outside and slammed the door behind her.

Huller swirled his beer can and said nothing. Tears streamed down Wallace's stubbly cheeks into the corners of his mouth. "It's her all right," he said softly.

Huller looked at him while he folded the top of the paper.

"It's Canny," Wallace said, his wet eyes straining at the words over the picture. His mouth struggled silently with each syllable.

MISSING! SINCE AUGUST 30, 1980.
CAROLINE ANNE BIRD. 18 MONTHS OLD.

"What's that say?" asked Wallace, pointing.

"Caroline," Huller answered, with a faint smile. "Caroline Anne Bird."

Wallace brought the poster close and peered inquisitively at it; then he frowned. "She said 'Canny,' so that's how we always called her." He glanced self-consciously at Huller. "She didn't talk too good acourse."

Huller held out his hand for the poster.

"Jest baby talk," Wallace said.

9

It was ten o'clock in the morning. Huller was supposed to pick Alma up at the hospital at eleven. The kitchen was a shambles again. The girls had emptied the box of toys all over the floor, which was tracked with mud from the rain-soaked yard. The sun had come out, but too hard, too bright, too suddenly, like crazy laughter after tears.

Canny was banging on the locked kitchen door. "Krystal's hungry!" she called, with her mouth at the glass.

"A couple more minutes!" Dotty yelled back. She lit a cigarette off Jiggy's.

"But she didn't have breakfast yet!" Canny called. "And her pants're all wet."

"I said in a minute, dammit!" Dotty hollered. Canny stood on her tiptoes and peered through the glass. Wallace looked away guiltily. Dotty got up and closed the curtain.

"So, the whole thing's timing," Huller was saying more to himself than either one of them. "The phone call, the drop-off point, the pickup, and giving them the kid."

Dotty leaned close.

Huller laid his cigarette pack on the table. "This here's the car with the kid in it," he said, pushing the cigarettes past his beer can. "This here's the pick-up point. Check the dough," he said, easing the pack alongside Wallace's coffee mug. "Then let the kid out," he said, pointing to the mug.

Dotty frowned. She looked between the mug and the cigarettes. "Who's driving?" she asked.

"Pops." Huller grinned. "He's in the car with the kid. We're here," he said, pointing to the matchbook. "In the truck. Soon as the money's . . ."

"But he'll get lost!" Dotty interrupted. "I told you how he gets lost."

Huller's eyes flicked at hers. "No, he won't," he said firmly. "We're gonna dry run this a few days ahead."

"He's not gonna remember!" Dotty groaned.

"Look! Everything I say, you gotta argue with, and I'm getting sick of it!" Huller snapped. He wiped the sweat from his neck with a dirty dish towel, then threw it down on the table.

"I'm sorry," Dotty said. "It's nerve-racking, that's all. Jesus, every time I even think about cops, I get sick inside."

"Well don't think about cops then. Think about all that money." Huller smiled and puckered his lips at her. "All those soft green dollar bills . . ." He glanced quickly at Wallace and his smile faded. "What's the matter, Pops? You scared too?"

Wallace nodded. He started to say something, then shook his head weakly.

"Say it . . . c'mon!" Huller gestured with his fingers. "Get it out! Now's the time."

Wallace shrugged uneasily. Huller gestured again.

Finally, Wallace said, "If'n we ask for money, don't that mean we . . . we're like kidnappers?"

Huller snorted. "Well you are, aren't you?"

Wallace's eyes went wide. "Not real ones. Not like on TV or nothing."

Huller bit his lip. "Oh yah? How do you figure that?"

"We didn't do it on purpose," Wallace said. He shrugged and glanced almost shyly at Dotty. "The tailpipe was loose and we stopped and I said, 'We ain't got no money and no food, and we gotta head back.' And then she took off, I guess for money, but, acourse, then I thought she just took off and I was gonna too, but she took the keys and then she was back with a little tiny girl in her arms and a jar of dimes. And I said, 'Who's that?' And first she said how she found it, and then she said some lady paid her to take it, and, acourse, she was scared and she kept saying, 'Just go! Just go!' Course, I was so scared too. . . ." Even now his face was papery white and his voice trembled with fear.

Dotty laughed nervously. "He's got a thousand versions. Every time, he tells it different."

Wallace looked hurt. "No, I don't." He scratched his head thoughtfully. "Fack, I never even told it before now."

Huller had been watching Dotty. His mouth plumped over the rim of the beer can in a slow, sullen smile.

"Don't look at me like that!" she spat.

"Like what?" Huller laughed, all wide-eyed and innocent-looking.

"Like you got everything all figured out!" she said.

10

Sometimes when a Pampers ad came on TV, Alma would sniffle some, but otherwise she was in good spirits. Of course, having the house so clean helped and having Jiggy around so much more now was nice, she was telling Wallace as he washed the breakfast dishes. He had made pancakes, Canny's favorite. Tonight he was planning on mushfries, which were the leftover pancakes cut up and deep-fried.

"Probably it was too soon," Alma said from the table. She was lighting another cigarette. Even with the window open, the kitchen was dim with smoke. Alma could smoke all she wanted now. It didn't make her sick to her stomach anymore. "It was just like when we were married. He'd want to go out and I'd be too tired and then my feet got so swellen I couldn't stand up even. And, acourse, relations was out of the picture, me being so big and so sick and all." She laughed. "The littlest movement'd make me want to throw up. He'd just sit down on the bed and I'd start to gag. . . ."

The water gurgled down the drain. Wallace wrung out the dish rag and bent low over the sink and wiped water spots from the faucet. His face was red.

"Which is rough when you think about it," Alma went on,

" 'cause relations is all newlyweds really got going for them. It's how they get to know each other. 'Course, it takes a lotta years. . . ." Her voice trailed off and she stared at her empty coffee cup a moment. "Dotty says you were married a long time. . . . I mean to your wife—the one before Dotty. Was the first one like Dotty? I mean, you know, as pretty like her?"

Wallace had not moved from the sink. He started wringing out the dishrag again.

"Probably not, huh?" Alma sighed. "Probably she was like me, all wrung out and fat and so miserable, you couldn't take no more. And along came Dotty and that was that and you just couldn't say no, so off you went. . . ."

Wallace muttered something.

"What?" Alma asked, leaning forward.

"She warn't fat," he repeated softly.

"Was she all wrung out and nagging all the time at you to stay home?" Alma doused her cigarette in the saucer's coffee puddle. From the box in her lap, she scooped a fistful of Chees-its.

"Nope," Wallace said uneasily. "I was always 't home."

"Didn't you ever go out with the guys?" Alma asked through a mouthful of crackers.

He turned and shook his head.

"Bowling? Or even just hanging out?"

He was shaking his head.

"Really? Jeez!" She regarded him with a curious, puzzled expression. She shrugged. "Well, what'd you do?"

"Nothing," he said.

Alma's eyes narrowed. "She run around?"

"Nope. She warn't like that."

"What was her name?" she asked, and when he told her, she repeated it. "Hyacinth. That's pretty. I never heard that before."

"All her sisters had flower names," he said, blinking. He had forgotten that. "There was Rose and Daisy and Marigold . . . and one that died, Daffodil."

From outside, now, came Kelly's piercing scream. When he

did not move, Alma rose slowly from the chair and waddled onto the porch. She was still passing clots. Dotty said some were as big as grapefruits. After Answan was born, Hyacinth couldn't walk for two weeks. Her mother moved in. Mrs. Kluggs had a harelip and a fine blue tint to her skin that marked her as a Mooney. Way back, all the Mooneys had been blue, blue as ink and proud of it, Mrs. Kluggs boasted. His mother-in-law hated his guts. She put his boots out on the porch to fill up with snow all night long. She used to go into the bathroom after him and open the window. If that didn't work, she'd tie a handkerchief over her nose. She even got Arnold to do it. Sometimes his whole family would all be sitting around with masks on.

He felt weak. He was remembering too many things. He looked around the kitchen, at the headless doll next to the sagging trash bag and the mud-caked sneaker by the dog's water dish, in which a black fly floated. For a moment, he could not remember whose house this was or why he was here. His eyes focused on the fly—on its hard, hairy head and its dark wings, inert and iridescent. "I got lost," he whispered. "That's what happened."

Out in the yard, a woman laughed. Alma was laughing, but it was Hyacinth's laugh that slashed like a razor down his back; her and all her Kluggs relatives, all laughing, slapping their knees and holding their sides from splitting over such a crazy story. Whoever heard of such a thing? *Went off to work one morning; comes dragging back five years later, saying he got lost. Come on Wallace, Tell us another one. . . .*

A week had passed and, as far as Wallace could tell, Alma knew none of the truth about Canny. She seemed content to smoke and watch her soaps and complain to Dotty about what a lazy little slut her fifteen-year-old sister was. Ellie had moved in three days ago, after a slapping match with her mother.

Jiggy and Dotty and Wallace were in the cabin now, working on the "plan." Alma was in the house, taking a nap. Right after breakfast this morning, Ellie had taken the three little girls into the woods to wade in the stream. Ellie was a big, bony girl whose breasts lifted against her thin cotton shirts like hard little knobs. Though she was prettier than Alma, Ellie's eyes were of the same dull stone.

Dotty sat on one bed in the cabin's heat, rubbing baby oil on her legs. She had been lying in the sun all morning, and her thighs were a fiery pink. Jiggy sat on the edge of the other bed. Between them, on the wooden chair, rigid in his silence, was Wallace. His hands capped his knees. As they talked, he nodded mutely, barely listening, his eyes blurred and still. Their voices hummed with words of a strange, bright fluidity, bobbing up and down and back and forth, glinting easily past him.

Jiggy was saying that Wallace should make all the telephone calls. "Then they'll think it's just one guy they're dealing with. It can't be me. I'm known."

"He gets all screwed up on the phone," Dotty said, tilting the bottle of oil against her fingers. She stroked the oil along the inside of her thigh. She glanced up at Wallace's remote expression. "He gets scared talking when he can't see who he's talking to."

"I'll tell him what to say," Jiggy said.

She shook her head. "He'll forget. Guaranteed," she sighed.

"I'll write it all down," Huller said.

"He can't read," she said, in the same flat tone.

Huller looked up at Wallace. The little man's jaw twitched. His eyes had a hazy cast. Huller's voice dropped. "What the hell am I getting into? Jesus Christ!"

Dotty shrugged. "He can read easy stuff that's printed." She laughed lightly. "Canny can read as good as him now."

Huller got up and went to the door. He stood looking out across the dusty driveway. "You should see the house they have, Canny's family," he said.

"I already seen it," Dotty said. "I was in it. Remember?"

Huller turned and seemed to be studying her, as if he were trying to make up his mind about something. "Weren't you scared, just walking into a strange house and taking off with their kid?"

"Not then. Not inside." She laughed. "I was gonna tell whoever came to the door I was collecting for cancer or something and then when nobody came, I just opened the door and went inside, straight on into the kitchen. There was a glass jar on the counter with dimes in it and then all of a sudden I remembered how hungry I was and I opened the fridge and stood there looking in at all the food, and then I heard this baby voice saying, 'Hi, hi,' and over the door of the fridge, I could see this tiny little girl. She was in the other room, in her playpen, you know, with her face pressed to the side, all cute and pudgy through the holes. The phone started to ring and she kept saying, 'Hi, hi,' louder and louder like she wanted me to say it back. Like if I didn't, she'd cry or something. So I went in and I said, 'Hi.' And then when I started to go, she started hollering it, 'Hi! Hi!' "

Dotty drew her knees to her chin and smiled. Wallace was looking at her now, and listening carefully.

"She wouldn't shut up and then the phone stopped ringing, so I grabbed her and then I thought I heard footsteps upstairs so I ran outside and when I got to the truck, Aubie started peppering me with questions. That's when I got scared! All I could think of was getting the hell outta there. I didn't think of nothing else, I swear. I mean, if I'd've planned it, wouldn't've gone so smooth." She sighed and rubbed her chin over her greasy shoulder. "Course, try to tell the cops that. How it was just one of those crazy things that just happened. And then I couldn't just ditch her in the middle of nowhere and then, after a while, Aubie was getting such a crush on her that when I'd tell him to stop the truck so I could leave her off someplace, he'd just keep on going. He wouldn't listen to me."

Wallace leaned toward her. "You never said stop, Dotty. I woulda if you did."

"Oh yah!" she laughed uneasily. "You really remember too!"

She rolled her eyes at Huller. "He can't remember what day it is, half the time."

"I 'member that day," Wallace said, gazing into the shadows in the corner of the cabin.

Huller was leaning against the door frame with his arms folded, watching the two of them.

"I 'member what you had on and what Canny had on. I 'member ever'thing that day."

From the woods came the little girls' whoops as Ellie chased them home. Like Ellie, whose tee shirt and shorts were slapped to her body, they were all dripping wet.

Dotty got up and stood next to Huller, who was staring at his sister-in-law. "She's gonna be a bag if she don't watch it," Dotty scoffed. Huller didn't answer.

"Don't be mad, Jig," Ellie called up to the cabin. "I'll get them all in dry things, I promise!"

Huller opened the door. "I'll give you a hand," he said, stepping outside.

"Bastard," Dotty muttered, watching them go into the house.

"Dotty?" Wallace said, and waited a minute. "Dotty?"

"What?" she asked, wheeling around, her arms folded tight across her bosom. "What the hell do you want?"

He hung his head and took a deep breath. "I'm scared."

"So what else is new?" she said, grabbing her cigarettes off the bed. She started for the door.

"Something bad's gonna happen," he said. He looked up at her, his face twisted with dread. "I know it is."

"Shit!" she groaned and flew toward the door, but then stopped suddenly and came back to him. The hard little line of her mouth wavered. "In my whole life, Aubie, you're the only guy I ever seen cry." She shook her head. "You're like a little kid. The first day I saw you, I thought that. It was like no matter what I said or did, you were gonna stick with me. But I was just a kid then, Aubie. I ain't a kid anymore. And in a few years, Canny ain't gonna be a kid anymore. . . ." She laid her hand on his cheek. "We're all getting growed up, Aubie." Her voice softened. "All but you. . . . You know what I mean?"

He shook his head. Truly, he did not.

"No." She looked at him. "Course you don't. I could spell it out black and white and you still wouldn't get it."

After she left, he continued to sit in the straight-backed chair, watching the tide of shadows that rose from the floorboards to his ankles, to his knees, then waist high. Of all the voices from across the way, he could make out only Canny's. He listened carefully. He knew he had to remember this, the way she laughed, and now, the way she was giggling, and then he thought, *Just like them two boys of mine, I ain't never gonna see her again.*

The next morning, Jiggy and Dotty left early. They were headed to Stonefield to go over the route Jiggy had in mind. Wallace was still in bed when Canny came into the cabin. Laughing to see him all curled up under the covers, she ran and threw herself on top of him. "You're getting lazy as Momma!" she scolded, trying to tickle him through the blanket. "Sleeping till noon! Not even getting up to eat or pee. . . ."

"Lemme be," he growled, pulling the pillow over his face.

Canny sat up and lifted the corner of the pillow. "You drunk?" she asked, peeking in at his gaunt, whiskery face.

"Course not!"

"You sick?"

"Nope."

She stared down at the lump in the pillow and scratched her head. "You mad at me?"

"Nope."

"Yes you are. You're mad 'cause I been sleeping over the house, huh?"

"I said I ain't mad."

"You sound mad."

"I ain't."

"Then get up . . . c'mon," she said, tugging at the covers.

"Don't. . . . I ain't dressed." He pulled back on the sheet. "Leave me alone, dammit, Canny!"

"I know why you're mad," she persisted.

"I ain't mad!"

"You think Momma's doing it with Jiggy now, huh?"

"Watch your mouth," he said, raising up on one elbow. He clutched the sheet to his chest. "Or I'll wash it out for ya!"

"Well, that's what you been thinking and I know it. But Poppy!" she squealed, breaking into a grin. "It ain't true. Least, not anymore. After Momma came over last night, Jiggy and Ellie were kissing on the couch."

"They was?" Wallace asked eagerly.

"Yup. I saw 'em through the hole in the floor." Canny smiled. "But then he turned out the light." She hopped back on the bed and sat cross-legged, facing him. "So, there's nothing to worry about, Poppy," she said solemnly. "It's gonna be just like always. Momma'll get sicka him or he'll dump her and then we can leave."

The early sun pierced the window in a fine, thin tube of light. Wallace gazed after it, his eyes distant again. Canny picked at a thick scab on her knee as she whispered stories about Alma and how she'd hate being her kid or Jiggy's, they were both so mean to Kelly and Krystal. "So, I guess I'll keep you, Poppy," she giggled, scrambling next to him. With her head at his chin, she curled close. She smelled like a milky little kitten. "That is, unless something better comes along," she said, in her gravelly voiced imitation of Dotty.

Jiggy had gotten a street map from the Stonefield town hall. He had the map spread out now on the cabin floor. He knelt over it, and with a red crayon drew a line down different streets. Dotty squatted next to him.

"What's that?" she asked, pointing to the X he had just made.

"The graveyard I showed you," he said, pausing to sit back on one knee. "Down behind these train tracks. From here, the graveyard," he said, running his finger along the map, "to here—the Birds' house . . . only takes five, maybe seven, minutes. . . . So, soon as the money's dropped, Pops brings the kid. . . ."

Wallace's eyes shot to Dotty's.

"I told you," she said. "He's scared of graveyards! Scared shitless!"

Huller looked up at Wallace's gray face. "That true? Pops?"

Wallace nodded.

"What the hell's to be scared of?" Huller snapped. "Everybody in there's dead. Dead people can't hurt you, right?" At the sight of Wallace's constricted eyes, Huller's tone eased. "Right?"

Wallace only shrugged miserably. He fiddled with the rim of his baseball cap.

Dotty drew her finger along the map. "Why not here?" She looked at Huller. "The dump. Aubie's used to dumps."

"Too far away," Huller said. "The graveyard's only a couple minutes from the kid's house."

"What the hell's the difference?" she asked. "Five minutes, ten minutes. . . ." she said, wiping polish remover onto each scarlet nail.

Huller snatched up his map. "You're starting to sound stupid as . . . ," he snarled, then, with a glance at Wallace, caught himself. "Time's all we got here. Once he makes that call, I gotta fly."

"Whatd'ya mean I? Where the hell am I gonna be?" Dotty broke in.

"In the truck, of course." Huller smiled sweetly. "With me." He winked.

She glanced uneasily at Wallace. "And then after he gets the money, he leaves off Canny and drives over the tracks to meet us," she said, in a loud, exaggerated tone.

"Something like that," Huller said, spreading the map again. "The fine points come later."

"Hey Jiggy!" Ellie called from the driveway. "Let's go!" Huller made a move to rise, then rocked back into place. Dotty was still talking. "How much later?" she wanted to know.

"A day or two."

Wallace's head jerked up. "You mean mebbe tomorrow?" His chest rose and fell in a little pant. "You mean we're gonna be bringing her back so fast?"

"No, no," Huller said, patting Wallace's shoulder. He folded up his map. "I just want to get it all figured out by then. That's why I keep going over the different routes."

"Hurry it up, Jig!" Ellie hollered from the driveway.

Huller went to the door with Dotty right after him. He turned and jabbed the map in her chest. "Where the hell do you think you're going? It's Ellie's old lady's birthday."

"Want some hot dogs?" Wallace asked, clearing the beer cans and cigarettes into a paper bag. "There's some left from last night." He knelt down and picked up the cap to the polish remover. "I could cut 'em up in sauce like you like." He had to press both hands onto the bed in order to rise. His knees were swollen and stiff with the cabin's dampness. "And after," he coaxed, "we could go for cones."

She stood in the doorway, hugging her arms, watching Canny come toward the cabin.

"Mebbe if you want, we could go for a ride after," he said. She shook her head.

"Mebbe we could find a drive-in movie. . . ."

"Shut up! Will you just shut up!" She ran outside past Canny, and sat up on Huller's porch, on the top step, tight in the right-hand corner, where Wallace usually sat, the one spot from which you could see the bend in the road.

Canny came in and flopped down on the bed. She said she was glad Alma had taken the two girls with her and Ellie. "They just suck's all they do," she sighed, scratching her head with both hands.

"Watch your mouth!" Wallace said, spinning around. He grabbed her wrists. "And stop that scratching!"

"You leave me alone!" Canny suddenly shrieked up at him. Her eyes were fierce with rage as she tried to pull her arms free. "You bastard!" she screamed, writhing and kicking up at his face. "Let goa me, you stupid little prick!"

He dropped her arms and just stood there, looking down at her. He wasn't mad or even hurt; he was afraid. "Listen to me, Canny," he said, pulling the chair close to the bed, where she lay curled in a ball with her back to him. "I gotta tell you something. Look at me, Canny . . . will you just do that for me, please?"

She turned and looked up guiltily at him. He took off his cap and scratched his head, then set the cap back on. "You see. . . ." He rubbed his nose until the tip was red. Her eyes never even blinked or flickered away. Finally, he was the one to look away. "No more swears," he said, gruffly.

"I'm sorry," she said, in a small voice.

"You better be."

"C'mon!" Dotty said through the screen door behind him. "Let's get the hell outta here."

Canny had already eaten her cone. Wallace could feel her eyes following every lick he made on his. "Here," he said, handing it over the seat.

"You sure?"

"I'm all full up on Big Macs," he assured her. "I ate mine and your Momma's too, don't forget."

"You're such a hog!" Canny laughed, starting in on his cone.

"A hog!" Wallace cried. "Who's calling who a hog that ate two herself, asides a cone, and then mine!" He turned to Dotty, who hadn't said two words since leaving Huller's. He cleared his throat. "Where you feel like going?" He cleared his throat again.

"Don't matter," she sighed. "Anyplace's fine with me."

He gave it a little gas and felt the motor's rush and all the old tappets tapping right up his leg and into his chest like a great surging heartbeat.

"Want the radio on?" he asked hoarsely.

"No."

He winced, not daring to breathe. Not daring to take his eyes off the road; not daring to break the spell. She sat with her head back on the seat and her eyes closed.

Maybe this was it, he thought. She'd just sit there and let him drive all night. And then come morning, she'd wake up and every sign'd say WEST . . . WEST . . . to Hollywood, California. Even Canny could sense it, sitting back there on the edge of the seat, watching him through the mirror.

"Take that left," Dotty said suddenly. Twenty minutes later, she directed him onto a highway, then through a set of lights past a college with a big statue out front. . . .

His hand sagged on the wheel. Ahead, the sign said, WELCOME TO STONEFIELD.

"Look familiar?" she asked, pointing him through the next set of lights.

He didn't answer; his mouth was too dry even to swallow. His eyes burned with every street light. He crouched so low in the seat he could barely see over the wheel.

"Down there's the graveyard. Really there's two, one on each side of . . . Take that left. Jesus!" she squealed as she jerked the wheel left to make the turn.

They were on a wide, tree-lined street. Every house was enormous and all the windows glowed with lights. A young girl and boy were walking up the hill, holding hands. The boy glanced over his shoulder at the rattle of the approaching motor.

"The school's up ahead," Dotty said. "That's where to turn!" She pointed. "Right before the school!"

"What school?" asked Canny. "Is it gonna be my school?"

"That's it!" Dotty cried, as the old car lumbered around the corner. "The one with the big round porch!"

"Looks like a bandstand," Canny said, as they passed by.

"Looks like a big old boat to me," Dotty said, kneeling on the seat and peering back. "Like Noah's ark with the railing all around."

The house, long and sectioned, with black roofs at uneven heights over its peaks and ells and dormers, was no more than a streak of white past Wallace's frozen vision.

She made him drive around the block and park at the corner. Wallace stared at the road ahead.

"How come we're stopped?" Canny wanted to know. "Who lives there?"

"I went right up the porch and in that front door," Dotty was saying. "All the doors were glass and I remember there were mirrors all over the place. White rugs and mirrors and I kept seeing myself and it made me laugh and then I heard, 'Hi, hi.' Every place I turned you kept saying, 'Hi, hi,' " she was telling Canny, who glanced uneasily at Wallace. "Like one of them talking baby dolls that only says one thing over and over till they wind down. . . . Son of a bitch!" Dotty said suddenly. "Who needs the bastard anyway. Thinks he's so goddamn smart, calling me stupid. . . ." She opened the door and Wallace closed his eyes as she darted across the street.

"Momma!" Canny called. The back door clicked, but before Canny could get it open, Wallace had driven off.

When he came back up the hill, Dotty was waiting on the corner by the stone wall.

"You crazy?" Wallace shouted, as soon as she ducked into the car. "What to hell you tryna prove? You don't give a damn 'bout nothin', do ya?" He kept it up for miles, sputtering and shaking his head and saying things he'd never even thought of before. Canny was huddled in the back, sucking her thumb and regarding the two of them with half-closed, inward eyes.

"Just get somethin' in your head and you do it! Don't matter that nobody else's ready or wants to, you just go on and do it or say it. . . ."

Dotty just sat there with her arms folded, stiff and pale, and dry-faced as a china statue.

II

It was late afternoon and three days into a heat wave that had shriveled the leaves on the trees and dried the grass to tinder. The big red dog panted under the porch. His eyes glowed through the dark lattice strips.

Down in the yard the three little girls sat in a sagging plastic pool with their knees drawn to their chins. They were pale and limp with the heat. Their Barbie dolls floated face down in the murky, grass-flecked water. Kelly said they were all drowned. She said their car crashed and rolled off the cliff and into the pond. Canny and Krystal had given up arguing with her. They drooped against each other in the pool and watched listlessly as Kelly tied stones to the dolls' necks to make them sink.

"They're all dead," she crowed. "Whole goddamn bunch of them!" Canny rubbed the bridge of her nose at a mosquito bite that was raised and white.

Up on the porch steps were Ellie and Dotty in sweaty halter tops and skimpy shorts. Dotty sat on the top step unbraiding Ellie's long black hair.

Alma and Wallace sat inside at the kitchen table. From time to time she glanced out the door toward the road. Jiggy had been gone since early morning. "He's up to no good," she said, lighting her cigarette with a butane lighter that hissed and flared so high it singed her eyebrows. Sweat matted on the dark hairs of her upper lip as she bent over the gray, shapeless bra she was mending. Wallace looked everywhere but at the bra.

Alma had been at the table since breakfast. She had spent most of the morning cutting out coupons from a stack of old magazines while she watched her favorite game shows. Every time Wallace tried to leave, Alma thought of something else she wanted him to do. After he had dried the lunch dishes he swept the kitchen floor, and then, when he thought Alma wasn't looking, he made it as far as the porch. She called him back and insisted he sit down and rest while she got him a cup of coffee. That was an hour ago and he still hadn't gotten any coffee.

"Once," she was saying, "him and this guy he knew, they were gonna hold up a liquor store and he acted just the same as now. Mean and nervous and gone all the time." She knotted the thread and bit it off and spit the long end onto the floor. "And when he's home, he's cleaning that damn gunna his all the time." She glanced up at the clock and Wallace knew it was almost time for her soap operas. She stubbed out her cigarette and poured a glass of cherry-powdered drink. She took a sip and made a sour face. "You forgot the sugar!" she said.

"I just put half in," Wallace answered. "Too much ain't good for ya."

Alma reached for the sugar bowl and tipped it over the glass. "I'll bet your first wife hated losing you," she said, as the sugar ran into the bright red drink. "This place is starting to look like one of them magazine pictures. So clean, I'm afraid to move." She slid the sugar bowl across the table and Wallace centered it between the salt and pepper shakers and the ketchup bottle.

"Lookit you," she laughed. "Mr. Neatfreak himself!"

Ellie's voice carried in from the porch. "I got a heart-shaped face," she said. She had pulled her hair back from her face and was looking up at Dotty. "Which is the best kind . . . well, easiest for different hair styles, that is."

Dotty's reply came in a strained voice. Alma shook her head.

"All she thinks about is that hair of hers." She lit another cigarette. "Spoiled brat," she said, through a cough.

Ellie came inside then. In a cold voice she asked Alma if she could borrow the scissors. They had barely spoken since Alma caught Jiggy and Ellie splitting a six-pack while they watched the late show together. Of course, Wallace had gotten another version from Canny. What Alma had come upon in the middle of the night was her sister fast asleep on the floor next to Jiggy with the "Twilight Sermonettes" flickering from the television, revealing Ellie's bare bottom through her nightie. Jiggy had looked up at Alma standing over them, her foot poised, ready to kick her sister's back again, and he said, "Kick her again and I'm gone." This, Canny had reported eagerly, adding, "If only he'da gone, Poppy, we'd be all set. We'd be gone now too."

"What do you need scissors for?" asked Alma, rolling her eyes for Wallace's benefit.

"For my hair," said Ellie, picking up the scissors from the coffee can that was Alma's sewing kit.

"Your hair! You ain't cut your hair since you was ten."

"Just the ends," Ellie said. "Dotty said they're all split and shitty looking. She's gonna trim 'em for me."

"She oughta trim something else while she's at it," Alma muttered. Ellie stalked outside and slammed the door.

Wallace got up and headed for the porch. He was sick of being stuck in here all day with Alma. He wanted to sit on the cabin steps and watch Canny in the wading pool. As foul-mouthed and mean as the Huller girls were, he still enjoyed watching Canny play with them. He loved the way her voice curved through the hot dusty sunlight as lightly as wings.

"You better plunge that tub again," Alma said, as he opened the door. "Last night's water still ain't down."

He closed the door. Ellie was back on the steps. Dotty had begun to snip the ends of her hair. From time to time their heads moved close and the giggly buzz of their talk seemed to drain Alma. She sighed when Wallace came out of the bathroom and told her the tub had already emptied.

"It's hard being the oldest," she said. "'Specially to that one." She shook her head. "Wild! That girl was born wild. If she was mine, I'd tie her in the cellar till she was calmed down or old enough to know better. Course, she don't listen to a word I say. It's a good thing Dotty's here. Least she'll listen to her."

She got up and turned on the television, then padded back to the table. Her soap opera was starting. She leaned on one elbow and squinted in at the set. "That's Myra," she said, nudging Wallace. He leaned forward and pretended to look, but from this distance the screen was just a smear of color. "She's the doctor's wife," Alma said in a quick aside. "The one that used to be a go-go dancer." She covered her mouth with both hands and made a whimpery noise. On television, a woman wept. "She's had magnesia," Alma whispered. "She can't remember the past. No matter how hard she tries, it's all a blank." Alma made the same whimpery noise again. "Can you imagine?" she sighed. "Not remembering anything that ever happened to you?"

All at once this picture came to mind. It was just like television in his brain. He was seeing Hyacinth when she was a pinch-faced, weedy little thing who used to work next to him on the jar line at the pickle plant. None of the other workers liked her, but then none of them had ever been very nice to him either. At first he and Hyacinth hardly ever talked. For four years, they had worked side by side, packing the dills eight to a jar, cut sides in, with their conversation consisting mostly of hellos and looks like rain, mebbe—with her doing most of the conversing and, eventually, the proposing, though it had been on his mind for months previous, he confessed after they were married in her uncle's twelve-pew church.

"Well, why didn't you say something?" she wanted to know.

"I dunno," he said softly, his brain all mushy and fogged with love and tenderness. He could feel the warmth of her hand on the armrest between them. Before her, he could remember the touch of no other human being. He couldn't stop grinning at his new bride, Hyacinth Wallace. He was part of something.

He had no sense of her belonging to him. It was more that he now was hers. He would settle into her life with the same eager trust that had so long before allowed the heavy metal brace to be fastened to his leg and would, in the years to come, propel him up and down countless highways, with Dotty beside him, her eyes as wild as her laughter, and between them, sleeping with her head on his lap, would be the tiny little girl, Canny, who would love him and trust him and believe in him more than anyone else ever had or ever would.

Hyacinth had looked at him, her hand no longer on the armrest, but white-knuckled on the lunch box she had packed for them to eat on the bus. They were on their way to Burlington, their honeymoon trip. A weekend at the Green Mountain Boys Motor Lodge; breakfast included and all the ice you wanted. He had had two bags delivered before he realized he had as little use for ice as Hyacinth had for him.

"Why'd you make me do all the finagling?" she had persisted.

"I dunno," he answered truthfully. He had no idea why she had ever spoken to him in the first place one day at the time clock when they were both punching out. He had no idea why she had walked down the steps with him, then kept walking along the bright dusty road, all the way into town to the shoe shop, where he had lived upstairs in the same dim room all the ten years after the Home; lived there alone without ever once in all that time having had a visitor or having heard a voice within those hard, airless walls but his own; had lived not only alone, but lonely, so lonely that he had begun to imagine that parts of him were breaking off, falling away, and missing. He was conscious of his thousands of different pieces. His brain had grown staticky and sore with the effort of having to keep track of all his parts. The sense of loss he felt was both strange and frightening. And sad. When he slept, he would dream the saddest dream of all, the dream of the missing brace, that one most conscious part of him that kept him whole and safe. In his dream, he would float right up off the bed, through the ceiling and the roof, drifting like a balloon through the thickest clouds and thinnest air, unanchored and weightless, clear off the face of the earth, with nothing or no one to yank him back.

And so she had asked him one more time—in the motel room right after they had tried to do it and had failed. He had known about that part of it, what it was they were supposed to do together. What he had not known for sure was how actually to get that part of himself inside her. Since neither one of them would touch anything with their hands, it wouldn't work. He had felt bad. Especially because Hyacinth seemed so mad. She asked him again. "How come you never let on? How come you never said nothing about us marrying and let me do all the chasing? Was your plan, wasn't it?" she cried, pummeling his back until it was black and blue. "To make me look foolish . . . to make them all laugh and say how my mother was right. . . ." She had pushed him off the bed and onto the floor, where he spent the rest of the night.

It hadn't taken long for a clever girl like Hyacinth to root out his limitations and his faults, which weren't so much things he did, but all those things he was incapable of doing. Most of her unhappiness began when she got pregnant and had to quit work and make do on one paycheck. She started hating the room they lived in over the shoe shop and hating not having a car, and went on to hating his mumbling and hanging his head when they met her people after church, to hating the smell of his feet and the brine in his hair and the way he gripped his fork, until, finally, she admitted how she had made a terrible mistake. It was him she hated, and, more than that, the fact that she knew he'd never change, couldn't change; because what she'd gone and done was thrown her whole life and all her chances (the few a homely girl like her'd ever have, she cried) away on a retard. And he wasn't to cry and feel a bit bad because it wasn't his fault. That's just the way God had made him, was all.

It was all her fault, she bitterly admitted. Her fault for wanting to get out from under her mother's thumb so bad, she'd gone and done exactly what her mother'd warned her against—thinking the first man who treated her decent was the one. She was the one to blame, not him, she wrote in all her goodbye notes, and had to print so that he could read them. She wrote the third note longhand and he was too ashamed to show it to anyone, so he just folded it up and slipped it into the secret compartment of his wallet.

Three times that first year she ran home to the Flatts. Twice he went after her and sat out on her family's front steps until she finally came out and said she'd go back with him. The third time, her daddy, big mean Hazlitt Kluggs, came after him, secured him a job with the county road crew, and moved them and the little they had into the four-room house renting dirt-cheap across from the Kluggs place.

Soon after that, Answan was born. Two years later, Arnold came along. The boys got bigger. Hyacinth took in ironing and mending and squirreled away every cent, going so far as to spend Sunday afternoons, after she made all her wash deliveries, downtown, checking telephone booths, as well as the stubble around the parking meters in the town lot, for change. Summers, she went through the park, up and down the paths, back and forth over the lawns, her eyes alert to the slightest glimmer in the grass. People started saying she was odd. Her back got a hump to it, which her own daddy said was the direct result of her foraging. He said, "Hyacinth ain't seen the sky in ten years, least not on a Sunday afternoon," which all the Kluggs split a gut laughing over. But damned if Hyacinth hadn't had the last laugh on them all.

She had put enough aside to buy the little house they lived in, which was something Hazlitt had never been able to do. She was the first Kluggs to become a landowner, and she was proud of it. Yes sir, it was dignity she was earning, through frugality and cleanliness and serving the Lord every Sunday, singing all three services in her uncle's church. Yes sir, those boys might have the name of Wallace to contend with, she'd sigh, and in the next breath she'd rattle off, like a grocery list, the misdeeds and failures of every last one of their Wallace cousins and uncles and grandpas, drunkards and welfare hell-raisers, and, most shameful of all, that one whole Wallace brood of six boys, all retarded and crippled. But it was Kluggs blood in her boys' veins, she'd insist, with a piece of thread quivering between her teeth. "Kluggs blood!" she'd say, and then pound the table with her shear handles.

And then as now, Aubrey would always turn away. For one thing, he was scared those shears were one day going to land in his heart, and for another (the second reason being the cause of the first), those two boys looked like Wallaces—not only talked and walked and smelled like Wallaces, but had report cards and mattress stains to prove it.

The commotion out on the porch confused him now. When the door burst open, he half expected to see one of Hyacinth's flower-named sisters leaping toward him. But it was Ellie, screaming and holding her hands to the sides of her head. After her raced Dotty, the scissors gleaming in one hand and a slender rope of long black hair in the other.

"Oh Ellie," she cried. "The scissors slipped. I'm so sorry," she called through the bathroom door, but Wallace could see how hard she was trying to keep a straight face.

After supper, Dotty tried to even out the rest of Ellie's hair, but each new trimming only left it more chopped looking. Finally, Dotty gave up. "You'll just have to have it all cut off the same," she said before she raced down into the driveway where the dog barked at the explosion of dust and pebbles that met Jiggy's squealing brakes.

Ellie's wails could be heard in the cabin even though Jiggy had shut the door and closed the window. It was dusk and the cabin's stale heat lay like a veil across Wallace's face. He kept blinking and lifting his chin to see better through the misty vapors. He was surprised that neither Jiggy nor Dotty was smoking. It must be their words, he thought, their voices snagging on his whiskers like dust or soot settling in all his pores.

He sat between them on the chair, his spine as rigid as the chair back. They talked back and forth across him. Dotty was sulky now and hot looking. Damp tendrils of hair curled at her temples like little red feathers. Wet little bird, he thought. Minute the air clears and morning comes, she'll be gone. "Where to now?" he'd ask, stretching his legs out long and sure over the pedals, feeling the highway's heat boiling up through the floor mats. "Anywhere," she'd sigh, her heart so much a part of her voice that the words bled and ran her disappointment all over him and Canny, who would pass secret smiles through the rearview. They'd have her back, same as always. And for days after, she'd need the two of them, him and Canny, the way she needed air to breathe. And his own heart would pound in his ears so loud he was sure she could hear it too. And he could think straight, and Hyacinth and those two boys and the long, pine-dark mountain road would be as distant and as dim in his thoughts as the man in the moon.

Dotty kept glancing up at him. Jiggy was telling them how he had driven each of the possible routes over and over until he had finally settled on the safest and the quickest. The money would be left off in the cemetery—in a sand bin that was next to a certain vault. And that way, Jiggy added, Wallace wouldn't have to worry about waiting in the cemetery. However, it was clear from his tone and the quick way he looked at Dotty that he had fixed it so *she* wouldn't have to worry any more about Wallace getting scared in the cemetery. Jiggy said he would be there himself. All Wallace had to do was give Canny a sleeping pill to knock her out, then drive to the town forest, which was on the outskirts of Stonefield, where he would leave her in a shack, sound asleep. Like a sleeping princess, the soft-eyed little man was thinking.

After that, Wallace was to go to a telephone booth and call the Birds and tell them where they could find their long-lost daughter, the baby girl, little Caroline, the pale-haired shadow in the picture, the fairy baby whose image had begun to glow behind his eyes like faint yellow candlelight.

Jiggy smiled proudly and Wallace's head swayed dreamily. Dotty was looking for a cigarette. She emptied her purse out on the bed and scratched through candy wrappers and lipstick tubes and the bright slivers of a shattered compact mirror. All she could find was a broken-off filter. On the other bed, Huller had the map open. He was drawing a black line from the cemetery to the town forest. He bent close and measured the line with his two fingers marking the inches. "Almost eight miles," he murmured. "Maybe nine. . . ." He measured again.

"Got a butt?" Dotty asked, sliding her legs between the beds and reaching into his shirt pocket. She fished out a piece of paper and when she saw the flush of anger on Huller's face, she giggled nervously and held the paper in front of her, dangling it as if it were in flames.

Huller bellowed and lurched for the paper. Dotty screeched and jumped onto the bed to get away from him. For her it was still a game, a way to get his attention. She shook the paper open and held it close to her face.

"I was saving that," Huller said uneasily. "I was gonna show you later." He gestured weakly and looked at Wallace. "Thing's exaggerated all to hell," he said.

Dotty's breathing seemed to stop as she read. Her shoulders curled close and she sank to her knees onto the bed. Her eyes rose and fell from line to line.

She looks like a little girl, Wallace thought. And in the last trail of daylight, with her head bent forward like that and her hair frizzed close to her sweaty temples, he was for some crazy reason reminded of the little Johnson girls who lived back through the woods, just up from Carson's pig farm. The hairs on the back of his hand stood on end and he felt goose bumps scurry up his spine like hard little feet. His head swirled. Suddenly he was remembering all kinds of crazy things. The yellow and pink squares in the quilt Hyacinth kept folded at the foot of the bed, but would never use; some things were just for show. Into his mind came faces and names he hadn't even thought about since that day, flying down the mountainside next to such a creature as Dotty was, wild and laughing with tears streaming down her cheeks.

"Jesus Christ!" Dotty gasped, still reading. "Her father's a bank president . . . holy shit!" She looked up at Jiggy and made a face. "The F.B.I." She shuddered. "The F.B.I.!"

Wallace was grinning as he remembered something else, them sugary baked beans Hyacinth always made from scratch. Saturday night was beans and franks and brown bread she did up and baked in cans.

"They always call the F.B.I.," Huller said, looking quickly at Wallace. "No big deal."

"No big deal!" Dotty said, shuddering again. She thrust the paper out at Wallace. He smiled and glanced at it. Now he was remembering her scalloped potatoes and all them soft fat raisins swimming in the cheesy sauce. . . .

"Take it, damn it!" Dotty was saying. "Here!"

He went slowly, sounding out each word. Most of them he had to point to so Dotty could tell him what they were. His stomach felt queasy the way it used to in school when he had to read out loud with the teacher standing over him, sighing, while the whole class snickered.

TOT FEARED KIDNAPPED

Police tonight are investigating the disappearance of Caroline Anne Bird, the eighteen-month-old daughter of Louis and Martha Bird. The child was reported missing at 2:10 this afternoon. Mrs. Bird said that it was shortly after 1:30 that she first discovered her daughter's empty playpen. Mrs. Bird said she was upstairs in the family's 8 Trenton Street home for only a few minutes while Caroline was in her playpen in the family room at the back of the house.

The distraught mother, who is nine months pregnant, told this reporter that she panicked and ran up and down the streets, calling the baby's name. "It was like being in shock," Mrs. Bird said. "I couldn't believe that she could be there one minute and gone the next. I still don't. I kept hoping one of the neighbor's children had taken her out to play. I just kept looking and looking and hoping. It never occurred to me until I called Lou at the bank that she might have been kidnapped."

Relatives and neighbors, along with local police and a National Guard unit, as well as fifty Boy Scouts, were still combing the area at press time. At 3:30 this afternoon, "Bunti," a four-year-old bloodhound, was brought up from the Georgetown State Police barracks to help in the search for the missing toddler.

The child is described as fair, blue-eyed, and blond. She was wearing a yellow and white pinafore, soft-soled white shoes, diapers, rubber pants, and a narrow white ribbon in her hair.

Stonefield Police Chief Daniel T. Mismanno said the F.B.I. has been called into the case.

Louis Bird has issued the following statement: "Caroline's family anxiously awaits any communication as to what is expected of us. Until further word, we are offering a twenty-five-thousand-dollar reward for the safe return of our beloved Caroline."

Louis Bird is president of the Stonefield Savings Bank and Martha Bird is a Paxton Academy faculty member and former town selectwoman. Caroline is the family's only child.

"What's that mean?" Wallace asked.

Dotty looked at the word. "Faculty member—means she's a schoolteacher."

He thought about this and when he spoke there was a note of wonder in his tinny voice. "I always knowed Canny was real smart."

Huller rolled his eyes. "Is he for real?"

Dotty giggled nervously. Huller folded up his map and went to the door, then paused and said softly to Dotty, who was right on his heels, "He's not . . . you know, retarded or anything, is he?"

Dotty laughed and tried again to make light of the little man hunched intently over the copy of the newspaper article he could barely read. Huller's face was tight with worry as he looked back at the strange mixture of pleasure and fear that played over Wallace's features.

"I mean, I can't be betting it all on a loonie—you know what I mean, Dot?" There was fear in Huller's tone.

Wallace's lips moved silently as his finger traced an arduous path from word to word.

"It's like the way he drives," Dotty said. "He gets there. It just takes him a while."

Huller muttered something. Dotty closed the door softly and followed him outside into the warm, damp twilight. Down in the driveway her voice slipped into the silence like a stone through water, quick and smoothly appeasing. "He's the least of our problems," she was saying. Huller went into the house without answering.

Now, the moon was round and white as a pearl in the black night. Wallace was still reading; the same words over and over. The little words triggered his recall of the bigger, harder words. It was just like a real story. Only he was in this one. Someplace. His hands trembled and the paper fluttered as if a vein pulsed through it. The words were magic. The letters had powers. They moved and scrambled all over the paper, then reset themselves so that all at once he could see everyone. They were all here; Hyacinth and himself and the two boys and the hot-top crew and Canny. He looked up, swallowing dryly. He could not imagine a day without Canny. What would he do? Who would he talk to?

He slid from the chair now onto the bed, where he lay on his side with his knees jackknifed to his chest. The moon rose higher and higher, its stark light flowing through the doorway and window. When it was exactly over the cabin's tar-paper roof, Wallace closed one eye and then the other and soon he was asleep; but the sleep swirled through a black vaporous tunnel that pushed out from his soul into the farthest part of the night, ending in that bend in the dark hallway with his cheek pressed to the damp wall and his eyes sewn tight like dead men's eyes, while in his ears Hyacinth's harsh voice told of the great horned beasts that crouched in the tangles of bed sheets and window shadows, ready to sink their razor-sharp fangs into the soft warm throats of naughty little boys who peed in their beds in the middle of the night.

VANISHED

All through the night, he stood by their door. Never once, in the dark of sleep or the deep pain of his dreams, did he leave them unguarded. When morning came, he sat up suddenly and felt the mattress wet against his thigh. Just then, a gust of early morning wind caught the door and blew it shut and he screamed to have the thing so near.

12

He thought it was July; sometime in July. The days were a bright web of women's voices shimmering in the porch heat and a blur of tires spinning dust in and out of the driveway and the late-night slamming of doors on children's nightmares, from which could burst the sudden clear scream of tears, children's tears, his, the little girl . . . Answan . . . Arnold. . . .

The cabin door banged open. "Give it over," Huller said, eclipsing the square of morning light. He gestured with his fingers. "I need it!"

Wallace pretended to sleep. His big toe twitched.

"Jesus Christ," Dotty groaned from the other bed. Hugging the sheet to her bosom, she rose up on one elbow, her face puffy and dully white.

"Wake him up!" Huller barked. "The article, I need it!"

"He lost it! He already told you," Dotty said.

Huller was at the foot of the bed now. Wallace lay so still that he felt dizzy, suspended in air.

"Wake up!" Huller demanded. "I don't have all day." He shook the bed, then kicked it. The impact vibrated in a ringing metallic shudder through the bed frame. Again, he kicked it, and this time the bed jumped.

"Jesus Christ," Dotty groaned, holding her head.

Huller bent over Wallace. He reeked of stale booze and old sweat, the smell like a bad taste, like spoiled meat, sour and wormy. Wallace's eyes seeped open. Huller's skin was dry, scaly. Flakes of it lifted at the cracked corners of his mouth. His eyes were bloodshot and pouched with circles.

"You awake?" he asked.

Wallace nodded.

"You find that clipping yet?" he asked. He kept wetting his lips. His chest rose and fell in wheezy gasps.

"Nope," Wallace said.

"You better find it," Huller said. "You got until this afternoon!" He swiped his fist at Wallace's face, just missing him.

"Leave him alone!" Dotty said in a disgusted voice. "You're just taking it out on him!"

"I want that clipping!" Huller growled.

"Get another one then," said Dotty. "You said it was a copy, and besides, you said yourself it wasn't important."

"That ain't the point," said Huller, his voice flattening, the anger and panic reined in and tight as a fist. The dog was clawing through the weedy underbowels of the cabin, its snout snuffling up against the floorboards. "The point is carelessness and worrying every minute the dummy's gonna blow it on me, that's the goddamn point!" said Huller.

Dotty drew the stained sheet around her as she got out of bed. She yawned and her bare feet made sticking, flappy sounds on her way to the bathroom. "The point is, you're just taking it out on everybody 'cause you can't find out their telephone number." She went into the bathroom and sat down with a little grunt. Beneath the stiff plastic curtain her feet straddled the base of the toilet bowl. "Like it's our fault or something," she called over the gush of her urine.

Wallace was embarrassed.

She flushed the toilet. "Like it's our fault they got an unlisted number!" She came out, knotting the sheet under her arms. From the heap of clothes on the floor she picked up her pants and fished a half-smoked cigarette from the pocket. "Call him at the bank," she continued. "Say you got something private to discuss and ask for his home number. Say it's personal." She lit the cigarette, her eyes sagging heavily on the first deep drag.

"It's the fucking Fourth," Huller said. "Everything's fucking closed." He looked down at Wallace and gave the bed another kick. "I want that fucking article," he warned before he left.

"Call one of his neighbors then," Dotty said, following Huller down into the driveway.

Wallace could hear the scuffle of their voices. The truck door slammed shut and the motor sputtered, then came on with a roar.

"Don't forget about the cookout," Dotty hollered.

"Fuck the cookout," Huller hollered back.

As soon as the truck was gone, Wallace got out of bed. Completely dressed, he had even slept with his sneakers on. In the bathroom, he splashed water on his face, then peered into the cloudy pitted mirror. His eyes were strangely bright. He moved closer and his breath fogged the glass. In the center of each eye he saw a small square of light, opaque and gleaming like a sun-flooded window. He looked away and quickly left the bathroom. He sat down on the edge of the bed. Cocking his head, he listened a moment before he unlaced his sneaker and slipped it off his foot. He lifted the rancid innersole and pulled out the flattened clipping, its soft corners tattered and sweat-stained. He smoothed it out on his knee.

So it *was* July, the Fourth of July. He tried to find that in the story, tried to find some mention of firecrackers and night sparklers and icy watermelon slices. Was there a parade? Could they hear the band from that house? From the front porch? From that big round front porch with all the rocking chairs just barely rocking in a breeze? Or did they take her to the parade? Mr. Bird probably carried her; probably sat her up on his tall, wide shoulders, and held on to her skinny little ankles. Beside them stood Mrs. Bird with her arms folded on her big baby belly.

From time to time, Hyacinth appeared in the story. Some

days it might be only a fleeting glance of her that Wallace had, the long thin whip of her apron string as she turned a corner, or just her worn green hymnal on the black stand by the bed.

But today was different. It was the Fourth and hundreds of people lined both sides of the street to see the parade and he was on one crowded corner and there on the opposite side was Hyacinth, all done up in her blue Sunday dress with the iridescent glass buttons sparkling on her chest and the black tie shoes she always wore because high heels put too much of a strain on her curving, bony back.

His breath quickened.

Her eyes scanned the crowd. She was searching for someone. For him. Of course, for him. What would he say? How would he ever explain it? Five years, she'd say. Five years.

The band was coming. His heart beat with the drums of the approaching Boy Scouts. Fifty Boy Scouts marching by; fifty Boy Scouts with bright orange scarves knotted at their throats and tan caps peaked on their dark-cropped heads; fifty Boy Scouts still combing the area at press time. . . .

Today was the Fourth of July and Huller had said he wanted it done by the seventh, but because he didn't know the Birds' telephone number, they couldn't be called. Wallace stared at the paper, at the letters that scrambled in and out of words. He couldn't think straight—not about Canny, not about ransom money and cemeteries and laying her limp body down on the forest floor. None of that was near enough to be real. It couldn't be real until it was happening. His only bridge between the past and the future had become this paper and, in the most frightening way, Canny.

The door opened and his head shot up.

"What's that?" Canny asked, squinting as she stepped from the wall of hard bright sun, here, into the dimness. She sat on the foot of the bed. Her cheekbones glistened with gritty sweat. "What's that?" she asked again. Wallace looked at her a moment and then he folded the clipping and put it back in his sneaker.

From across the way came Dotty's laughter. Alma was dragging the kitchen chairs onto the porch, where Dotty sat on the floor, cross-legged, surrounded by record albums. Ever since Ellie had gotten sick last week and gone home, Dotty had been her old breezy self.

"We're gonna have hot dogs and hamburgs," Canny said, gesturing toward the house. "They got the grill," she said, meaning the rusted, legless grill he always kept in the trunk of the car. "Momma's picking out her favorite records. Ellie's bringing her stereo back."

Wallace got up and scooped an armload of Dotty's clothes from the floor and set them on the chair. A pair of her red nylon underpants fell and Canny picked them up, idly twirling them on one finger as she spoke. "I got some good news," she whispered. "But you can't tell Momma."

He snatched the twirling panties and stuck them in his pocket.

"Ellie's coming back with all her stuff in a suitcase and they're gonna hide it in the barn and then they're gonna run away soon as he gets the number."

"What number? Who?" Wallace asked.

"Jiggy and Ellie!" Canny came and stood close by him. She rubbed his hands. "Ain't that great?" She grinned. "Ain't that the best news yet?" Her jaw trembled and suddenly she was crying. "I got bugs," she said, gesturing at her dull, tangled hair.

"It's just hot," he said. "Ever'thin's all itchy."

"One fell out," she whispered, leaning close.

"Probably a beetle flew on you."

"It was flat. And it had a lotta legs and I couldn't hardly see it."

"Then it was a tick!" he said, smiling at her. "A tick's flat and it's got all them legs. And ticks just get on you one at a time. They don't grow on you like hair bugs does."

She bent forward and with both hands scratched her scalp until her eyes watered. "I'm so itchy, my stomach feels puky," she groaned.

"C'mere," he said, taking her into the bathroom. He wet her

hair in the tiny, brown-stained sink and lathered her with hand soap. He filled the plastic cup with water and kept pouring it over her head. Little beads of light shone on every hair. He rubbed her neck with the towel and when she stood up straight, he rubbed her head with his hands through the towel. Still the hair glistened. He looked closely, sifting one by one through the fine yellow strands. She was loaded with nits. Her scalp crawled with lice.

"I do, don't I? I got bugs," she said with a shudder. "You're looking at the bugs!"

"You got a rash is all," he told her. "One of them itchy heat rashes."

"You're lying to me, Poppy," she said, batting away his hand and turning.

He looked at her. "Don't say nothin' to your Momma," he warned, and she nodded somberly.

Last spring when he had found a bug in Canny's hair, Dotty just took off. Those two days alone with Canny in the tiny, airless apartment had been the most frightening time of his life. Without Dotty, he couldn't think what to do, couldn't seem to make connections. When they ran out of milk, he and Canny drank tap water. When they ran out of bread, they ate just the bologna rounds. When the lady from the first floor banged on the door, hollering that she needed to use their bottle opener, he and Canny just sat very still and looked at one another and never said a word.

"I'll get some stuff for it," he told her now. "Some kerosene or something."

"There's some out in the barn," she said. "In a red can."

They both looked up at the sound of Dotty's voice.

"She's calling you," he said.

"Canny!" Dotty kept calling. "Jesus Christ, get out here!"

Canny ran outside. Dotty wanted her to find the rest of her records. He stood by the door and watched Canny search under the front seat of the old car. She pulled out a hubcap and a bag of Dotty's shoes and the bottle of whiskey from the motel room.

"What's that?" Dotty called, leaning forward.

"Booze!" Canny answered, holding up the bottle.

"Whee hoo!" Dotty cried, shaking both fists over her head.

Alma came out of the house and they both ran down to take a quick swig from the bottle.

A little while later, Wallace was sitting on the porch, watching Canny digging treasure holes in the yard, when a battered red station wagon crawled into the driveway on low, squishy tires. Kelly and Krystal and Ellie got out carrying the speakers and the turntable, the three of them attached by wires and the same slack-jawed languor.

The driver was tall, with long, thin hair and bony, tattooed arms. He approached the house with his head bent and his shoulder angled as if against a singular, biting wind. His front teeth were pitted and stained and pointed like fangs and Wallace knew at once that this was Carl, the brother. The blood drinker. The vampire. The monster in all of Hyacinth's stories.

The night was muddy with damp heat and flecked with a few distant stars. They sat up on the porch, Alma, Ellie, and Wallace, and, down on the top step, Dotty with the three little girls. She wore a satiny red dress split up to her thigh and black glittery stockings. She looked sad and as out of place as if she'd been dropped off at the wrong party. At her feet were a paper cup and the last of the whiskey.

Jiggy had missed the cookout as well as the firecrackers that Carl was busy setting off below them in the driveway. Each fizz of light made the little girls gasp and giggle. Under the porch, the dog whimpered and growled, its hard tail beating the wet black soil. Alma got up and stood over the girls. "Who wants the last hot dog?" she asked.

"Save one for Jig," Ellie called, and Dotty poured herself another drink and leaned back with her elbows on the porch floor.

"He had his chance," Alma crowed. She slid the charred,

withered hot dog into a roll and made a show of giving it to Wallace. He didn't want it, but he ate it anyway. She sat next to him and called down to Carl for a sparkler.

"They're gone," Carl said, as he lit the last firecracker. Its thin red whizz spit and fizzled into the darkness like an arrow suddenly deflected.

"Shit," Alma said. "I been cooking all night."

"Well don't blame me," Carl said, wiping his nose on the back of his hand; his eyes, nose, and mouth were now irritated and raw from the fumes, while his skin in the night had the odd bloodless sheen of a slug.

"You coulda saved me one," Alma pouted, crossing her jiggly, sunburned arms over her chest.

Dotty took a long drink. She leaned back and sighed. Ellie had gotten up to put on another stack of records. The night grew hot and lush, deepening with the din of the music. Ellie snapped her fingers and her head jerked back and forth to the beat. "I been ba-a-ad. I been ba-a-ad. . . ." Lips pursed, she shimmied her shoulders, and then suddenly her head shot up. "Since I been born!" she sang in a growl.

The little girls were up on the porch now, giggling and dancing. Their hard bare feet were crusted with dirt. In an effort to imitate Ellie, they snapped their fingers and twitched their hips and shouted with her, "I been ba-a-ad, a real bad ass!" And then on 'ass,' they giggled, staggering into one another. A half-grin came over Wallace. His eyes were on Canny. Dotty kept her back to them. She took another drink, staring all the while at the distant road.

"Like this!" said Ellie, demonstrating how to rock their pelvises back and forth. "Pumpit!" she laughed, as her own narrow hips undulated. "Hey!" she laughed.

"Hey!" the little girls called back.

Headlights moved through the tree line. The dog crept out from under the porch and began to whine. Dotty got up then and turned the volume as high as it would go and she began to dance with Ellie and the three girls. The music crashed and beat at the night like a monstrous, clanking engine that was slowly consuming them. Goose bumps rose on Wallace's arm. Even Alma was dancing. The porch floor trembled. "Hey!" Dotty called, and gestured down to Carl. He shook his head, self-consciously. Dotty ran down the steps and, grabbing his arm, forced him onto the porch. She bumped her hip into his and danced around him. His two sisters were limp and wet-eyed with laughter. With her knees pinned together, Alma crouched low as if she were trying not to wet her pants. "Oh God," she gasped, as Dotty's arms slithered like snakes round Carl's bony neck and sunken chest. His eyes began to burn and his cheeks warmed with color. Dotty stuck out her tongue and wiggled it at him. He lowered his eyes.

The dog was the first to see Jiggy's truck come into the drive-way. The dog and Ellie, with her chopped, boyish hair. She leaned against the railing and smiled at Huller, who sat in the truck, watching Dotty advance again on Carl, shimmying against him, backing him up against the wall of the house. She whacked her pelvis into his, then stepped away, her face twisted and sharp, and suddenly haggard as if she were going to be sick. The music was over; the record still turned, in a soundless rasp. Dotty went into the house and let the screen door slam after her. Following her Huller passed Ellie with an imperceptible nod. He and Dotty stood just inside the door. His voice was low and coaxing. Wallace leaned back, listening.

"Fuck off," Dotty kept saying. "Just fuck the hell off."

"Four-seven-six-two-one-nine-one," Huller said. "Now tell me to fuck off."

"How'd you get it?" Dotty asked. A match hissed and cig-arette smoke streamed through the door screen.

"I got it," said Huller. "Don't I always get what I need?"

"What about her out there? You said she wasn't coming back."

"I can't make her not come. She's Alma's sister."

"Little bitch gets on my nerves," Dotty muttered.

"Umm," Jiggy sighed. "You feel good. . . ."

"Yah?"

Just then, Wallace saw a long white Lincoln come into the driveway. The black tinted window on the passenger side rolled down and a woman stuck out her platinum blond head and asked the three little girls if this was Huller's place.

"Jig!" Alma warned from the railing.

Huller came out to the top step. The car door opened then and Wipes Callahan got out and Huller hurried down to greet him.

"Hey!" Callahan said.

"Hey!" Jiggy said, starting to nod.

Though Callahan hadn't seen her, Dotty stood just inside the screen door.

"I been hearing things," Callahan said, his head bent as he spoke in a low voice. "I been asking around. You know, that thing the girl said. Well, there were some bucks involved. Still are, from what I hear. There was nothing—no clues, no leads, no nothing. It was like the biggest thing ever around there. I mean, we're talking major. The thing went on. Pictures. TV. The papers. I mean, it. . . ."

"Forget it," Huller said. "She just . . . you know."

"She here?" Callahan asked.

Huller glanced up at the empty doorway. "Nah. She was flipped. You know. I'm sorry she took your time."

Callahan was staring at the three children who sat on the porch railing. "Cute kids," he said. "They all yours?"

Wallace's eyes locked on Canny.

"All mine," Huller said.

"Hey!" Callahan jabbed Huller's arm. "Keep in touch." He drew a card from his shirt pocket and handed it to Huller. "Case anything comes up." He glanced up at the little girls and then back at Huller. "I got a knack for smoothing troubled waters."

After Callahan left, Alma kept playing more records, but nobody wanted to dance. Carl straddled a kitchen chair, backward. Six empty beer cans stood at his feet. Ellie dozed against the railing and Krystal lay against her, asleep with her head on

Ellie's hip. Kelly lay in a ball, curled like a sleeping cat. In her sleep, she scratched at her head and moaned softly.

"Carl," ordered Alma, "bring Kelly up for me, will you?"

Wallace watched Carl untangle himself from the chair. He bent over Kelly, and when he lifted her, she stiffened and her eyes opened wide. "No, Uncle Carl!" she screamed. "No, I don't wanna!" Her scream thinned through the house.

13

It was morning and he felt as if he hadn't slept at all. He got out of bed and went to the bathroom. Bits of things stuck to his feet. Dotty's snoring rose and fell in a soft, hoarse rattle. On the chair between the beds was a plate of sodden potato chips peppered with cigarette ashes. It had been long after midnight before she'd finally fallen asleep. Callahan's visit last night had set them all on edge, especially Huller, who had herded the two of them into the hot cabin. Again, he had wanted all the details of the day they had taken Canny. He had paced back and forth, firing the same questions at Dotty. What had the Birds' house looked like inside? Exactly what time had it been? Where did they go when they left her house?

"I don't know for sure," Dotty had said.

"What street? What road? What highway?"

"Shit! I don't know!" Dotty had roared back. "We just went. I told you that!"

"Just went's not good enough!" Huller had said.

"Why?" Dotty had said, her chin out, her eyes hot. "You don't believe me? You think it's bullshit?"

"Maybe. Isn't halfa what you say bullshit?"

"Yah? Is that the way it is?"

"How do I know!" Huller had said. "How do I know she's not just some kid you're saying is the Birds'. I don't know who you are or him! I mean I could get fucked here in a big way!" His voice had quavered as he ran his arm across his wet forehead.

"You just gotta believe me," Dotty had said. "There's nothing else I can tell you I haven't already said."

"Dotty, you heard Callahan! That kid disappearing was the biggest thing that ever happened there. And I don't understand how the two of you, you and him, especially him, ever in a million years pulled it off. I mean, you slipped right past them, the F.B.I., cops, troopers, bloodhounds, a fucking manhunt! Jesus Christ, how'd you do it?"

Wallace had looked at her. He remembered the endless driving, Canny's tears every time she woke up and saw him, and through it all Dotty's voice, as hard and sure as the road passing under the tires.

"Simple," Dotty had said in an obvious effort to calm both herself and Huller. "Number one, nobody saw us; number two, we were only there a few minutes; and three, what'shername friggin' brilliant Bird didn't even call the cops for what? Forty-five minutes?"

"Forty minutes," Huller said.

"By that time we were long gone." She had laughed. "I mean we were in orbit. We didn't stop. We didn't talk to anybody. We just moved out of one life into a whole new one. We never bought a newspaper and we didn't even have a radio in the truck. We didn't know anything that was going on. We just kept going till we got to Florida. When we needed gas, I siphoned it. When we needed food, I took it."

"It's screwy," Huller had said. "The whole thing. Just screwy."

"No," Dotty had said. "It's luck. I've always been lucky."

From across the way now, a door creaked open. Looking up, he saw Canny tiptoe onto the porch and then glance back inside the house before she scurried down the steps to the small, sagging barn, where she had told him there was kerosene. Wallace started for the door, glad that Dotty was still asleep. This would be a good time to soak Canny's hair. By the time everyone woke up, they'd be done.

Before he could open the door, he saw Carl come out of the house. His shirt was undone and he buttoned his pants as he came off the porch, leaving the zipper open. Still dull-eyed and limp with sleep, he headed toward the barn, moving close to the house through the trough of early morning shadows that rippled and swayed like dark water. With his hand raised to the barn door, he glanced back over his shoulder before slipping inside.

Wallace waited, but in a few minutes when Carl still had not come out, he left the cabin and passed quietly up to the barn door, which was slightly open. He cocked his head, blinded by the bright slant of dust-riddled light that sieved through the opening. The air against his cheek was hot and dry.

"Just touch it." Carl's voice was thick and glutinous. He was short of breath. "I'll give you a quarter like I do Kelly."

"No," said Canny, her voice a faint rustle, like a page turning.

"I'll give you two quarters."

"I don't want two."

"Just touch it."

"No."

"C'mere. . . ."

"Let goa me. . . ."

"Gimme your hand . . . just p . . ."

"You let goa. . . ."

"Don't!" Carl growled. "Uhhh! You little . . ."

"Poppy!" she screamed. "Poppy!"

At that, he scurried back to the cabin, and with his hands on her sweaty back, shook Dotty, pumped her up and down on the bed, pumped her as if she were a drowned body, pumped the sleep from her sleek, wet back.

"He's gonna kill her . . . gonna suck her blood and drink it and kill her. . . . Wake up, Dotty. Please! Oh please!"

She sat up trembling, but her eyes wouldn't open. Propelled

by the terror in his voice, she staggered blindly to the door in just her underpants and bra. Wallace ran back and grabbed the sheet from the bed and threw it around her as they came to the barn. With Wallace close behind, Dotty slid the door open. Up in the rafters, a family of mourning doves shot from their warm, dark perches, their wings beating like the crackle of flames.

"You bastard!" she bellowed, lunging at the shadowy mass that knelt over the struggling, groaning child, his hand clamped over her mouth.

Before he could stand, Dotty was on his back, tearing fistsful of hair from his scalp. Canny sprang at Wallace. Blood trickled from her nose and mouth. Wallace swept up the sheet from the floor and tried to stop the bleeding. He tried to find the vampire's bite, but his eyes were blurred with tears.

"Poor Canny," he bawled, and hugged her close. "Poor baby Canny."

The barn door swung completely open and in the sudden gash of sunlight, Dotty's arm rose and fell with a sick thud. The rusty shovel she had snatched from its nail on the bin caught Carl on the shoulder. Moaning, he lay curled on the floor in an oily smear.

"What the hell's . . ." It was Jiggy, blotting out the sun, the startled dog raging at his heels, snapping, while Wallace continued to dab the sheet corner at Canny's streaked chin.

"What're you . . ." Jiggy had grabbed Dotty's wrist, snaring the shovel in mid-blow.

"Kill him!" Dotty panted. "Kill him and kill him. . . ." She lunged for the shovel, and, with his open hand, Jiggy slapped her, hitting her so hard that her head snapped back and trembled on its stem.

Carl huddled against the bin with his arms scarfing his head. He whimpered like a child.

"It's okay. It's okay; it's okay," Wallace continued to whisper in Canny's dry, brittle hair, though he knew it was not; for now the worst had happened. From the pages of fairy stories of lost princesses and fairy babies, down the long, dark, wet corridors of nightmare, had stepped this monster, this blood-drinker, Carl. And, as in his dreams and the long-ago times (lurking with his ears to the cold, hard wall) he asked himself over and over: What had he done, what had he done, what had he done. . . .

14

"How's this sound?" Dotty asked, her head bent over the paper. "Hello, Mr. Bird," she read. "How are you? I would like to take just a few minutes of your time if you don't mind. . . ."

"Sounds shitty," interrupted Jiggy, as he penciled a short line on the map, and then, turning it sideways, drew a longer, intersecting line.

Her eyes had dark circles under them. She glanced at Wallace, who sat on the edge of the bed. Ever since the incident with Carl this morning, Dotty had seemed on the verge of something; whether tears or laughter or hysteria, Wallace couldn't tell, but something would boil over in her soon enough. This was the tenth time Jiggy had belittled the dialogue she was writing for Wallace to use on the phone.

"What's wrong with it?" she asked.

"Same as before. Sounds made up. Fake." Jiggy leaned over the map.

"I don't know what the hell you're talking about! Course it's made up. I'm making it up!" She threw the paper and pen onto the bed and stomped across the cabin and stood by the door. After a moment, she wheeled around and pointed at Huller. "I know what's the matter!" she said in a tight voice. "You're still pissed about that brother-in-law of . . ."

"Shut up," Jiggy said. "Sit down and shut up!" Carefully, he drew another line on the map, this one in ink, blood-red ink. He smiled and darkened the line.

"Well you are!" she said. "You been on my ass all day and I'm sick of it!"

Jiggy looked up and smiled. "Yah, I guess you're right. Only you got the reason ass-end-to. You see, the thing that really bugs me is getting out there too soon—before you split the fucker's head in two."

Dotty sighed. She shrugged nervously and sighed again. She blinked and her eyes were filled with tears.

Huller tilted back in the chair and shook his head. "What the hell're you doing? You chop the hair off one of my in-laws, and then you try to chop the balls off the other. Who the hell's next?" He smiled.

Dotty laughed uneasily. She picked up her purse from the end of the bed and began to search for cigarettes. "Son of a bitch," she said through the cigarette she was lighting. "Doesn't deserve to live." She took a deep drag that wheezed in her chest. For a moment she stared into space. "Some don't, you know. Once I knew this girl. She was just a kid, really. Fourteen, I think she said. She never had nothing. All her life, nothing. Not even her own bed. Her daddy was just the meanest cocksucker around. I mean, *mean*!" She shivered and hugged herself. "He was always at her. Just all the time, every minute on her case. 'Do this! Don't do that! Help your Ma! Take them kids out for a walk!' He never let her be a little kid herself, you know what I mean? Him and her mother, they just used her. Only he was the worse; he used her the worse way of all. First, it was touching. Then, it was all the way. Poor kid. She was only ten and then when she was thirteen, she went to her Ma and told her. And her Ma said, 'You dirty, lying, pig tramp, saying such things about your own Daddy.'

"And her Ma slapped her and punched her and kicked her

and just went crazy, beating on her and screaming, 'Pig tramp, dirty little pig tramp. . . .' Beat her so bad she couldn't go to school for a week till the sores and cuts got better. So then this girl I knew said, 'I'll fix her! I'll show her!' And she waited till just the right time, till he was drunk and half mean and half sexed up and winking and rubbing himself against the corner of the table and getting that blindy look he'd get like a flabby-donked old bull, tryna talk sweet, but only could think of dirty words like a little kid.

"Only that time she didn't steer clear of him. She didn't leave the house or the room even. Her Ma was due home from cleaning the pigman's place any minute and all her little sisters were on the floor watching TV. She sat up on the chair staring down at the backs of their heads and she thought how if somebody didn't do something, if somebody didn't stop him, then he'd be on one of them next, on one of those sweet little girls she loved so much like they were her own even. So she just sat there and let him keep on and keep on and keep on. And so just when she figured it was time for her Ma to get there, she looked up at him and she smiled and, for the first time, she didn't try to run or anything.

"He grabbed her and she just got up and never once pulled back and went in the room there and never said a word. He was just getting ready and she heard the shed door open and close and then she heard her Ma's voice saying hello to her little sisters. Right then he started on her and once he got going, he didn't care if the whole county came by. 'Ma!' she hollered. 'Ma! Come and get him off me. Ma! Help me, Ma!'

"And you know what happened then?" Dotty smiled, almost amusedly. "The TV just got louder and louder and louder and then she just stopped screaming and fighting and just laid there and waited for him to finish. And she knew then how it was the same for her Ma in a way. How it was up to her, she knew, to keep him off all of them.

"After that, if she said anything, all her Ma ever said was, 'I can't do nothing. Run away then. Take off.' And by then she had a boy she liked, this older guy she used to tell about her and her Daddy to, only she said how it was someone else she knew. And this guy said, 'Tell your friend, some bastards don't deserve to live.'

"And then one night, right after that, it was a boiling hot night and she was sleeping on the couch with just a shirt on and in he came in the middle of the night. It was so hot and sticky and, to tell the truth, she was kinda high herself and had just a while before snuck in from her date with the guy she liked; and he kept shaking her, tryna wake her up, and just when he was gonna lay on her, she rolled off the couch and ran outside, and he took off after her with his bottle in his hand. He caught her, and when it was over, he sat up and lit a cigarette and took a swig, and all of a sudden she grabbed the bottle and she just let him have it. Over and over on his head and his face, and when the bottle was just the broken neck left with blood in her hand, she picked up a big rock and kept on going. Then, just so there wouldn't be any doubt, so her Ma'd know, so everyone'd know, so he'd know, she lit a match and tried to set him on fire—there. The matches kept going out but she could smell his hair burning. So she kept lighting them, one after the other, till the book was empty."

Dotty looked at the cigarette she was stubbing out in the litter of potato chips and ashes. "The weird thing is, she wanted more matches. That's all she could think of, how she needed more matches. But when she got back to the house, the door was locked. So she slept in the shed and then, the next morning, he didn't come back, so she knew he was dead. When her Ma left for the pigman's, she got more matches and went back and tore off his shirt sleeves and put them on his belly and lit them, but the fire kept going out. So she figured she better get going, only she got lost in the woods that day and night and maybe even the next. And she could hear men's voices, sounding mean and hot and mad, and she could hear dogs baying and snarling, and she knew they weren't gonna listen. It hit her how it was probably gonna be just like all those times with her Ma. They'd call her dirty names and they'd never believe her."

Now there was silence. Wallace stared at her and Jiggy stared at her and the only sound in the cabin was the drip of the bathroom faucet. She looked so young right then, like a little girl, Wallace thought. It was the kind of youth that emerges from dreams, from sleep, disembodied and fragmented.

"She get caught? The men ever find her?" asked Huller. He had wedged a matchbook cover to a point, which he was using to dig out the grime under his thumbnail.

"She never said," Dotty answered brightly, her voice like the jangly glass pieces that used to tremble in the wind on Hyacinth's front porch.

"You mean they might still be looking for her?" He held up the thumbnail and, frowning, examined it from every angle.

"Who the hell knows." Dotty stretched back and yawned. "Or cares."

"I do." He had said it so softly and yet so deliberately that Dotty jumped off the bed and stood over him. "Why the hell should you care?"

"What's her name?" Jiggy shot back.

"I forget." Dotty shrugged. "Look, just drop it, will you? I only met her a few times and half a what she said I never believed anyways, she was such a liar."

Huller had turned to Wallace. "You ever meet her before, the one she told about?"

"Nope." Wallace shook his head and thought hard. "But I heard of her. Some place-ter-other."

Dotty's story had confused him. After she and Jiggy left in the truck to get milk for Alma and to find a suitable telephone booth for their call to the Birds, Wallace took out his clipping. Only a few of the letters would come together, just the easy ones like *and, the, me.* He stared at the print and tried to remember how the story went. But Dotty's story kept intruding, so that Canny was sitting in a dimly lit room in front of the television set, while in the distance the pigman's hogs squealed, which was crazy, because the only pigman he ever knew was back in the Flatts. And Buntie the bloodhound was licking a dead man's face. Blood and gore trickled down its drool, and from the fleshy detritus assembled a face, bleary-eyed and black-whiskered, a face he knew, had known, had seen, feared, avoided on the mountain roads and down by Ida's on Fridays. And Canny held up her arms and screamed, "Poppy! Poppy!" And when he went to pick her up, the dog sprang and its fangs tore into his throat, into the soft underflesh of his jaw, where a mouth began to suck, began to work, to suckle his blood.

The door banged. Framed by the harsh glare of the doorway were Alma and Canny.

"She got bugs?" Alma demanded. Breathless and furious, she pushed Canny out in front of her.

"I ain't got bugs!" Canny said indignantly. "Tell her I ain't got bugs." Her eyes widened on Wallace's for confirmation.

"She ain't got bugs," he said.

"Then how come she's always scratching her head and what the hell'd she want kerosene this morning for?" asked Alma.

"Her head's itchy." Wallace shrugged. He looked at Canny. "How come your head's itchy?" he asked softly.

" 'Cause of the heat," Canny said, jerking her bare shoulder out of Alma's rigid grasp, which left the indentation of deep, colorless half-moons where her nails had been. "Makes me itch."

Alma's eyes narrowed. "Well, what'd she want kerosene for?"

"What'd ya want kerosene for?" Wallace asked Canny. A look of panic came over her. "I was thirsty," she told him. "It was hot and I was thirsty."

"She was hot," repeated Wallace, looking to Alma. "And she was thirsty."

"You were gonna drink it?" Alma asked.

"I thought it was cider," Canny said, with clear, wide eyes.

Alma sniffled and drew the side of her sweaty face across her shoulder. "You're not a very smart little girl," she said. "Causing all this trouble just 'cause you're stupid." And then, as if un-stoppered, a great weeping cry drained from her. She sagged onto the edge of the bed and bawled. She sat with her feet so far apart that Wallace could see her huge white panties. He stared at a point behind her head, at the yellow knothole that bled through the whitewashed pine boards.

"Everything's just falling apart," she cried. "My whole life's just falling apart."

"What time is it?" Dotty called out to Jiggy. "Six," he answered.

It was suppertime, but no one was very hungry. Jiggy sat on the front porch, tilted back in a wooden chair with his feet propped on the splintered railing. On the floor beside him was the six-pack Dotty had just brought out from the refrigerator. She wore black shorts and a white halter top that kept slipping down. She couldn't stay still. Alma was in bed, complaining of a bellyache, so Dotty was frying bacon and scrambling eggs in a black iron pan. She kept going out to the porch every few minutes to see if Jiggy needed anything else.

When it was time to eat, Wallace turned off the television and trailed the three children into the kitchen. He noticed that in the space of only a few minutes they had all scratched their heads. Dotty set the pan of eggs and bacon directly on the table and told them to help themselves. She went to the door and leaned against the frame. "What time is it?" she asked.

"Six thirty-five," Huller answered.

She sighed and pressed her forehead against the screen. Wallace bent low over his plate. Suddenly, Krystal spit her eggs into her plate and burst into tears. Kelly had kicked her under the table. Canny went on eating and said nothing. She reminded Wallace of a small gray mouse. Once or twice she glanced at him. Everything about her seemed lifeless and dull. Only her eyes shone.

"She kicked me!" Krystal charged.

"Liar!" Kelly sniffed.

"What time is it?" Dotty asked again.

"Six forty," Huller called back.

"Gross!" Krystal gasped and pointed at her sister. "She's showing her food!"

"Fuck face," Kelly leaned forward and whispered, eggs frothing between her teeth.

At that, Krystal took up a fistful of eggs that had catsup on them and flung them at her sister, missing the mark entirely and, instead, hitting Dotty's bare back. In a blind rage, Dotty flew at the little girl and slapped her.

"Mommy!" Krystal ran upstairs screaming, the mark of Dotty's hand hot on her cheek. Her screams knifed through the house.

"Jesus Christ," Huller muttered from the porch. He sat forward and, one by one, hurled the empty cans at the dog, who had been sleeping in the driveway.

"Now I gotta change!" Dotty cried, running between the bathroom and the porch door. "What time is it? I got time to change? Goddamn, I didn't mean to hit her . . . oh shit . . . oh God, I feel like my head's gonna blow fuckin' off, I'm so nervous. Wipe me off, Poppy." She stood with her back to him so he could clean away the mess. "You're such a little bitch," she scolded Kelly, reaching behind her back to shake out the halter top. "You're just the meanest little bitch I ever knew!" Her voice was shredding, falling apart.

The child's face hardened and her eyes seemed to sink into her skull. "I can't wait till you get arrested," Kelly said, and held out her chin and did not flinch or blink when Dotty bent over her, but continued to stare up coldly at her ashen face.

"What're you talking about, arrested?" Dotty demanded. "You tell me what the hell you mean by that!" She grabbed Kelly's shoulder. The child began to scream for her mother in a voice of such grating terror that Dotty lurched back and held up her hands in submission.

"What the . . ." It was Huller in the doorway.

"What's she mean, I'm gonna get arrested?" Dotty demanded.

"Ma! Ma!" the child screamed, beginning to gag. Her chest heaved and fell and her eyes rolled and her lips darkened to blue. Suddenly her head jerked back on the chair and her legs stiffened in front of her. She fell writhing and thrashing onto the floor. Spittle foamed in the corners of her mouth.

Wallace was horrified. He looked at Canny, who continued to eat. It was only when Alma came running into the room that she laid down her fork.

Alma knelt over her daughter. "Gimme a pillow!" she cried. Krystal ran to get a sofa pillow, which she slid under Kelly's head.

"She said I'm gonna be arrested," Dotty kept trying to tell Jiggy as he bent over Alma and Kelly.

"She's having a fit!" he said, batting away Alma's hands as she attempted to hold down the child's kicking legs. "Let her alone!" he said.

"She's dying!" Alma shrieked, pushing him away. "She's dying and it's all their fault and I want them out!"

"She's not dying, you stupid ass! She's having a fit," he screamed at his wife over the little girl's wracked body.

"Listen to him," Dotty begged Alma. "Listen to Jig!"

"Don't die," Krystal was sobbing into the front of her undershirt. "Please don't die."

Canny slipped off her chair and went into the living room and turned on the television. She sat facing the kitchen, but she didn't look in. Her gaze never wavered from the screen. Every now and again she scratched her head. She's too quiet, Wallace thought. He knew he had to say something about what had happened in the barn. But every time he looked at her and thought of it, he was too ashamed.

"Gimme some water," Kelly murmured. Her eyes opened slowly. Dotty sat next to Wallace. She slumped in the chair. Her hand trembled as she lit a cigarette.

Alma stood up while Jiggy picked up Kelly. He carried her upstairs, followed by Alma, who was insisting that they take Kelly to the hospital.

"It was a fit," he said again. "I seen a lot of fits."

"You saw what happened," Dotty said to Wallace. "I never laid a hand on her, right, Aubie? You were there. You saw what happened."

She got up and stood at the foot of the stairs, listening. She paced back and forth between the worn wooden treads and the table. Every now and again, she reached over her shoulder and scratched her back. "Can still feel it," she said under her breath.

Upstairs, the voices grew louder.

". . . business . . . ," came Jiggy's voice.

". . . Your own daughter? . . . more important than that?" came Alma's voice.

Dotty looked at Wallace and before she had said a word, he knew that the time had come. It would be tonight. Dotty made a move toward him, but Jiggy and Alma were on their way downstairs.

"They come and they go," Jiggy was saying, as they came into the kitchen.

"Listen to Doctor Huller here!" Alma announced. "Well my aunt had fits and swallowed half her tongue once and they had to pull it out and sew it back together!" She glanced at Dotty and Wallace for support.

"She might never get another one," Huller said, washing his hands in the sink.

"Yah, and she might get ten more tonight!" Alma retorted.

"She'll be okay," Dotty said. "Really."

Alma ignored her. "Please, Jig," she begged. "It won't take long."

He was wetting his comb under the faucet. Just as he began to slick back his hair, she grabbed his arm.

"Listen to me!" she shrieked. "You listen!"

He pulled away and wet the comb again. He drew it slowly through the wet, darkening wave on the crown of his head.

Alma looked sick to her stomach. "I know what's going on!" she cried. "Don't think I don't. I can see," she said, tapping her temple. "I got ears! I can hear!"

Drawing his fingertips carefully after the comb, Huller flattened the wave.

"I know what you're up to!" Alma said, and Dotty's face froze. She, too, stared at the back of Huller's smooth yellow head.

He turned. "Look," he warned, shaking the comb at Alma. "You just shut up! You just shut up and get out of my way."

With her arms folded and her sagging chin quivering, she stood directly in front of him. "I seen the stains," she burst out. "And the look she gets around you. . . ."

"Alma . . . ," Dotty began.

"Well I'm telling you, mister. You're just as bad as Carl. Only worse, 'cause poor Carl's got a problem and you . . . you just don't care who you screw." She stepped closer then and swung her fist, catching him on the chin. "You son of a bitch," she bawled as he began to laugh.

"Go ahead," she sobbed. "Laugh! You'll see how funny it is when I call your probation officer and tell him about your fifty fucking thousand dollar big deal you and El . . ."

"Shut up, you pig!" Huller bellowed, clamping his hands on her throat, squeezing and shaking her. "You fat, miserable pig!"

15

The truck sped through the night. Bugs splattered the windshield. Dotty chain-smoked and drummed her fingers on her purse. Next to her, Huller squinted over the wheel, his face cold and impassive.

"Here," he said, when they were still on the highway. Ahead, over the treetops, was a huge sign that said EASTPORT MALL, I MILE. He turned on his directional. "All you have to say is what's on the paper," he spoke loudly over the clicking. "And if Bird asks any questions, just say them back . . . repeat them." He glanced past Dotty at Wallace, who slumped in the seat with the baseball cap low to the bridge of his nose. "That way we can give you the answers." Huller nudged Dotty. "Tell him what I said."

"He heard you," she said dully.

Wallace did not move or speak.

Huller snorted. "Hell, this is gonna be a piece of cake, Pops. Nothing to worry about." He kept glancing over at Wallace. "You're doing them a favor. You got what they want and they're willing to pay for it." Huller laughed. "It's the American way." He laughed again as he sped onto the exit ramp and over a bridge, where they turned left into the shopping center.

Huller parked at the far end of the lot, where the three empty storefronts had FOR RENT signs in their windows. He pointed at the telephone booth on the edge of the parking lot. His voice thinned as he explained how hard it had been to find a telephone booth that stood alone; most of them came in twos or threes and were attached to stores. He had even taken the precaution of removing the light bulb from this one. He had thought of everything. As he spoke Dotty unzipped her purse and removed two sheets of lined paper.

"I'll go in with him," she said, reaching past Wallace for the door handle.

"Wait!" said Huller. "One more time, read it."

"You make me nervous," she said.

"I won't say a word. I just want him to hear it again," Huller said.

Dotty began to read in a lifeless monotone and Huller nodded eagerly with each phrase.

"You listening, Pops?" Huller interrupted.

"Yup," Wallace said.

"The important thing here is to convince Bird that you know what you're talking about. That you're the kidnapper," Huller said.

"But I ain't," Wallace said.

"Yes you are," Huller said, in a soft warning slither.

"Not a real one. Not really," Wallace said, as he got out of the truck, but neither Dotty nor Huller had heard him. Huller gave Dotty a handful of change and then he walked to the phone booth with his arm on Wallace's shoulder. "It'll be over in a minute," he said. "Just be cool, Pops."

Wallace and Dotty were pressed against one another in the airless booth, which was littered with dusty yellowed newspapers and Styrofoam cups. Dotty inserted a dime, listened, and began to dial. In Wallace's hand was the paper she had helped him memorize. Over his shoulder, she trained a small flashlight on the paper. The phone was ringing. Dotty's quick nervous breath tickled the back of his neck. Huller leaned in the doorway, gripping the frame of the booth with both hands. Wallace stared at the words Dotty had printed. His toes curled over the wadded lump in his sneaker and he couldn't remember what it was, just as he couldn't remember why he was here. In fact, if someone had asked him at that moment, his honest answer would have been, "I got to read this paper here. Why? I dunno. What's it mean? I dunno. I just got to, that's all. Don't mix me up. Don't ask me nothin'."

The phone continued to ring. A mosquito was biting the back of the hand that held the receiver.

"C'mon! C'mon!" Dotty growled, jiggling anxiously against him.

"Shit!" Huller said, tapping his fingers on the metal door strip. "Hang up. We'll go sit in the truck a while."

It was at the moment that Dotty clicked off the flashlight that all of the darkness was consumed by an oddly familiar voice in his ear.

"Hello?" the child repeated. "Who's this? Hello?"

"Hang up," Dotty said, reaching for the receiver.

"Hello?" said the child.

"Hello," Wallace said, the speech coming from memory. "Hello, Mr. Bird. I am calling about Caroline. . . ."

"She's dead," the child said. "You want my Daddy?" she asked, and Wallace nodded as she began to call, "Daddy! Daddy! He's in the pool," she confided into the phone. "We're having a party. . . . Daddy! Daddy!"

Dotty had turned on the flashlight. Its trembling beam made the words jump out at him.

"Just a minute," the child said, and the phone fell with a clunk. There were footsteps. A door slammed.

"What's going on?" Dotty whispered fiercely. She jabbed his back. "Who're you talking to?"

"Nobody," he gulped, shaking his head.

"DADDY . . . ," the child's shouts were drifting back, ". . . a man on the phone . . . Caroline. . . ."

"You're talking to . . . ," Huller began.

But to his ear came another click, this one more distant. The child's voice was still in the air, in his mind, imprinted like crickets, like rustling leaves.

"Hello!" came a man's voice, angry and breathless, and, as he spoke, all the voices around him, all the splashing and laughter and conversations and tinkling glasses, ceased. Wallace could feel, could almost see, the men and women frozen, their faces all Kluggses and Mooneys. It was Hazlitt in his ear, his father-in-law lodged there like a sharp stone, Hazlitt wanting his truck back after all this time.

"Hang up!" the voice commanded, and Wallace thought he meant him and his hand moved toward the phone. "Elizabeth! Hang up the phone!"

It clicked. The child was gone. What child? Did the Kluggses have Canny? Dotty shook the papers at him.

"Who is this?" the man demanded. "What the hell do you want?"

In the background a woman gasped "Louis!" and Wallace's eyes widened. He imagined another woman on the line and, connected to her phone, another, and another, like the paper doors in a picture book Canny used to have, one door opening onto another smaller door that opened onto an even smaller door and so on, until the last door opened, and there was a tiny mirror in which you could see yourself.

Dotty hissed and slapped the papers at him.

"Hello," he said. "Is Mr. Bird there, please? Can I talk to him? Thank you, I'll wait."

"What do you want?"

"Is Mr. Bird there?" Wallace repeated in his faint singsong tone. He was horribly confused. His brain felt stuck and there was nothing he could do to make it work right.

"Is this supposed to be funny? I'm Mr. Bird. . . . Is this a joke?"

Dotty had pressed her ear to the receiver, listening. Now she cupped her hand over the mouthpiece. "It's him!" she said. "Tell him!"

Wallace looked at her. Tell him what? All Kluggs wanted was his truck back. The truck was gone. They had sold it.

"It's Canny's father!" she said, backhanding her fingers against his head. "I am calling about Caroline," she coaxed, rolling her hand expectantly.

"I'm calling about Caroline," Wallace said, his voice trembling, the words jumbled and run together. "I am the person August thirty, nineteen eighty, that took her and I still have her. She is fine. I want to give her back to you if you will give me the reward money."

"You're the same nut as last summer! Well, this time I'm prosecuting," said Bird, and he slammed down the phone.

Wallace just stood there, while Dotty and Huller both fired questions at him.

"What'd he say?"

"He sound like he believed you?"

"He ask any questions?"

"He wanna know about Canny?"

"He hung up," Wallace said, the receiver still in his hand, which gripped it like a claw.

"What'd he say before he hung up?" Huller asked.

"He said he was a prostitute," Wallace said.

"A what?" Huller demanded in a high voice; Wallace repeated himself.

Huller hollered all the way back. "All he had to do was keep him on the phone. Keep talking, that's all he had to do! Is that so hard?"

Dotty didn't answer and Wallace stared out the window. They were on the highway. The truck could go no faster. Huller pressed the pedal to the floor and the speedometer trembled on 75, 76. . . . The truck shimmied and the steering wheel vibrated loudly. Dotty popped open two beers, one for herself and one for Huller.

"I got to do everything myself? Get the maps! Get the number! Write the speeches! Jesus Christ, I might as well call Bird myself; might as well tell him I did it!"

"Huh," Dotty murmured.

"I might as well. Might as well for the little he can do!"

"It's phones," she said, turning her head toward Huller and lowering her voice. "I told you. He gets all screwed up on phones."

"Yah?" Huller said, taking a long black capsule from his shirt pocket. He flipped it into his mouth and washed it down with beer.

"You had one on the way," Dotty reminded him.

"Fuck off!" he snapped, slowing as they approached an empty rest area. Huller pulled in and parked directly in front of a telephone booth. He guzzled the last of his beer, then jumped out of the truck, giving the door a vicious slam.

Wallace and Dotty watched him insert his dime. He dialed, hung up quickly, dug the dime from the coin return, and dialed again and again.

"He's getting shit-faced," Dotty said, under her breath. "He scares me when he gets like that."

"We could go," Wallace said. "Tonight. There's gas in the barn."

"Go where?" she sighed.

"I dunno. Someplace."

"We been every place, Aubie."

He thought a minute. "You said Hollywood before."

"Aren't you tired, Aubie?" Her head rested back on the seat. Her gold-lidded eyes were closed. "Aren't you just . . . tired?" She sat up suddenly at the angry roar, which was followed by shattering glass. Huller had just heaved a large rock through the telephone booth.

"Fuckin' phone's off the hook," he muttered, pulling back onto the highway. He held out his hand for another beer and swore because Dotty was having a hard time opening the can. The tab had broken off. "Gimme the opener," he growled. "In the glove compartment!"

Dotty leaned past Wallace and fumbled through the greasy

maps and wadded napkins. "What's this?" she asked, holding a newspaper clipping to the light of the dashboard.

"Gimme that!" Huller commanded.

"It's about Canny." She glanced up at Huller.

"It's the same one," he said.

"No," she said, peering at it. "It's different. It's a picture of her father." She bent low to the paper and began to read, "It was announced this morning at . . ."

"I said give me that!" Huller roared, snatching the paper from her. "Don't do that!" he exploded. "Don't be such a pushy broad! Don't just grab things," he said, as he folded the paper into his shirt pocket. With a quick glance in the mirror, he changed lanes. They had come to another rest area with a telephone booth. The truck squealed in on two wheels and Huller jumped out. The line was still busy. He was about to drop in his dime again, when he dashed out of the booth instead. He stood by the window on Wallace's side and leaned in with a crooked smile.

"How 'bout if I bring you there in person, Pops?" Under the tall arc lights, Huller's face glowed with a pinkish, luminous sweat.

"You crazy?" Dotty gasped.

"That way, you could tell what happened. . . ."

"You're kidding!" Dotty said. She leaned past Wallace. "What're you, nuts?"

"How 'bout it, Pops? What d'ya think?" asked Huller, ignoring her.

Wallace shook his head and looked at Dotty.

"You could tell him what happened. No phones, no thinking. . . ."

Wallace continued to shake his head.

"Cut it out, Jig!" Dotty said.

"You got the balls for that?" Huller asked, grinning.

Suddenly the door opened and Huller was grabbing Wallace's arm and pulling him out. He stumbled and staggered into Huller, who clamped both hands down on his shoulders. "You got any balls at all?" Huller spat at him.

"Leave him alone," warned Dotty, scrambling to get out of the truck as Huller grabbed the front of Wallace's shirt in his fist.

"Don't you touch him!" she screamed, and ran at Huller's back and grabbed him around the waist with her hands locked on his belly. Roaring, Huller spun around and around, and like a doll, Dotty flew with him, her feet dragging in the dust. Huller's laughter had the crack of a fist. Like a sprung bow, he arched and broke free, throwing her backward onto her hands.

"C'mere . . . c'mere. . . ." He gestured in Wallace's face. "I won't hurt you, little man. I just wanna see your balls."

"Bastard," Dotty moaned, getting to her feet.

Huller had Wallace by the front of his shirt again. With his fist jammed into Wallace's chin, he backed him toward the line of dark trees where the woods began. Dotty ran toward the truck and grabbed the two unopened cans of beer from the floor. Wielding them by the plastic connecting circles, she swung them at Huller, hitting him on the back of his head and his shoulders. "Let him go," she cried. "He never did anything to you," she panted. "He never did anything to anybody. . . ."

16

The next morning, Wallace waited until Jiggy drove off before he left the cabin. When he came into the kitchen, Alma was sitting at the table. The dark hairs of her upper lip were flecked with potato chip crumbs. She crumpled the empty bag and threw it at the paper trash bag. It missed and rolled across the floor by the stove.

"I gotta talk to you," she said. She took a wad of toilet paper from her breast pocket and blew her nose. "I gotta know what's going on."

He could barely hear her. There was still in his ears the child's sibilant lisp, as familiar and comforting a sound and yet as startling to consider as the pump and flow of one's own arteries, as one's own heart.

There had been the man's voice. Canny's father, Dotty had said. His eyes were wide, filled with an image of Mr. Bird, tall and thin with a gold watch chained across his dark vest. Caroline was a pale golden child in white with her arms raised toward Mr. Bird's narrow shadow. Caroline was the child of Mr. Bird, Canny's father, Dotty said. But he was Canny's father. That's why Mr. Bird hadn't cared or understood last night. They had been talking about two different children. Mr. Bird didn't know

Canny; that was it. It was almost clear to him. Almost. Alma's voice kept trampling through his brain and muddying his thoughts.

"I woke up with this awful feeling," she was saying. She was spooning grape jelly onto sugar cookies. With quick, covetous movements, she piled her dish with them. "Like something bad's gonna happen." She shivered. "Like there's evil in the air," she said, licking a tremble of jelly from the back of her hand. "It's something bad. I can feel it. He's so weird-acting. Like last night, he got up out of a sound sleep and started cleaning his gun. I could hear him, whistling and kinda laughing to himself." She looked at Wallace. "Where'd you go last night, you and Dotty and him? What're them maps about? And what'd that guy in the white Lincoln want? You gotta tell me! Please!"

Huller's truck could be heard rattling down the road. Alma got up and hurried to the door. "It's him," she said. She shaded her eyes with her hand. "Oh shit! He's got Ellie with him again."

All day long Wallace stayed close by Dotty and Canny. Ellie lay on the couch. There was a large wet stain on the pillow where she had drooled in her sleep. She shuddered as the front door opened and banged shut. Dotty had just come in from sun-bathing. She wore tight black shorts and a man's tee shirt with the sleeves rolled up. She and Alma took out their cigarettes and sat down at the table. With Ellie back, both women had forgotten their harsh words of the day before. They sat with their heads bent close. From the confusion on Dotty's face and then the quick shake of her head, Wallace guessed that Alma had just asked her the same questions about last night.

"Get off me," Ellie suddenly groaned, as Krystal climbed over her curled legs.

"Not until you get up," Krystal said.

"I don't feel good," Ellie warned. "I'm gonna puke."

"Go ahead," Krystal laughed.

With that, Ellie sprang up, catapulting Krystal onto the floor, and, with her palm cupped to her mouth, she raced wide-eyed past the two women, into the bathroom.

"I hope I don't get it," Dotty said, holding the back of her hand to her brow. "I feel like I'm burning up."

Just then Huller bounded onto the porch and into the house. He was wiping his hands with a greasy rag. He banged on the bathroom door, then stepped back quickly when he heard Ellie moan.

"She's sick," Alma said, with a narrow stare. "Me and Dotty were just saying we hope we don't get it."

Huller made a quick move toward the stairs.

"Don't tell me you're sick," Alma said. "Don't tell me you and her both got the same bug now."

His head jerked around, but he smiled and said, "I'm too mean to be sick." He flipped the oily rag at her. She ducked and it caught on the door screen.

"Bastard," she muttered, and Dotty laughed.

It was mid-afternoon and Huller still wasn't back. He had left at noon, refusing to tell Alma where he was going.

From the bathroom, Wallace could hear the two women talking.

"I oughta call his probation officer," Alma said.

"What good'll that do?" Dotty said nervously.

"Maybe that way I'll know what's going on."

"I told you," Dotty said. "He's just tryna help me and Aubie out of a mess. Well, tryna help Aubie," she said, in a low voice. "It's real bad. I mean, he's in some real bad trouble."

Dotty winked at him as he came out of the bathroom and sat at the table. She was working Alma's lank, dull hair into a crown of thin, wet-looking braids. Next, she curled Alma's eyelashes, which were so short the curler only caught the tips of them.

The three little girls had come in and they sat at the table, each waiting her turn to be made up. Canny opened her eyes wide as Dotty gently eased the curler's rubber base pad to her pale lashes.

Watching Dotty, he could almost believe that nothing was wrong, that last night hadn't happened.

"I probably would've had my own shop by now," she was saying, in that soft, distracted voice of women in the midst of making something. She was curling Krystal's lashes now. "After I got Miss Florida, my head got so swelled, I couldn't buckle down," she sighed, wetting her little finger and lifting the corner of Krystal's lash to the curler.

Wallace smiled, squinting a little in the bright blur of her voice.

"And now's the blush," she said, dipping a brush into a little glass pot of glossy pink cream. "Smile!" she commanded, then drew the brush in bright dabs high on Alma's flat, round cheeks. She went on to each of the girls.

"If they let me use my own, this is the shade I'm wearing in the screen test," she said, working the color into Kelly's hairline. The little girls were so pleased with all this attention they could barely speak. Their eyes shone.

Canny lifted one cheek to the tinted brush and then the other. "Oh," she said softly, as Krystal passed her the round, frameless mirror. "I look like a teenager," she sighed.

"Now, who's this ugly broad?" Dotty laughed and pretended to study Wallace. "Lemme see what I can do," she said. "A little color here," she said, drawing bright circles high on his stubbly cheekbones before he could push her hand away.

The little girls giggled.

"Oh Poppy!" Canny cried. "You look just like a clown!"

Dotty turned back from her assortment of makeup and looked at him. "He does!" she said, unscrewing a tube of red lipstick. "You know, Aubie, you do!" she said, bending close and slashing a ring of lipstick around his mouth. "You're perfect," she said under her breath. "Just perfect." She dragged deeply on her cigarette. "You've got that look," she said, in a rush of hot smoke that blinded him.

With eyeliner, she drew broad eyelash strokes, and out from both corners of his red-circled mouth, she penciled long, thin cat whiskers. "Just like clowns do. You know, happy and sad all at the same time. Like any minute your heart's gonna break. . . ."

Alma couldn't stop laughing. She hung on to the edge of the table. "Oh my God . . . oh my God," she wheezed. The Huller girls were also laughing. Canny's smile had weakened. Now Dotty was drawing a bright blue star, which glittered on his forehead.

In the other room, Ellie began to stir with all the laughter and the stench of the women's cigarettes. "Put out them butts," she called. "I told you the smoke makes me sick."

"Go sit on the porch if you don't like it," Alma hollered back.

Again, Ellie begged them to put out their cigarettes. "I'm gonna throw up," she warned.

"Go ahead," Alma yelled. Dotty had just lit another cigarette. Wallace looked up as he heard Huller's truck outside. Smiling, Alma also lit a cigarette. Ellie began to swear and call her sister names. Both women inhaled deeply and blew their smoke directly toward the living room. Ellie screamed and flung one of the girl's sneakers into the kitchen.

"Goddamn it," came Huller's voice from the porch.

"Please don't smoke," Ellie moaned.

"Put it out," Huller said first to Dotty, then to Alma. Outside, the truck's engine raced.

"Tell her to sit on the porch," Alma sniffed, with a conspiratorial glance at Dotty.

"I'm telling you to put it out," he snarled.

Again, Alma looked to Dotty for support. "Nobody cared when it made me sick. You smoked all the time I was pregnant."

At that, Huller snatched the cigarette from her lips. He threw it on the floor and ground it out. There was a brief hiss as Dotty doused hers in her coffee.

Alma stared up at her husband, her face not only white under all the makeup, but waxy. She shuddered and looked as if she were the one who was going to be sick. She kept staring at her husband.

Huller had taken a piece of paper from his hip pocket. He gestured to Dotty with it. "C'mon," he said. "You too, Pops . . . ," and then his mouth fell open at the sight of Wallace's painted face. "For Chr . . ." He looked in amazement at Dotty. "Will you tell him to do something about it? Please?" He went to the door. "Please?" he said again, and the door slammed after him.

"Wash your face!" Dotty snapped, and suddenly Wallace felt foolish.

"He did that to me," Alma said in a small voice. She looked toward the darkened living room at the thin form that huddled on the sofa, Ellie with her knees drawn to her chin, her ragged hair blunt-ended and thickly capped over her ears.

"It ain't fair," Alma said. "It just ain't fair to go through all I been through and then have it end up like this."

"Alma . . . ," Dotty started to say, but the horn was blaring outside.

"It ain't fair," Alma was still saying when Wallace came out of the bathroom and ran out to the truck. Traces of the makeup clung to the rough hollows of his cheeks and his eyes were smudged with black.

"I want some questions answered," Dotty was saying as he climbed up into the truck. "And I want them answered now!"

"You know all there is to know, doll," Huller said, pulling onto the road and shifting into gear. "Tonight's the call. In a few days they go away for vacation." He held out the paper. "Have him read . . ."

"No!" she said, pushing the paper back. "You know what the hell I mean."

"There's nothing to say, dammit!" The heel of his hand hit the steering wheel with a thud. "Now make him read it. This time he does it right! I'm warning you. . . ."

Dotty flipped the paper onto Wallace's lap. He stared at it. Sweat began to bead on the bridge of his nose.

"Nobody warns me," she said. "And nobody, but nobody, screws me either."

"Aw c'mon," Huller said, clamping his hand over her knee. She batted it away.

Huller wet his lips and smiled at her. "Read it to him, will you, doll? C'mon," he coaxed when she still didn't move. "We got big fish to fry." He winked. "Look, relax. This time it'll be easier for him. This time I did a little scouting around first."

"What do you mean?" she asked.

"I called him myself," Huller said. He flicked on the directional. "Just to set it up. So Pops won't blow it again."

"I thought you weren't going to make any moves on your own," Dotty said. "I thought we agreed on that."

"Look, I'm sorry," said Huller. "It was just an idea I got when I was out."

"I get ideas, but I don't just go do them," Dotty said, her voice rising.

Wallace was trying to pay attention now. Blinking, he tried to focus on what they were saying, but the fear he sensed in Dotty caused his own to stir.

Huller was telling her that all Wallace had to do was give Bird a few details. For this, Wallace was glad. He didn't understand Dotty's anger.

"What details?" Dotty was asking.

"Like what the baby had on and where you went after. . . ."

"What the hell's that got to do with anything?" she asked. "That's none of his business where we went."

"I know," Huller said. "I know, but we just have to humor the guy. We have to convince him. I mean, why should he leave twenty-five thousand bucks out in a bag somewhere just because we *say* we've got his kid. Mr. Louis Bird wants to be convinced. And believe me, I could tell, he's ready to be convinced."

"What do you mean?"

"He just sounded tired. You know, like he's been through this a million times before and now he just wants it over."

"So do I," Dotty sighed. She lit a cigarette and sighed again. "I'm tired too."

Huller lit a cigarette. He took three quick drags and then he flipped it out the window in a trail of red sparks. When he came to a small grocery store, he pulled off the road and parked beside the telephone that stood at the far end of the parking lot.

"One more thing," Huller said, turning off the motor. "Bird wants to talk to you too."

Dotty grabbed his arm. "Why? Why's he want to talk to me? How's he know about me? What the fuck did you tell him?"

Huller snatched her hand from his arm. "He said he wants to talk to the one that actually took the kid, the one that went in the house." He shrugged and tried to smile, but the smile stayed small and cold.

"Why? What's that going to prove?"

"Do I know?" Huller said, his voice tightening. He drew his hand across his greasy forehead. "But that's what he said."

"No," she said, her eyes wide. She was smiling. "I'm not talking to him."

"Yes, you are," Huller laughed. "Oh yes, you are."

She turned to him and lowered her voice. "You said he didn't have to know there was more than one. You're the one that made such a big thing out of it!" Her voice was a whisper, scratchy and insistent. Wallace imagined he was hearing her through a window screen. "You said Aubie'd do all the talking. You said it had to be that way."

"Well, now it's gotta be this way." Huller pinched her chin and drew her face close to his. "First he talks to you. And then he talks to Pops. All you tell him is what happened. That's all."

She jerked away. "I'm not talking to him, Jig!" She stubbed out her cigarette and lit another.

"You b . . . ," Huller started to say.

"Don't push!" she spat, pointing the cigarette at him. "I mean it! Don't!"

He grabbed her wrist. "I'll push," he snarled. "I'm in so fucking deep now, it's all I can do!"

Wallace stared out the side window.

"Get your fucking hand off me," Dotty warned, her voice cracking with pain. "You don't fool me. I know what you're doing! You think you're fooling me; well, you're not!"

Huller's hand fell away. His tone softened.

"Course you know what I'm doing, Dot. Course you do. It's what we planned. Only sometimes we got to make a few changes." He smiled.

A half hour had passed. Because Dotty would not speak on the phone, Huller had to rewrite everything. He seemed desperate to appease her. She watched him write and she smoked and said nothing.

Wallace twisted the button on his baseball cap. He felt as if he should also be mad, but all he could really feel inside was fear. When Huller had finished, Dotty went over the speech with Wallace, pointing to each word as she read. He nodded and continued to turn the frayed button.

Dotty and Wallace were squeezed inside the telephone booth. Huller stood outside with his hands on the frame and his head hung. His faded jeans sagged low on his hips and the thick hairs of his chest were matted with sweat. When Dotty had dialed the last number, she listened, then quickly put the phone to Wallace's ear. It was answered on the first ring.

"Hello!" cracked a man's voice like a gunshot, resounding over the line (distantly, "hello . . . hello . . . hello . . .") "Hello!" he said again, almost shouting.

"Hello," Wallace muttered softly, reading with Dotty's finger under each word. "This is the same person you talked to before," he read hesitantly. "I have your little girl. . . ." He pulled the paper closer.

"Caroline!" Dotty whispered.

"Caroline," he said. "And I want to give her back. She is. . . ."

"What does Caroline look like?" Bird interrupted.

Wallace bent close to the paper, searching for the answer. Dotty pressed her ear to the receiver, listening.

"What does she look like?" Bird asked again.

Dotty flipped her hand at him to speak. "Tell him," she mouthed. But he was blank.

"Tell him what Canny looks like," she whispered.

"She's little. And her hair's long now, and her eyes're blue."

"What color is her hair?" asked Bird.

"It's . . . it's . . ." Wallace couldn't think of the word. He squinted at the hairs on Huller's chest. "Yellow!" he said, as suddenly as it came to him.

Huller nudged Dotty and whispered in her ear and then Dotty shook the paper at Wallace. Again, he began to read.

"The day I took her was August 30, 1980. On a Saturday. It was just about noontime. I went right in the front door and through the house and in the kitchen. She was in her playpen in the back room. I took a loaf of bread out of the refrigerator and a blue mason jar of dimes off of the counter and then I heard the phone ring. That's when I took her. When the phone stopped ringing. I took her and I went out the front door. . . ." He kept glancing entreatingly at Dotty. This was her part to read, not his.

"Go ahead." She nodded.

"And then I drove away," he read. "And no one saw me. . . ."

"Did she have anything with her?" Bird broke in. "Something in her hand? Was she carrying something?"

"Jest a spoon," Wallace said, remembering. "That's right. I forgot about that spoon!" He looked eagerly at Dotty. " 'Member that spoon?" he asked her. " 'Member how she wouldn't let go of it?" Dotty nodded and held her finger to her lips. There was an odd silence. All he heard in his ear was breathing, a strange breathing, like the pant of a lung or the beat of a heart.

"What kind of a spoon was it?" Bird finally asked, his voice strained and weary and small.

Wallace shrugged and looked at Dotty. "I dunno. Jest a spoon, I guess . . . a fancy spoon—it had a word on it . . . no, not a

word . . . a . . . a . . . a . . . a A. It had a fancy A on it. I
'member now 'cause my na . . ."

Dotty clamped her hand over his mouth and groaned softly.

"What? What did you say?" Bird called loudly. "I can't hear
you. Where's the spoon? What did you do with the spoon?
Don't hang up, please don't!"

"I threw it out the window," Wallace said.

"The spoon? Where?"

"At a red light. We was stopped and I threw it out."

"Why?" Bird asked.

"I was afraid she'd get hurt," Wallace said. "The way she
was banging it. . . ."

"Is her . . ." Bird was saying as Huller took the phone.
"Okay?" Huller said gruffly, then nodded as he listened. "All
set then?" Again, he nodded, smiling now, his face gleaming
with sweat. "Yah . . . yah . . . ," he murmured.

Dotty stared at him, her eyes narrow and bright in the dark.

"That's what he wanted to hear, Pops," Huller said, slapping
his back as they headed for the truck. "That spoon did the trick.
That was never in the papers. Never. Nobody knew about that
spoon."

"He told you about that? About the spoon?" asked Dotty
when they were in the truck.

"He never said *what* it was. Just that there was something
only one person could know. . . ."

"And you never said nothing to me," Dotty mused. "I guess
you figured I'd blow it or something, huh?"

"I knew you wouldn't blow it," Huller said, turning and
looking over his shoulder while he backed the truck out into
the lot.

"Or maybe you still thought I was lying about the whole
thing. That's it! You had to prove it to yourself too!"

"C'mon, Dot. . . ."

They drove in silence for a few miles. Wallace could feel
Dotty's foot tapping next to his. She bit her lip and sighed. "I
don't know if I can do it," she said.

"Do what?" asked Huller.

"Give her back. Five years is a long time," she said in a funny voice. Wallace listened carefully. He knew that voice. That was the shivery voice of the crazy girl, the one with blood cuts on her wrists; the voice that ran from tears to bright jangly laughter and back again so that it was all the same, screaming, talking, laughing, crying, all the same, saying the same thing, skimming the sharp blinding edge of a jagged, glassy cliff. . . .

"I love that kid," she was saying in choked, stuffy gasps. "Maybe I don't show it all the time, but I do."

"What're you getting at?" Huller asked, veering sharply into the breakdown lane. He stopped the truck and stared at her. "What the hell're you saying?"

"Just that it's gonna be hard." Tears blubbered down her cheeks. "She's all the family I got," she sobbed, and blew her nose in a tissue. "Her and Aubie." She lifted her head and looked at Wallace and then sobbed even more. His own eyes were filmy with tears.

"Look," Huller was saying. "She'll be better off. They're loaded. They'll give her everything."

Dotty continued to cry. Wallace's chest ached with the pain of containing his sadness. Huller's calloused finger tips tapped on the wheel. Dotty's weeping grew louder.

"And don't forget," Huller said exasperatedly, "she's their kid. Not yours."

"I need a drink," Dotty sobbed. "Or one of them pills or something, Jig. I gotta calm down." She blew her nose again. "I'm going to pieces. Jesus Christ, I'm falling apart." She held up her hands and the sharp silver tips of her nails glinted. "Look how much they're shaking." She stared at her hands as if they weren't part of her.

"Here," Huller grumbled, stretching his legs and stiffening himself to get at his hip pocket. "Just one," he said, dropping a brightly speckled capsule into her palm. "Just to get you over the hump," he said, and then he put one in his own mouth and swallowed with a gulp. From her purse, Dotty withdrew a half pint of gin. She washed down the pill with a long, thirsty drink, then passed it to Huller.

Wallace's eyes were glassy with tears. He stared blindly down at passing traffic. Everything came at him too loudly and vividly. The red of a passing truck caused him to cringe and his insides to tighten. The sweet scent of gin engulfed him. Dotty's voice was smothering, like a drunken kiss, careless and wet and sickening.

". . . think I'll have some more," she was saying, unscrewing the cap.

"Next twenty-four hours are gonna be crucial," Huller warned.

"I just keep thinking how close we been," she sighed.

"Yah, well," Huller said.

"Just so she knows why. I mean, what if she tells stuff like about Carl?"

"Don't worry."

"Or times I had to hit her. Oh Jesus! She'll tell so much about me, they'll know right where to find . . ."

"Stop it! Stop it!" Huller had been saying, as her hysteria grew. "I told you I'll take care of that part."

She was drinking from the bottle. "But how? You don't tell me how."

"Don't worry," he said, laying his hand over her knee. "I'm gonna take care of all that."

"Oh shit," she cried softly. "How much more time?"

He looked at his watch. "Less than thirty-six," he said.

"Thirty-six what?" she asked, laughing nervously. "Days, weeks?"

Huller glanced at Wallace, who was still turned to the side window. "Hours," he mouthed.

"Shit," she said. "Oh shit, I'll never make it."

"You'll make it." Huller said, and he laughed lightly.

17

All night long he tossed and turned, waking, and with one eye charted the pale moon's descent. Thirty-six hours, he thought. Thirty-six more; that was all.

By morning the thirty-six had been whittled to twenty-four. In twenty-four more hours Canny would be gone. The back seat would be empty. There would be no more stories; no one to watch television with. He would eat alone. But what then? What would it all mean? Would the pain in his chest ever go away?

He sat on the edge of the bed, lacing his black sneakers, staring at the bright spring of light that welled up from the hole in the floorboard. He searched through that small quiet place inside himself where Hyacinth and the two boys were, where his father swilled Carson's pigs, where a little boy leaned against a fence post, snapping a stick against the metal bone that grew outside his leg; searched, and came upon the lacerated thumb of Camelia Crebbs, and also Hyacinth's church dress, dark blue with square glass buttons and a wide lace collar that ruffled over her shoulders; searched, but could find neither Canny nor a place where she might eventually be.

All his life, that's what his trouble had been—knowing A,

knowing B, knowing C; but never being able to put them into meaningful form. Parts were always missing. As a child and even later as a man, a father himself, drawing for his boys and more recently for Canny, his pictures always showed a man without an arm or a face without a nose or a dog without a tail.

In the past few days he had hardly spoken to Canny. The lump in his shoe, the article, now so softly frayed that it shed papery flakes each time he unfolded it, had become more real than Canny herself.

On the bed opposite, Dotty groaned. Her eyes fluttered and then her hand shot up to cover them. The morning light seemed to have seeped, not from the windows, but up from the knothole in the floor, rising higher, so that no corner of the cabin was free of its glare. Dust floated in the currents of sunlight and nowhere did a breeze stir or a shadow fall.

With one hand Dotty fumbled blindly through her purse on the floor until she found her white-rimmed dark glasses and her cigarettes. She put on the glasses and lit a cigarette, inhaling as she sagged back, coughing softly against the stained pillow. She asked Wallace for a glass of water, which she used to wash down another of the brightly colored pills he had seen her take last night. She barely bent her head to take a sip. She handed back the glass and her hand shook so that water spilled on the side of the bed.

"My head's ready to blow," she said after a few minutes, lighting a second cigarette off the first, which she stubbed out in the saucer on the chair.

"It's them pills," he said. "They make you crazy, you know they do."

"I'm already crazy," she said. "I was born friggin' crazy."

"It's them pills," he said again. " 'Member that other time?"

Her mouth trembled and then she bit her lip. She stared at him. He couldn't see her eyes behind the black glass lenses, but he knew she was staring at him. He shrugged self-consciously. "Them pills made you crazy," he said softly. "You took a knife and you locked yourself in the room with Canny. And you said you was gonna kill her and you. And then you fell asleep and Canny took the knife and got open the door. . . ."

She was laughing. She blew out more smoke and laughed.

"Oh Aubie," she said, and then he saw her wipe at the tears that leaked out from the dark glasses. "You think she'll remember stuff like that and tell?"

"She was awful little," he said.

"Maybe you could talk to her," Dotty said. "Or maybe I could write a letter or something. Just so they'll know we didn't mean to hurt her. I could just stick it in her pocket. After you give her the pill to keep her asleep. Jig wouldn't have to know."

"What if the pill's bad for her?" he asked suddenly. "What if it makes her sick?" This bothered him. He had never forgotten the time she started running around in circles after he had given her a spoonful of cough syrup. She had banged her head into the wall and thrown things and acted so crazy he finally had to tie her arms and her legs. He had held her like that, struggling and kicking so much that the ropes rubbed her legs and arms raw.

"It won't," Dotty said. "Jig musta made sure it's not too strong."

"What if he don't know?" Wallace asked.

"He knows!"

"What if he thinks he knows, but it ain't right and she g . . ."

"Damn it, Aubie! Will you cut that out? You drive me nuts when you start that stuff."

"Yah, but what if the . . ."

"What if the world stops spinning, Aubie? What if the sun explodes? Jesus Christ!" She took off the sunglasses and squinted at him. "Do you understand what's happening here, Aubie? I mean, really?"

He just looked at her. He couldn't tell if she really meant the question or if she was building up to a fight.

"Do you understand that tomorrow morning you get Canny

dressed and ready and then you feed her and make her take the pill and then we drive to Stonefield in our car and Jig follows us in the truck. We take her to some woods, to this cabin he's got ready. We leave her and then he goes and picks up the money. And if it's all there, Jig calls the Birds and tells them where she is. Then he . . ." She paused, her mouth opening and closing wordlessly. He could feel the gears turning, the wheels spinning. From across the way came Canny's voice, raised and angry. "I did not! She did! No, I didn't! You shut up!" And then she screamed suddenly. Wallace started for the door, then turned back with a helpless look at Dotty.

"Listen to me, Aubie!" she said, calling him back. He kept looking at the door.

"This might be our last chance to talk," she said. "I gotta say this. I . . . I feel like this real old lady sometimes inside. Like I'm dying. Like I will, if I don't take off. I gotta get off on my own. But the thing that stops me is you, Aubie. I always get this feeling it wasn't just Canny I took that time, but you too. That's what's giving me the shakes—not just Canny going, but you too, Aubie. The thought of it's . . . I can't stand the thought of anything happening to you. . . ."

The front door of the house slammed and then came the familiar roar and skid of Huller's departing pickup.

"She'll probably take you back," Dotty said. "You could tell her you got hit on the head and you been all this time trying to figure out who you are." She sat forward eagerly on her crossed legs. "I saw that once in a show and the guy was gone for ten years and his family spent all that time looking for him. I'll bet she's been looking for you all this time, Aubie. I'll bet she hasn't slept a night since you been gone." She smiled. "Why don't you call her, Aubie? Call and say, 'Hey, Hyacinth, I just come to and I know my name now and I wanna come home.' "

He had been shaking his head. "I wanna go with you," he said. "Like we said."

"Yah," she sighed. "Well, remem . . . think about what I said anyways. Keep it in mind." She got up from the bed. "Shit," she muttered, wrapping the sheet around herself. She lifted the plastic curtain and went into the bathroom. When she came out, she was dressed in a red skirt and a baggy black tee shirt that said MIAMI BEACH in glittery pink letters.

"I'm gonna get something to eat," she said at the door. Across the way, the children's screaming had begun again. Alma screamed back at them. Dotty turned from the door and took a pill from her purse and slipped it into her pocket. "My head's gonna goddamn blow," she said, lighting a cigarette for the walk over. "I can feel it."

He began to straighten up the cabin. Every corner was heaped with her clothes. He picked them all up and dumped them on one bed. Each thing he folded, he laid on the opposite bed. When all her clothes were folded and stacked, the colored shoes lined up in pairs, he reached under the bed for the empty bags and boxes they never threw out, but kept. All them moves, he thought, all them times, town to town. . . . Suddenly his arms fell to his sides and he sank onto the wooden chair. This time she means it, he thought. She'll be gone and Canny'll be gone.

"Quick, Poppy!"

He looked up to see Canny pushing a square red gas can through the torn flap at the bottom of the door screen.

"For the bugs," she hissed, stepping quickly inside. Even as she spoke, she scratched her head. "The kerosene!" she groaned, lifting the can with both hands and bringing it into the bathroom. She came out and shook his arm. "I got it, Poppy! I got the can!"

She wore an old green shirt he had never seen before. Threads hung from the armholes where the sleeves had been cut. The blue pants she had on were torn at both knees. Her feet were black with dirt.

Can't go back like this, he thought.

"Poppy!" She shook his arm again. "Do my hair! They're all watching a show!"

She took his hand and tried to pull him up from the chair. "Please, Poppy! They're all itching and Alma just told Momma they either got chicken pox or bugs. Please, Poppy. Alma's mad as hell!"

He pulled the chair into the middle of the cabin and sat Canny on it and covered her shoulders with a cut-out plastic trash bag. Using an old sock dipped in the kerosene, he patted each matted clump of hair until her whole head was soaked. Her eyes were bloodshot from the fumes and her nose ran. He pulled the oily strands of her hair between his thumbnail and index finger, trying to scrape off the pearly white lice eggs. When it pulled, she winced and wiggled her shoulders. "Ow," she said softly. He parted the back of her hair and was sickened by the rash of sores there. Her scalp looked like raw hamburg.

"You got 'fections," he said, peering close. "They's all pussy. After, I'll put some of that 'fection stuff on," he said, working more carefully now. "Make it feel better," he murmured. "Get ridda the hair bugs and the sores . . . make it all better. . . ."

"I love you, Poppy," she whispered. She tilted her head and looked up at him. "You love me?"

He nodded and she grinned.

A crow cawed and high leafy breezes swept over the cabin roof, flapping the tar paper up and down like wings. Just then Huller's truck hurtled into the driveway and screeched to a stop.

"Ellie's pregnant," Canny said in a rush. "Alma told Momma if she gets his gun she's gonna shoot 'em both."

"Who?"

"Ellie and him. Jiggy."

"What'd Momma say?" Wallace cleared his throat. The fumes reddened his eyes.

"Nothin'." Canny shrugged. "I think she's drunk or getting there. She's having breakfast. Beer and pretzels." Canny grabbed his wrist as he started to work on her hair again. "Poppy, I'll bet if you say we're going now, she'll go. She looks so sad."

When he didn't answer, she said, "And you know what else? All of Ellie's stuff's in the toolbox back of Jiggy's truck! I think they're taking off!" she whispered happily. "I saw them putting the stuff in last night. Late, after Alma was sleeping and the cabin lights went out. She said, 'Thirty-six hours. I don't think I can wait that long.' And he said something about 'the rainbow.' "

At the sound of Huller's truck, they both looked toward the open door. With the old red dog barking after it, the truck raced around the circle and onto the road. Wallace bent close and skinned another strand of nits from her hair.

The rain began at noon. It fell in soft, warm waves, each time subsiding for a few glaring minutes of wet sunshine, only to sweat down from the hard blue sky again. The children had been inside most of the day watching television with Alma and Dotty.

When it was almost suppertime, Ellie came across the way to the cabin door. She brought her small white face against the screen.

"The kids're getting hungry, Pops." She shaded her dull, close-set eyes and squinted. "You in there?"

He nodded, then added, "Yup."

"Well, Dotty's asleep and the kids're starving and Alma says everyone can go screw, she's not cooking for a hotelful no more and I tried, Pops. But just looking at the cans is making me sick, much less cooking. . . . Think maybe you could fix something?"

He got off the bed and followed her. In the front room the television set sputtered with static every few minutes. Dotty slept on the couch with her mouth wide open and an ashtray heaped with butts on her chest. Canny and the two Huller girls were on the floor trying to watch cartoons. Light and shadows from the screen flickered on their faces. Krystal and Kelly both scratched their heads. Canny glanced at him uneasily. Her hair hung to her shoulders in greasy, wet-looking clumps.

Huller was in the barn and Alma was nowhere to be seen, but every few minutes, like the far-off thunder, her shuffle rumbled overhead. Wallace opened two cans of Spam, which he sliced thin for eight, then added to the onions already frying in the pan. There were no potatoes, so he boiled macaroni. When that was cooked and drained, he added it to the Spam and onions.

Ellie ran into the bathroom and slammed the door. Even with the water running, he could hear her retching. Outside, the sky blackened suddenly with another storm and lightning flashed. The dog crept up the porch steps and huddled close to the door. With every tremble of advancing thunder, it whimpered and pawed the chicken wire that held the bottom door screen in place. Wallace looked at the dog and wondered why it didn't bark to be let in or just push in the door. The dog looked back through heavy wet eyes.

Wallace went to the door and through the safety of the screen murmured, "You're a dumb dog, you know that, don't ya?" The dog pointed its snout to the muddy sky and howled softly. Wallace chuckled and held open the door. The dog darted inside and ran under the table.

Huller was coming up the steps. He wore a big yellow rain poncho and his boots were smeared with black greasy mud, which he tracked into the kitchen. He pulled the dripping poncho over his head and threw it back out onto the porch. "Been working on the truck," he said, gesturing back at the barn. "Just about ready to roll," he said, with a conspiratorial clamp of his hand on Wallace's shoulder. The minute he stepped past Wallace, the dog charged out from under the table and, snarling, caught the cuff of Wallace's pants in his jaw.

"Get outta here!" Huller snapped, booting the dog's rump until it fled back under the table.

Wallace could feel the thud of his heart in his ears.

"What's this shit?" Huller said, lifting the lid of the frying pan.

"Supper," Wallace said, conscious of the dog's dull, filmy stare.

"Well, let's eat then," Huller said. "Alma!" he hollered up the stairs. "C'mon, everybody! Chow's on!"

They all crowded around the table, hot and sullen-faced. Dotty's eyes were bright and blank as a bird's, the pupils so big they looked ready to seep out of the sockets. She hadn't wanted to get up, but Huller had insisted. She ate nothing. Instead, she smoked, filling her plate with ashes and matches. Huller was in the best mood Wallace had ever seen, cracking jokes and teasing his daughters.

Alma hadn't said a word. First Kelly began to scratch her head, and then so did Krystal. Alma's lashless little eyes moved between the two of them. She glanced at Canny. "What's that in your hair?"

"Nothing," Canny said, lowering her face to the plate.

"How come it's so greasy-looking?" Alma asked, her two daughters scratching frantically now.

Canny shrugged and looked at Wallace. Alma's eyes widened. "She got bugs, don't she?" She sniffed in Canny's direction. Canny's face was almost in her plate.

Alma sniffed again. "That's why," she said, looking from Krystal to Kelly. "That's why they're so itchy." She began to scratch her own thin hair. "We all got bugs!"

Ellie touched her own chopped hair and examined her fingertips.

Dotty burst out laughing. She buried her face in her hands and tears ran from her eyes. She shook her head and gasped with wild laughter.

"All of us!" Alma exclaimed. "And it's all your fault," she said to her husband.

"Shut up and eat," ordered Huller, pushing back his own plate in warning.

"Lookit her laughing," Alma said to him. "She don't care."

"Shut it," Huller snarled.

Krystal had begun to cry. "I can feel the bugs," she said, stiffening in her chair. "They're biting me all over!"

"They're gonna eat your head up," Kelly said, and Krystal screamed. "And then," Kelly continued, "they'll eat your neck. . . ."

Ellie got up and ran for the bathroom, her hand over her mouth.

Alma stared at Dotty, who was still laughing. "Stop it," said Alma. "Stop laughing like that."

This made Dotty laugh harder. Alma's lip trembled. "You get out!" she said to Dotty, with a quaver of fear in her voice. She took a step back and looked at Huller. "Make her go," she said, so low it was almost a whisper. "Make her go before something happens."

Kelly had stopped tormenting Krystal; they watched Dotty's ragged, teary laughter.

"Momma," Canny started to say, but Huller was standing over Dotty now, telling her to go next door and sleep it off. He put his hand on her arm and she pushed it away. Her eyes were slick with rage. "You bastard," she kept muttering. "You don't fool me, you bastard."

"Give me a hand, Pops," said Huller. He grabbed her arm, but again she shook him off. She stood up and her chair crashed backward. Still muttering, she staggered outside.

Huller sat down and pulled his plate back into place. He scraped his bread through the hardening grease, unmindful that he was the only one still eating. Canny got up and came around the table, headed for the door. Huller grabbed her wrist and pulled her close to his chest. "Where you think you're going, princess?" he said through a mouthful of bread.

"See how Momma's doing," Canny answered, stiffening away from him.

"She's okay. She just needs a little sleep," he said.

Canny strained back. "I'll just go see," she said. She pulled back, but he still held on to her wrist.

"Let her go," said Alma. "Let 'em all the hell go."

Huller smiled at Canny. "I'll tell you what," he said, wiping his mouth with the back of the hand that held hers, wiping it back and forth as he spoke, "I'll go check on your momma. That way you can play with the girls some more."

"Not with me," Kelly said, screwing up her face.

"Not with me," echoed her younger sister.

"And she ain't sleeping with them either," Alma said. "Not with bugs she ain't."

"Yes she is," said Huller, still holding Canny close. "She can sleep on the couch." He smiled and patted her narrow backside. "I'm going to take special care of this little package here." He patted her again and now his open hand held there. Wallace's eyes burned with sweat. The light bulb grew too bright. He stared at Huller's hand and a voice boomed in his head, *Get your hand off her!* But no one had heard it.

"Hey, Pops! Go check on Dot and whatever's she's taking, see if you can't hide it on her."

"I'll go look too," Canny said, making a move toward Wallace, but Huller held her back.

"Pops can take care of it, princess. And that way, I can take care of you," Huller said, patting her again. His smile was not a smile so much as a quick, wet slither that curled Wallace's toes in his sneakers, causing him to lurch across the driveway. His breath came tight and as sharp at his rib cage as the beaks of pecking birds.

The cabin was empty. Wallace turned from the doorway to see Huller watching from the porch. At the same moment, with the same surprise on their faces, they both looked toward the barn, from which Dotty had just emerged, staggering down the rutted incline. A long piece of paper trailed from her hand.

"You bastard," she hollered, as Huller ran off the porch.

He snatched the paper from her and stood close, speaking to her in a low, urgent, placating voice.

"... double-crossing, two-bit, sonofamotherf... ," she rattled over his talk.

Huller had her by the arm. He was trying to pull her to the cabin, away from the house where Alma's face floated in the doorway. In an upstairs window was Ellie, her cheek limp on the screen like a flattened curtain.

Each time Huller grabbed her, Dotty jerked free in a torrent of curses. For a moment he seemed almost afraid of her. Now he had her again, his thick fingers cuffing her wrists as he half-steered, half-dragged her toward the cabin. Wallace had to jump off the wobbly cinder blocks to get out of their way.

"Quick, Aubie," Dotty screamed, as Huller forced her up the steps. "You and Canny get outta here before the . . ." She screamed with pain then as Huller clubbed the side of her head.

"Get the hell in there!" Huller growled, shoving her into the unlit cabin.

Wallace heard the thud of her fall and then her sob, sharp like the crack of a bone. Huller looked down at Wallace. "She's all screwed up," he said. "I shouldn't have given her anything. Let me cool her down. . . ." He glanced back into the cabin, where Dotty's voice snarled from the darkness.

"Let me get her straight," he said, snapping his fingers nervously. "Go on back to the house and let me get her straight." Huller's eyes were like Dotty's, as bright and depthless as black glass.

"I said go on back to the house!" bellowed Huller as he leaped from the step and jerked his hand up under Wallace's chin. He stood so close, Wallace could smell his sweat and the sweet liquor on his tongue.

"Fucking feeb . . . ," he muttered as Wallace quickly crossed the driveway.

He didn't go into the house. He stood in the middle of the driveway, listening to them scream at each other. All he could make out was his own name passing between them. He went back to the cabin and stood by the steps.

"Admit it," Dotty kept saying. "Go ahead, admit it!"

"You're so fucked up," Huller said, "you don't know what you're talking about."

"Admit it!" she said, her voice relentless and grinding. "Admit it!"

"Here! Take one of these . . . you're all fucked up . . . here. . . ."

"You and that Callahan, you got us all set up, don't you?"

"Are you crazy? Callahan? He'd sell me so fast!"

"What about the clipping?"

"You got it all screwed up!" Huller said. "You read it wrong."

"I read it right. Twenty-five thousand for their kid and another twenty-five if the kidnappers are caught."

"It sounds worse than it is." He tried to laugh, but it came out a cough.

"You . . . ," she began.

"I didn't want to scare you, that's all, babe." His voice softened. "I couldn't take a chance on you getting panicked, that's why! I figured on telling you after . . . when we were long gone and so rich, you couldn't . . . you wouldn't change your mind."

"What about Ellie? She coming too? Are me and her both gonna . . ."

"She's got nothing to do with this! I told you before—nothing!"

"Well, who knocked her up then?"

"If she doesn't know, how the hell should I!" Huller exclaimed.

"Alma thinks it was you."

"Look Dot, tomorrow morning we have to move. Tomorrow morning, there's no more Alma, no more Ellie, no more Callahan. There's nothing but you and me and all that money. Think of it that way. Forget all this other shit. It's all gonna come off like clockwork. I got it all laid out. I got every move, every second figured. There's nothing I didn't think of. And you got nothing to be scared of, Dot. I worked it all out perfect. Even Pops talking to the Birds. It was like a stroke of genius the way it worked out. He confessed! Don't you see? You were never mentioned. He did all the talking. . . ."

"But you wanted me to and I wouldn't," Dotty said.

"And that's when it all started to come to me," Huller said. "How it was just like putting the pieces of a puzzle together."

"But what about Canny?" Dotty asked in a faint voice.

"She was a baby. She doesn't remember. For all anyone knows he kidnapped you too. You were just a kid. He took you and then he took her."

Dotty was crying now. "You can't do this . . . not to poor Aubie. You don't understand."

"Understand what?"

"I don't know," she sobbed. "I can't explain it. But of all the people in the whole world, he . . . he's . . ."

"Look, that's the way it is," Huller said, his voice clamping over her sobs. The chair scraped and the hard heels of his boots moved hollowly to the door. "Everything's set."

"But what about Aubie?"

There was silence and then Huller said, "They'll be waiting for him."

"No!" she moaned. "Not poor Aubie. . . . Please. . . . Just let him head back home. Let him. . . ."

"Jesus Christ!"

"Maybe we could even ride him part of the . . ."

"Shut up!"

"No, you listen to . . ."

They stood just inside the door now. Huller had her by her wrists, holding her so rigid and so close that they were one writhing figure, caught in the last of daylight, frayed and ghostly behind the dirt-plugged screen.

She grunted and struggled. "You listen . . . ," she kept trying to say.

"You shut up!" he finally bellowed. "I'm getting fed up! Jesus Christ, I don't need you," he roared as she butted her head into his shoulder. "Just like I don't need the feeb. . . ."

"Shoot him then!" she cried. "You might as well! Shoot him and put him out of his misery!"

"Well, that's a thought," Huller laughed.

"Just give me the gun," said Dotty. "I'll do it myself." She laughed. "I'll blow all our fuckin' heads off," she panted. "Every goddamn one. . . ." Her voice rose hysterically, and in measure with her words came Huller's voice, deep and jagged.

He was saying, "All I need is the kid . . . and I don't even need her. I could bring her back dead, you hear me?" He was slapping her.

Wallace trembled with the sickening sound. He touched the rough outer board of the cabin and was surprised that the earth sat so perfectly still beneath his wracked body and their savage blows, that it could lay unjarred and heedless to this pain.

"Dead!" Huller grunted, slapping her again and again. "In a bag or a box or even just a handful of her teeth . . . or her hair," he said, yanking Dotty by the hair and throwing her onto the bed, which jumped against the plank floor and sent a shudder through Wallace's fingertips. Then came the steady thud, thud, thud of a dull, monstrous heartbeat. . . . Was he kicking her? Kicking the bed? She made no sound.

"All I need's proof she's found," Huller grunted with each blow. "And dead or alive's not going to matter . . . you hear me, you crazy bitch, you. . . ."

Dotty whimpered. Something crashed. The chair maybe. Glass shattered.

"I don't need any of you, so don't push! I'm tireda being pushed. . . ." He grunted. She grunted.

Something, a shoe or box, thumped against the wall, then fell.

"Don't," Dotty panted. ". . . bastard . . . goddamn. . . . Ohhh!" she moaned, and a slap of flesh struck flesh. Another and another. She moaned again and there was a crack, a splintered breaking apart that shuddered through the cabin frame.

There was no sound, not even silence, just stillness, and then the dry, rattly swish of a tree branch across the cabin roof.

I got to go now, he thought. She's gone. Dotty's gone. He did it to her. . . .

Above, the door flew open, back against the cabin wall. Huller's thick shadow loomed over the steps, the driveway. He was gone.

Inside, Wallace found her curled on the bed with her face to the wall. The back of the chair had been broken off, and in the bathroom doorway, the plastic curtain hung by one brittle shred. Everywhere were clothes and shoes, and underfoot, the crushed glass of makeup bottles, their dark liquids inking his footprints to her side.

"Dot?" He touched her shoulder and said her name again, relieved when she moaned. He bent down, listening to the congestion of her breath and tears.

"Dotty," he whispered. "Wake up! Wake up, Dotty!" He shook her and said it again. She swore and curled tighter.

"We gotta go," he pleaded. "He's gonna kill us, Dotty. He's gonna kill Canny. . . . Wake up, please wake up, Dotty."

She stirred, and when she turned, he saw the split raw flesh in her bottom lip and the blood that had run down her chin and jawbone to her ear, where it caked in her hair. Her right eye was swollen and bulging and when she moved her head again, he saw the pills that Huller must have thrown down at her in his final disgust. Like bright candies they were scattered over the stained blue ticking of the pillow and the soiled sheet. He picked them up, all that he could find, and put them in his pocket, and then he sat down on the other bed and watched her.

They would have to get out of here tonight, as soon as the Hullers were all asleep. He had to figure it out. He needed a plan. This time, the running would be different. This time, they would be running from someone who knew all about them. But he couldn't think about that. Right now, his biggest fear was that he wouldn't be able to wake Dotty up in time. In the past when she had taken pills, she could sleep twelve or fourteen straight hours. Maybe he could just carry her out to the car. Between himself and Canny, they might be able to do it. He could sit on one side of her with Canny on the other side and they would drape her arms over their shoulders and then lift her onto her feet. . . .

Canny, he thought, looking up suddenly. He had to get Canny over here with him and away from Huller. That was the first step. That's it, he thought. One step at a time.

"Don't get scared. Just figure it out," he spoke softly to

himself as he left the cabin and crossed the driveway. "Don't get scared. . . . Just go one step at a time. . . ."

"What'd you say, Pops?" It was Huller coming down the steps from the house. A can of beer hung from his fingertips. In the corner of his mouth was a cigarette. Its red glow moved up and down as he spoke. "She send you over? She was flipped."

"No," Wallace said. "I just wanted Canny over. For the night. For the last night."

Huller came off the step and with his tongue lifted the cigarette stub from the corner of his mouth, then spat it onto the ground at Wallace's feet. "Let her have a good night's sleep, Pops. She's gonna need it. It's best for her, Pops. Okay?"

Wallace just stood there. He didn't know what else to say. Canny had come to the door. Her forehead was pressed to the screen and her chin rested on the head of a fuzzy earless bear. "Poppy!" she called, and started to open the door.

"Stay there," ordered Huller. "Inside!"

As the door fell shut, a chill swept through Wallace. Huller's arm yoked his shoulder.

"Trust me," Huller said, walking alongside, steering him back to the cabin. "Don't worry about a thing. I got everything under control. Bird's gonna get his kid back and you're gonna come out of this looking like one hell of a hero. I mean, the way you took care of the kid, the way you care. Bird's gonna be so grateful, he'll . . ."

"But Alma don't want her in the house . . . not with bugs, she don't . . . ," Wallace blurted. He had finally thought of another reason for Canny to sleep in the cabin.

"What the hell're y . . ."

"She can sleep over here," he said excitedly. "She got 'em bad, ya know. They's so bad her head's all cut and I never seen so many nits. They's probably all gonna hatch tonight. Probably hatching right now." His eyes were bright on Huller's. "Probably looking for people to bite right now even."

"Slow down! Take it easy, Pops. Those're more words than

you said in a month. Canny'll be sleeping downstairs w . . ."

"She'll be scared," interrupted Wallace.

"Not with me down there," Huller said, with a hard pat of Wallace's shoulder. "No bogeyman'll get by me."

The two of them stood over her bed. Dotty's eyes were open, staring, the hardness of her face cold and set. She might have been blind or dead. Wallace heard the catch in her throat and then a sob, so thin and sudden and yearningly, sorrowfully wild, that it seemed to pierce his flesh.

"I'm sorry . . . oh . . . I'm so sorry," she wept. "Oh God."

Huller had sunk to one knee; his head was close to hers and his voice was gentler than Wallace had ever heard in a man. He almost sounded like a woman as he tried to comfort her.

"It's okay . . . it's okay . . . I lost my cool. . . ."

"Oh Jig," she wailed. "I'm so sorry. It's all my fault. I'm so fucked up. . . ."

"Hey, take it . . ."

"No, no, listen to me," she said, raising herself up on one elbow. "I shouldn't've argued with you. Whatever you do's okay. Even if . . ."

"Hey!" Huller said, standing suddenly. "We're all on edge. Even Pops here, he's all jeeped up, talking a blue streak. . . ."

She blinked then and peered up at Wallace through filmy, distorted eyes.

"This'll help you down," Huller was saying as he took something from his pocket and tucked it next to her cheek. "Here, Pops, you oughta take one too. Here." He held out his palm. "Take it!"

The minute the pill touched his hand it began to melt, so feverish was his flesh now, so sickened were his insides. She's gonna do it, he thought. She's gonna let him kill Canny and then she'll kill me. And she won't even care, he thought, hearing her sobs pitch suddenly and unaccountably into a burst of girlish laughter. "Oh Jesus, oh Jesus . . . Aubie'll be so strung out. I can't believe it. . . ."

She'll laugh, he thought. Even if she does care, she'll still laugh, just so she won't have to. Dotty don't like to care, he thought.

"Here!" Huller had turned on the light. He looked closely at a long yellow pill that was wrapped in cellophane, the two ends tightly twisted. "This one's the kid's," Huller was saying. "She'll take it a half hour before we go. It'll knock her out just enough so we can move her easy. . . . What's the look for, Pops? It's a sleeping pill, that's all. So she won't get scared."

"He's afraid it'll hurt her," Dotty said, laying back against the pillow, her fishy eyes closed now, her speech thick and weary. "Make her sick or something." She kept licking the split red flesh in her lip. In the hard glare of the light, her jarred, wounded face made him think of spoiled fruit.

"Oh no!" Huller said. "This won't make her sick. Tell him, Dot."

"Won't make her sick, Aubie." She licked her lip and started to smile. "It'll make her rich . . . make us all rich . . . that one pill's gonna make us all rich." Blood leaked from the wound of her smile.

18

If there was one quality Aubrey Wallace possessed beyond all others, it was patience. Enough so that his father could have said, "You just wait. It won't be long. Just do what you're told and I'll be back. It won't be long."

And he had waited; had done as he was told, had neither complained nor questioned, but had waited, as indifferent to calamity and doubt as the ice coated trees outside his window that first long winter in the Home. "Wait your turn," was the Home's prime rule with so many wild boys to manage. In time the words would bestow the numbing inculcation of prayer: wait your turn; wait your turn; just wait your turn.

He waited now. He waited for Dotty to sleep soundly, for the lights to go out in the house, for the dog to cease its sporadic barking. Once, he checked the car, then walked close by the house, under the window where Canny would be asleep on the couch. The television was still on. Its bluish light shimmered on the sagging sheet that curtained the window. The smell of cigarettes came from the same window. The dog barked and Huller swore. Wallace hurried back to the cabin and sat in the dark while Dotty slept heavily, her bubbly snore steady and deep as he waited.

Outside, the night teemed with firefly sparks and the dry ignition of cricket song, and across the bruised sky flashed the quick tremble of heat lightning, and every now and again there came, faintly, the rumble of long-ago storms.

All this time he had been thinking. The muddle had begun to clear. These were his facts like mileposts along a dangerous road: that come morning, Huller would turn him in for the extra reward. Dotty would go along with it and Canny might get hurt in the process. Or worse—and he remembered Huller saying all he needed was a bone, a handful of her hair, or just some teeth. Even if Huller planned on running away with Ellie, Dotty wouldn't believe him until it was too late. It's all changed, he thought. He would have to bring Canny back himself and then he would go home to Hyacinth. His eyes widened in the darkness. He sensed the orderliness in this plan, the rightness. All would be as it was before, long ago. He would say, "I went and it wasn't my fault and now I am back," and all that came between he would forget, and it would not matter. They would go their own ways again, all of them, him, Dotty, Canny, as once they had before, each as separate and apart and unknown to the other as planets in their orbits.

That it could be so simple astonished him. The certainty of what he had to do was like the clearest, brightest glass that, he knew, once tilted just a hair this way or that to the light could blind him. And so he sat, silent and still, not daring to move.

Because it seemed almost too simple, he sensed the need of a charm, an amulet; some complication to make it worthy of success, to shield them from harm; a mission like the knight's errant journey through hostile kingdoms of deadly dragons and barbed hedgerows. An explanation was needed, some way of telling his side of it and why it had happened; his acknowledgment that this senseless act had indeed been without plan, that no harm had been intended. He sensed that this might be enough, this ordering of the universe, this telling, this tale that seemed to begin, not with Canny as he had first thought, but with that day on the country road; no, not even there. It was more than that, wasn't it? It went beyond mere facts and dates. It was Mr. Bird, the voice in his ear, asking why. Why? Because the tailpipe had begun to rattle, because Dotty had been hungry, because they had no money, because a gate had been unlatched, a door unlocked; because at that moment a telephone had been ringing and whoever picked it up to say hello had not the slightest idea that two lives like blindly falling stars were moving closer, closer . . . the footsteps soft, the child watching; upstairs, the phone to an ear, perhaps even laughter . . . and closer, aligning themselves in that instant, in that convergence, that explosion that shatters, then makes a universe, that blindness that only later is pieced together, but can never be made whole or understood . . . upstairs, unseen, unheard, "Hello, I'm fine," while downstairs, in the room of light and mirrors, the baby, the unmet child, demanded a greeting back to its own, demanded it of the wild-eyed girl with dried blood under her nails.

And in that moment of impact, who were they but strangers who would never be strangers again, whether they met or never met, or never even knew the other's name, because as Canny was all of her family, so was he every Wallace and Herebonde and Kluggs (whereas in truth, in blood, he had not been, but in that moment of collision, of violation, became so—for all time) just as Dotty was all he had ever known of mystery and dreams and wildness and chance.

None of this could he understand, but, sensing its intricacy and its mystery, he was filled with the same wonder as one who, through the bright underside of stars, believes he can perceive the workings of all the night beyond.

In the cabin, he sat on the edge of the bed. Dotty lay with her back to the light and the pillow over her head. He stared at the pad of paper on the wooden chair. His brow furrowed and his mouth thinned as he read the first sentence he had written. It made no sense. He balled up the paper and stuck it in his pocket, then began again, slowly, painfully. "Dammit," he muttered. He forced the pencil to move. It was like trying to splice two wires together. He knew what he wanted to say, but the connection between his brain and his hand just wouldn't work right.

An hour later, he had finally printed:

> YOU DON'T KNOW ME. BUT THIS HERES YOUR LONG LOST LITTEL GIRL I HAVE BRUNG BAK AFTER ALL THIS TIME. SHE IS YOUR REEL BABY THAT A PERSON I NOW TOOK TO LOVE AND NEVER MENT TO HERT.
>
> I DONT NOW YOU SO I WOOD LIEK TO SEE THINGS LEF THE WAY THEY ARE LIKE THAT BECUS I NEVER DID NO WRONG. AXCEP BY NOT STOPIN THAT PERSON THAT WAS THE ONE TO REELY TAKE HER.

His fingers were cramped and locked on the pencil. Sweat filled his baseball cap. His head ached and a lump hardened in his throat.

He wrote:

> NOT ME. I DID NOT TAKE HER. I HAV GILT THOU BY NOT DOIN ANY THIN. BUT I AM MAKING IT UP BY GETTING HER BAK SAF AND SOND AND BY MY OWN PERSON THAT HAS TO COUNT FOR SOMTHIN.
>
> I HOPE YOU HAV GOOD LUK WITH HER. REMBER SHE IS YOUR REEL DOTER SO YOUSHOOD IF YOU WATE. SHE IS A REEL GOOD GIRL. I LIEK HER ALLOT. SOMETIMS I EVEN LOVE HER.
>
> I WOOD APPRESIT YOU NOT SENTING COPS ON ME BECUS I PROMIS NEVER TO DO A BAD THING AND REELY WHEN YOU STOP AND THING I NEVER REELY DID.
>
> PS I AM SORY FOR ALL THIS TRUBEL. TELL HER I WILL MISS HER.

He held up the paper and his face flushed. "Lookit that," he whispered in wonder. It was the first letter he had ever written. He turned out the light and stood by the door. Across the way, the house lay in darkness. He tiptoed down the steps to the car. With one hand on the wheel and his shoulder braced to the frame, he began to push. The car creaked and then he pushed with all his might, and pushed, butting his head to the frame, grunting softly, until, finally, it began to roll. He got the car to the mouth of the driveway, then turned it onto the road. He kept pushing until he had gotten a good mile, and then he made his way back. His every footstep seemed to thunder through the moonless night.

He stood outside the window. A breeze lifted the torn sheet and it billowed in, then fell against the screen. Behind it, he could hear Canny's ragged little snore.

"Canny!" he whispered, and scratched his fingers down the screen. "Canny, wake up!" He pressed his ear to the screen and listened. Just then, the sheet lifted and the dog's cold wet snout poked against the screen into his cheek. He sank to his knees and the dog growled. From inside, a child's sleepy voice scolded, "Cut that! You bad dog. . . ."

"Canny!" he hissed. "Put the screen up. Quick!"

And as she did, his eyes froze on Huller's wide back hunched over the table in the kitchen, sound asleep, his head on his arms.

"Take your second left to 495. And just watch the exit signs. Stonefield's about fourteen miles," the gas station attendant said.

"Where we going?" Canny asked when he got back in the car. He glanced at her. "I got to tell you something. You see, once, a long time ago, there was this little girl. She was a year old then."

"What was her name?" interrupted Canny.

"That ain't important. Jest listen," he said. He couldn't remember the name in the article and he didn't want to have to stop and take off his shoe to find out. "Anyways, she was little. . . ."

"Make up a name."

"Huh?"

"I like stories that all the people have names," she said.

"But this ain't a story, Canny." He looked at her. "It's a story, but it ain't."

"But you said, 'Once upon . . . once. . . .' "

"Damn, Canny, you're getting me all mixed up. You see, she was jest a baby. Not even two and this lady come along . . . well, she waren't a lady then. She was a girl, I guess you'd call her. . . ."

"Where's Momma?" Canny yawned.

"Sleepin'."

"She know we left?"

"Nope. Anyways, she . . ."

"How come?" Canny pestered. "This a surprise? Like that time we picked all them cans in the middle of the night?"

"Yup. So anyways . . ."

" 'Member that, Poppy?" she sighed. "We musta picked a thousand, huh?"

"Well . . . a lot."

"Can I lay down?" She yawned again.

"Sure," he said as she laid her head against his leg. "Anyways, she was just a girl. And the truck started clunking on accounta the tailpipe. And the guy in the truck says, 'The tailpipe's coming off.' And the girl, she says, 'So.' And she laughs." He grinned. "She was all the time laughing. Laughing no matter what." Wallace frowned. "Dammit, what's next? Oh yah, the tailpipe. So the guy says, 'The tailpipe's coming off.' He says he ain't got a dime and how he's lost and how back at home his wife don't know where he is." Wallace sighed. "I looked at her then and I told her, 'We're heading back. Soon as I get the tailpipe wired.' "

His eyes glistened over the wheel. "And I'm working on the tailpipe and all of a sudden she jumps outta the truck and takes off down the street and I said to myself, 'Go! Now's your chance!' So I get back in the truck, but the keys was gone. She took 'em.

"And I'm sitting there scared as all get out, thinking now

what do I do. When I see her running back like a bat outta hell. And she's got this little baby girl in her arms. . . ."

The sound of his voice through the darkness pleased him. As he told it, he could see it all as it had been that day. "And then next thing I knew we was outside Washington, the capital, and she's already got you calling her momma and me poppy; and she says, 'Two more days. Jest let's keep her two more days!' And we kept going and two more days'd be up and she'd tease, 'A coupla days more' . . . and then it was a week. 'Okay!' I'd say, 'A week. A month, okay.' And before I knew it, she thought she was your real momma and I was your poppy and after a time, you didn't know no better."

He glanced down at her, then back at the road. "After that, come winter and then summer and winter again and we just got in the swing of things, moving around. Taking care of you. Course, by that time, Momma started finding out the hard work taking care of a kid is. And she kept wanting good times, being so young. And all the moving and the being so scared started getting to her and I tried to do the best I could, taking care of you so she wouldn't have to, and taking care of her too. By that time I was jest so scared she'd take off on the two of us and then what would we do? You know what I mean, Canny?"

His hand groped over her face. "Canny? You sleepin', Canny? Ain't you heard a word?"

He veered sharply into the right-hand lane. Ahead, the sign said STONEFIELD, NEXT EXIT.

"Wake up, Canny! Wake up!"

To the east, the black sky was rimmed by a pale strip of silvery light. Canny sat soberly against the seat. She kept yawning.

"Was a right turn," he muttered, heading back toward the center of town. "We was on the main drag and we took a right." Now he was back on Main Street. He slowed to a crawl, creeping past the fire station, the library, through blinking red lights, past the post office and a string of fancy stores, and then he turned.

"We lost, Poppy?"

"I dunno," he said, driving slowly down the narrow tree-tented street. "Mebbe not . . . looks different in the dark." His eyes widened. Across the street, on the opposite corner, was the same white house he remembered. "Right here," he said, pulling in against the curb.

"But it's too early, Poppy! You can't haul junk when they're all sleeping."

He took the letter from his pocket. Canny yawned and scratched at her head with both hands.

"Don't," he said, looking at her, and he took away her hands. "You don't want them people thinking you got bugs still."

Her chin jerked up. "Maybe if they think I got bugs, they'll give us more stuff so we'll go." She laughed.

"Listen now. And listen good, Canny. . . ." The tone of his voice was frightening, even to him. "You're . . . I gotta . . . You see, I ain't always been . . ." He looked away and folded the letter again. "This is the street."

He opened the car door and got out. "C'mere," he said, beckoning her across the seat. Her eyes on him warily, she got out and stood close to the car, watching him back onto the sidewalk. "C'mon," he whispered, but she wouldn't follow. He went back and picked her up. Her arms fastened around his neck as he walked slowly down the street. "See that big house," he whispered at her ear. "The one with the round porch. All you gotta do's go up and ring the bell, or if they don't have one, knock on the door. But you gotta knock loud acourse . . . 'cause they'll be asleep." His footsteps scraped over the gritty sidewalk. "Give 'em this letter," he whispered, bending to set her down. Her legs roped around his waist. She buried her face in his neck.

"No," she murmured. She held his neck so tightly he felt dizzy and staggered against the thick, dark shrubs. He reached back to pry her arms loose. "Let go! Dammit, Canny! I gotta do this! You want a licking? You're gonna get one! Let go! Dammit!" he cried, finally parting her knotted fingers. He pushed her legs from him and got her down on the sidewalk. He tossed the letter at her, turned, and ran toward the car. Behind him dogged the quick flap flap flap of her rubber sandals on the pavement. "Poppy!" she screamed. "Poppy! Don't leave, Poppy! Please, Poppy! I won't be bad. . . . I love you, Poppy! I love you. . . ."

"Elizabeth?" came an anxious voice from the corner house.

Canny shrieked with terror and both she and Wallace turned to see an old woman with long white hair standing in the second-floor window.

"Poppy!" Canny shrieked, and flew at him. He clamped his hand over her mouth and pulled her close.

The screen rose in the window. "Elizabeth Bird! What are you doing out there so early in the morning? Does your mother. . . . Oh!" The old woman gasped as she leaned and peered down at the child in Wallace's arms. "Not again," she groaned. For a moment Wallace and the old woman stared at one another, frozen in open-mouthed horror.

"You're gonna dump me," Canny said between teary gasps. "Just like they said." Her chest heaved and fell. She sat close against him, her arms locked on his. The old car sputtered each time he accelerated. He drove with his eyes on the rearview. Any minute now, he expected to see a cruiser break through the darkness at him.

"Shh," he kept saying.

"You wanna dump me. You and Momma're sick of me. You hate me. Everybody hates me," she cried, her shoulders trembling with sobs.

"Shh . . . look for a phone. . . ." He could barely speak. The words hurt his throat. His tongue was thick and unpliant. Shoulda left her, he thought. Shoulda just run.

"Don't dump me, Poppy. Please don't!" she wept, squirreling her head up under his driving arm. She turned her face into his chest. "I'll be good. I'll be so good you'll think I'm gone."

Most of what she said he didn't hear, but the feel of her mouth working against him was like another heart beating into his.

He turned right and found himself back on Main Street. What's the plan? he kept asking himself. What's the plan? In his panic, he had forgotten. Bringing her back was all of it he could recall. If he couldn't drop her off, then he'd call the Birds and tell them where to find her. He'd leave her in the telephone booth. He'd tell her Dotty was coming; that she should wait for Dotty. He'd give her the letter to hold. The letter! He felt on the seat and realized he must have dropped it when the old woman called out the window. He couldn't even remember what he had written in the letter. Not a single word came to him.

From a distance came the sound of a siren. Ahead, there was a telephone booth on the edge of a parking lot that lay like a shoreless black lake between a dry cleaners and a ladies' dress shop. Wallace pulled in and parked close to the dress shop. In the streetlight, the window mannequins' sad, grainy faces all seemed to be watching him.

"C'mon," he said. He opened his door and did not even have to pull her after him, so tightly did she cling, her legs skittering with his. "Who're you calling?" she asked. "You calling Momma? Tell her I'll be so . . ."

"Shh . . . ," he said, pulling her against him so he could close the door on the booth. The siren grew louder.

"Tell her let's go," Canny hissed. "Tell her all Ellie's things're in the truck. . . ."

"Shh!" He fished in his pocket and held the handful of change close to his face. No dimes. All he had was a nickel, pennies, and four quarters. He dropped a quarter into the slot. The sudden buzz of the dial tone startled him. He pushed the button for the operator.

Canny was tugging at his shirt. "Tell her. . . ."

"Don't!" he said. "Don't do . . ."

The operator answered and his head snapped up. "Hello, I

need somebody's number." He tried to turn his back to Canny, but she turned with him. "Mr. Bird," he said. "Louis."

The operator asked him the town he was calling.

"Stonefield," he said, but he couldn't remember the street. "It's a big white house," he said into the phone. "With a big round . . ."

"I'm sorry, sir," the operator interrupted. "That is an unpublished number."

At the mention of the big white house, Canny had twisted her arms around his waist. She stared up at him. He lowered his voice and turned his head. "I know. That's why I need it."

"I'm sorry, sir, but I can't give it to you. . . ."

"But I . . ." He listened and realized she had hung up. His quarter rattled down into the metal cup.

"Who's Bird, Poppy?" Canny shook his arm. "How come you're calling somebody?"

"Shh. . . ."

"Call Momma! Who're you calling? You calling Momma?" she asked as he dropped the quarter into the slot and pressed the button.

"Hello," he said, when the operator answered. "I gotta make a call to Atkinson, Vermont, but I only got a couple quarters." He examined the change in his palm, held it close to the glass. Canny looked too. "Seventy-five . . . eighty-six cents," she counted, pointing to each coin.

"Eighty-six cents," he told the operator. "Okay," he said after listening to the operator's explanation. "But I don't know if she'll pay. It's been a while. She . . . Hyacinth Wallace," he said, and then in just giving her his old number felt a weakness in his joints that made his legs go boneless. The ground rippled under his feet. "Aubrey Wallace," he said, closing his eyes tight and hunching forward as the ringing began.

"Poppy. . . ." Canny kept grabbing his arm.

"Hullo?" came the distant voice, the flesh of it still too distant to perceive.

She'll know what to do, he thought, hearing the operator ask if she would accept a collect call. There was static on the line. It crackled in his ear like an electrical charge, like lightning. Maybe there's a storm there, he thought. The operator repeated her question.

"Aubrey Wallace ain't here no more," answered the voice he knew was Hyacinth's.

In the background he heard a man's voice, dark and muffled from beneath sheets, a pillow, from way down deep. At first Wallace thought two lines had crossed, that two different connections had been made. And then the old bed creaked. He might have been in the room, in that dark, square room, he could hear it so clearly.

"And neither is Mrs. Wallace. This is Hyacinth Farnham you got. Mrs. Henry T. J. P. Farnham," she added proudly.

"Poppy! It's . . ." Canny hissed.

"Damn," he whispered. Now why'd Hyacinth say that? He couldn't get what she meant straight.

Canny tugged on his arm. "Poppy!"

"I'm sorry, sir," the operator was saying in his ear. "Would you like . . ."

Click! And the phone went dead. It was that hand, that thick yellow-haired arm that shot past his face to press down the lever, then took the receiver from his hand, never saying a word, not one single word. Huller's gun nudged him out of the booth back to his car.

Behind him, he could hear Canny's voice far, far off in the night, scared and asking Dotty over and over what had happened. "What's wrong? Oh Momma, your face is so beat up . . . it's so sore. . . ."

"You bastard!" Huller snarled, and with vicious stabs drove the gun muzzle over and over into his spine as he went. "You stupid little bastard. . . ."

They were at the car. Huller opened the door. With the back of his hand, he hit Wallace's head and shoved him inside, down onto the seat. "Don't try nothing. Don't even think of it," he snarled, as Dotty climbed in next to Wallace. Her face was mashed and puffy and crooked. The red slits of her eyes were no more than glassy little blood cuts; the tip of her nose skewed crookedly sideways; and her lips were dark and thickly protuberant. It was a dead face, days dead and bloated and ugly, distorted and rippling in the glare of the passing headlights like a corpse floating face up. She didn't make a sound.

"She'll be in the truck with me," Huller said through the window. "Just keep that in mind. I got the kid and the gun."

They were halfway back before either one of them spoke.

"I was tryna call home," he said. His head ached and his chest hurt. He didn't dare tell her he had brought Canny to the street where the Birds lived. "I was gonna tell her I'm coming home. I was gonna take Canny and go home. I had it all wrote out."

She said nothing. In the darkness she struck a quick hissing match and lit the cigarette she held in the corner of her mouth that wasn't split.

"I told 'em how it happened . . . how it waren't on purpose, how . . ."

"Shut up," she said thickly, her jaw rigid and outthrust. "Just shut up."

"He said he'd shoot her. He said he could do that!" Wallace said, suddenly enraged. "I heard him say so!"

"He won't," Dotty said.

"And he's gonna get me arrested," Wallace said. "He'll. . . ."

"No, he won't," she said, in that same dull, level tone like a voice in the dark, beyond a wall, unreachable. "It's all different now."

So she still don't care, he thought. It's just him and her that matters.

In the dark quiet the house stood tall and depthless as an enormous headstone. A light went on in an upstairs window and then it went off. The curtain parted and a blank white face looked down at them. Huller pulled in behind them, parking sideways to block the mouth of the driveway. He got out and opened Canny's door and held out his arms to her. She jumped down close to the truck and, ignoring Huller, started for the car. He caught her by the shoulder, turned her, then steered her toward the house. When he opened the door to put her inside, the dog sprang onto the porch. Yelping gratefully, it came to run at Huller's heels in a low, slavish crouch. It whined and rubbed its matted coat against Huller's legs while he stood by the open window telling Dotty it was up to her now to keep this thing together.

She stared straight ahead, in profile her battered face strangely resembling Alma's.

"In a few hours, it'll be done," Huller was saying. "But you gotta stay tough." He reached in and lifted her chin. "I feel shitty about this . . . about hurting you. . . ."

She nodded in an almost imperceptible, trancelike, rocking movement.

"Of all people . . . after all you've done. . . . Jesus!" He kept it up, speaking to her in his low, smooth rattle.

"I need something," she said.

"No more pills. There's only a couple hours left. You've got to be sharp!" Huller said.

"The gun," she said, forming the words with difficulty. "I'm afraid." She gestured weakly toward Wallace. "I wanna gun. . . ."

Huller stared at Wallace. With his hand falling slowly from sight, he opened the door. "C'mon," he said to Dotty, his eyes never leaving Wallace's. "Go on inside," he said to her. "Let me. . . ."

"No!" she said, trying to pull back on the door. "I don't mean that!"

Huller held the door. The dog snuffled and pawed the ground near Huller's feet. "Doesn't matter," Huller said. "Mine or somebody else's. Either way's fine with me."

"I'm tired," she said. "He'll be okay. I just gotta sleep."

"Gimme the keys," Huller said, reaching past Dotty for them.

He came around to Wallace's door and opened it. "Out!" he said. "C'mon, little man." He pulled Wallace out and jerked him back against the car. The dog snarled and dove toward Wallace's feet. Growling, it nipped at his pant legs.

Wallace sank against the car. He wasn't afraid of the dog. He wasn't afraid of Huller. He was suddenly very tired.

Huller laughed. He turned and went to his truck, taking from the flat bed a ball of rope, which he unwound. Chuckling to himself, he told Wallace to face the car and put his hands behind his back. With the dog still snarling and nipping, he knotted an end of the cord around Wallace's wrists; the other, he slung tightly through the thong of the dog's stiff and shrunken leather collar so that there was no more than a foot of rope between them.

"You won't have any problems now," Huller said, laughing, because as the dog twisted and struggled to free itself of the rope, it pulled Wallace, his knees bent and back arched, backward after it.

"Poor old Red," Huller laughed, and then his face darkened. He leaned close to the dog and scratched its blunt head. "Poor dumb thing. Oughta put them both outta their misery," he said, with a trace of sadness in his voice.

19

The darkness didn't matter because she could barely see through her swollen eyes. It was her hands, trembling and graspless, that took so long untying the rope. Released, the dog sank against the door with its drooling muzzle on his paws.

Wallace could feel the animal's eyes on him through the darkness. Dotty sat propped like a broken doll on her bed. Wallace sat on his bed. From time to time his head bobbed with sleep. Outside, the crickets' cry thinned.

"I got to sleep," Dotty said desperately. "I just got to."

"It's almost morning," he said, noting uneasily the lightening sky, down now to one last scrim of gray. His throat hurt when he tried to swallow. Pretty soon, she'd go next door and then, after a little while, the door would open and Huller would tiptoe in and, in that club of a voice he used on the dog, would tell Wallace to turn over and then there would come the shock of cold metal, hard against his temple, the gun barrel dug into that soft, boneless depression he'd always been afraid to press on for fear of injuring his brain, of damaging it any more than the doctors said had already been done at birth.

He had just drifted into sleep when he felt Dotty climb next to him on the bed. She lifted his arm over her shoulder. "I wish

I was dead," she moaned against his throat. "There's no way out. There's nothing left, no place to go."

"Hyacinth got married," he said suddenly with a note of wonder in his voice at the way it had just dawned on him, had just burst out of him. "I never thought of that, of her getting married," he said.

"How do you know she is?" she asked, catching a sob in her throat.

"She told me," he said. "In the phone booth. She said she was Mrs. Hyacinth T. J. P. Farnham."

"And what'd you say?" She sat up and blew her nose on the corner of the sheet.

"Nothing. I couldn't think what to say."

She got up then and stood by the door. The dog scurried to lay between the beds. She was looking at the house. She lit a cigarette, took a few quick puffs, then dropped it on the floor and ground it out with her bare heel. A deep sob rose in her chest, then expired in a small moan. She pushed open the door, then eased it into the frame without its usual bang.

His head hung to one side. He closed his eyes, barely asleep again. His arms were numb and his legs were like metal rods, unyielding and cold like the old brace. His breathing seemed to stop and he thought he had been asleep and dreaming for a long time. I been asleep all this time, his voice said. I slept through it all. Canny's gone and Dotty's gone and Hyacinth's gone and so're them two boys. They's all gone. And so're you, the voice kept saying. So're you. . . . Gone. . . .

BOOMBOOMBOOMBOOMBOOMBOOMBOOM

He thought he could hear his heart that loud, like a hollow blast. But it wasn't his heart, because now it was gone. And here he was opening his gummy eyes onto the palest threads of morning light dangling through the thickly twisted trees. On the floor next to him, the dog's head shot up, and it howled.

"Jest gettin' up," Wallace announced, lifting his feet cautiously from the bed. "That's all," he said, his hand raised in appeasement. "Jest gettin' up. . . ."

From where he sat on the bed, Wallace thought he saw a flash of orange light through the quick-moving shadows of dawn. The dog too had seen it. It started back, then tensed forward in a powerful crouch of still, frozen energy, its taut haunches so ready to spring that its rump trembled and twitched.

Just then, the door flew open and the dog bounded out past Dotty, who ran inside with Canny. Canny wore the same clothes as the night before. Her hair hung in clumps and her tired eyes moved pinkishly behind a dull coating.

"Momma!" she kept saying, trying to get Dotty's attention. "Momma. . . ."

"Here!" said Dotty, flipping him the car keys. "I couldn't find his, dammit. You'll have to go around the truck." She ran into the bathroom and came out with her makeup rattling and bundled in a dingy towel.

Even standing still for a moment, she gave the impression of running, lurching. All the crazy disjointed movement was contained in her voice. She seemed to fizz and crackle with energy. Even her wiry hair sputtered with it. A faint charred odor wafted from her.

Outside, the dog continued to bark.

"C'mon," she said. "Let's go! Let's go! Jesus Christ, there's no time. . . ."

"Momma!" Canny said, grasping her arm. "What was that noise? They were . . ."

"Shit! I need shoes!" Dotty panted. "Find me some!"

Wallace grabbed her shiny red high heels and set them at her feet.

"Take them! Just take them!" she said, and he clutched them to his chest.

"What happened? Please tell me!" begged Canny.

"Nothing! Now go!" Dotty gave her a little shove. "You want your Poppy killed? You want him dead?" Dotty screamed.

"Move! C'mon quick!" She held open the door. Canny ran

past and after her came Wallace. It was then that he saw the gun braced against the sagging screen, like an extension of Dotty's hand, the long glinting finger that was the barrel of Huller's gun.

The dog had been running around the house, then up the front steps to the door, which it hurled itself against, with a cry of something that was dying.

Inside the car Dotty was laughing, softly and nervously. The light through the trees was jarring, so bright against the film of the windshield that he had to look away.

The car started up right away. He was surprised that Huller hadn't disconnected the battery. He backed up and turned, then drove to the end of the driveway that was blocked by Huller's big black pickup. He kept glancing in the rearview, expecting to see Huller charging after them.

"Go around it," Dotty said, leaning forward. "Just go around it!" she screamed.

So he did, turning the car into the woods that bordered the main road. Leafy branches and sharp pine needles battered the windshield and slapped through the open window at his face. "Damn . . . damn . . . ," he muttered, wincing as he steered with his right hand while he tried to shield his face with his left.

"There!" Dotty called, pointing ahead. "Take a left! There's the road!"

At that moment, as the car emerged from the woods into a shallow culvert below the road, an explosion wrenched the ground.

"Poppy!" Canny gasped at his ear.

At first he thought a rock had hit the bottom of the car. But when the car pulled onto the road with its old lumbering roar and the explosion came again, he glanced in the mirror and saw rolls of thick, black smoke churning through the treetops. Them poor little girls, he thought. He kept thinking that. Them poor, poor little girls.

"Poppy," Canny murmured, but when he looked back at her in the mirror, she said nothing.

Dotty turned down the visor. The old brittle clipping of the moon walk hung by one pin. She tried to tuck it up, but it kept slipping down. So with a savage swipe, she tore it off and threw it out the window.

Nothing in her expression had changed. Her eyes were still filled with that bright uneven light and her mouth seemed to quiver with that strange sense of motionless energy that charged the early morning air like electric sparks. It was her voice that was different, deep and fiberless, as if it issued not from flesh or ligament, or even bone, but from stone.

"Now get on the main road," she was telling him. The turn ahead was one he had never taken before. "And now, pull over!" she ordered, pointing to a boarded-up gas station. She had him drive behind the station and park close to the building.

"Gimme the pill," she demanded. "Jesus Christ . . . Jesus Christ," she groaned, looking around at the piles of worn tires and the rusty oil drums filled with water. He dug in his pockets for the wrapped pill Huller had given him.

She grabbed it from him and knelt on the seat, facing Canny.

"I ain't sick," Canny said when she saw the pill.

"You'll be sick if you don't," warned Dotty, as she pushed the pill against Canny's unyielding lips.

"No!" Canny said and fell back, so that to reach her Dotty had to hang over the back of the seat. She swore and drew back her hand and slapped Canny's face. She hit her again. "Get up here, you little bastard," she muttered, grabbing her hair and yanking her forward. Canny grunted and then she sobbed.

"She takes 'em mashed," Wallace said quickly. "You gotta mash it."

"Not this time!" Dotty cried, as she tried to force the long yellow tablet past Canny's stubborn lips. "Open up, goddamn you . . . little . . ."

"Here," Wallace said, taking the pill from her. Before she could get it back, he bit it in half and put it in Canny's mouth. "Swaller," he said, with a pleading glance.

She gulped and her eyes welled with tears.

He looked down at the remaining half in his palm. The pill was huge. "This okay for kids?"

"Don't start," she warned. "Give it to her. Fast!"

He turned on the seat. "Here," he said, and when Canny opened her mouth, he winked and pretended to give her the other half.

Dotty glanced over her shoulder.

"Swaller," he said, and Canny forced a loud gulp.

"Now lay down," Dotty told Canny. "And close your eyes and pretty soon all this shit'll be just a bad dream."

He started the engine and pulled onto the road. Dotty told him to stop at the first pay phone he saw.

Her eyes were closed. "I don't need him," she muttered with her head back on the seat. "I don't need anybody." Tears leaked from her eyes and down her cheeks, which were so bruised the flesh was beginning to blacken. She opened her eyes and looked at him. "What's wrong with me, Aubie?" she whispered. "What the fuck's wrong with me? All I do's hurt people."

He thought a minute. "You're bad," he said, nodding his head as if to pump out the thoughts. "But you're good too. It's jest your bad part's too . . . it's too strong for your good."

"There's one!" she said, pointing to a telephone booth in the parking lot of an Italian restaurant.

He watched her from the car. She bent over the telephone shelf and then suddenly she straightened, her hands scrambling the air as she spoke.

In the back, Canny sagged in the corner of the seat. Her chin lay on her chest and her head bobbed ever so slightly as if she weren't yet deeply asleep. He looked back at Dotty. Right now she was talking to the Birds. They were probably deciding how much they were going to pay. Last night he'd gotten too scared. He hadn't been strong enough. Today he'd do it right.

Suddenly, he thought of Krystal and Kelly and a wave of nausea washed over him. For a moment their plain round faces were all that he could see. He blinked and blinked until he saw past them, saw Dotty through the sunstruck, grimy glass of the phone booth—not Dotty, but a blur of gray, a shadow.

She ain't right, he thought, raising his hands slowly, one to the wheel, the other to the key. What he had said was wrong. She wasn't part good and part bad—not and do that; not and shoot two little girls, both younger than Canny—if that's what she did. . . . Maybe she didn't. Maybe those were jet booms and that's what the smoke was from too. He took a deep breath. Them poor little girls, he thought again. And poor fat Alma. His fingers closed over the key. Now! his brain commanded. Now! Just go! Leave her and go!

But she'll be all alone, he thought, watching her leave the telephone booth. Barefoot, over the pebbles, she walked quickly with her arms folded and the gun dangling at the side of her breast.

"They're waiting for my next call," she said when she got into the car. "The money's all set." She looked at him. "It's at a graveyard, Aubie, so I don't want you coming apart on me, understand?"

He nodded.

"You gotta do this," she said. "You can't fuck up, Aubie." She hugged herself and almost seemed to shiver. Beside her, Wallace was wet with sweat. It ran down his temples and over the bridge of his nose to channels underneath both eyes.

"First we go to the town forest." She was trembling. The map in her hand fluttered. "Then after we leave her off, we go get the money and we call them and tell them where to find her." She bent forward and rested her brow on the dashboard. "I feel like I'm gonna puke," she groaned.

He kept blinking as he drove. It was hard to see through all the sweat. As he drove it seemed that the car had never ridden smoother. The engine was almost silent. If there were bumps in the road, the tires must have been floating over them.

She said turn and he turned . . . left . . . right . . . right . . . left. Once she said pull over, stop, quick, I'm gonna be sick.

And he did. She opened her door and with both feet braced, she leaned over the road and he could hear it splatter onto the roadside. He could smell it and he could see her shoulders writhe and he could hear her bitter gasps at the end.

Then she sank back against the seat, thin and spent. She said she felt better now. "Get on the highway. Up ahead's the road," she said.

He was on the highway. He passed farmhouses and an apple orchard and, in the distance, like black spikes of a battered fence, rose in uneven heights factory smokestacks and chimneys. The highway here narrowed suddenly from three lanes to two. It was his lane that had vanished, so that there was nowhere to go until she jerked the wheel. All around him, horns blared and brakes squealed. Canny slept so soundly that not even the horns awakened her.

Soon they were off the highway on a wide road, deeply shaded by the thick pines that towered along both sides. There were no houses here. For miles there seemed to be only this pine forest.

"Up there." She was pointing to the right to a sign that said STONEFIELD TOWN FOREST in black letters. He turned onto the narrow dirt road and drove slowly past a parking lot littered with beer cans and broken bottles.

"Keep going," she said, "till you come to a fork." She looked at the map again, then glanced over the seat at Canny. "She better not wake up," she said. "There! Keep right now—off the road. And just keep going."

Here, the road became two rutted tracks. Weeds grew up from the high center mound. If he went over twelve miles an hour, the axle scraped against the jutting stones.

Dotty kept insisting that somewhere in here there was a shack that Jiggy had brought her to see. "Just keep going. It's way far in," she said. "He said nobody ever comes out this way."

After a couple of miles, the road narrowed even more. At some points, thorny vines dragged over the roof and against the closed windows. Dotty kept peering at the map in her lap, at a spot she kept marked with her finger. Under the map, the gun made a soft mound.

"Where we goin' after?" he asked.

"After? After what?"

"After the money. When they got her back," he said thickly.

"I don't know yet," she said.

"You still wanna go to Hollywood?" he asked.

She didn't answer.

"You still wanna go to Hollywood?" he called over the motor. She looked at him and suddenly she laughed, and he saw for the first time that her front tooth had been knocked out. The black gap sickened him. He looked back to the road, to the sagging, weathered shack coming up ahead.

He pulled into the newly cut clearing beside the shack. The front door was made of three z-braced boards, its shiny hasp obviously new. He opened the door and looked inside. It was a small, dark, airless box. A cobweb glistened from corner to corner. The smell of cold, wet dirt made him shiver. She'll be so scared, he thought. He could picture Canny sitting up suddenly in the pitch black and starting to scream, thinking it was a nightmare, thinking that any minute he'd come. What if something went wrong, he wondered. What if they never came for her? No one would ever hear her. Dotty was calling to him from the car.

"She's moving," Dotty called. "Quick! Get her in before she wakes up."

In the back seat, Canny's eyes fluttered. She tried to lift her head, but her eyes rolled and she fell limply back.

"Canny?" he said, ducking his head into the back seat.

"Where's my . . . ?" The rest of her words were too thickly slurred to be understood. He lifted her head and brought her face close to his. She looked at him for a moment and smiled a lax, drooly smile and then her eyes rolled to whites, seeming to sink back in her head.

"Canny!" he said, shaking her.

"Pull her out!" Dotty said. "Just pull her!"

"She's waking up, but she ain't!" he said, in a panicky voice.

"Then get her in there before she does! Pull her! Pull her out!"

He picked her up, easily lifting the small limp frame that seemed made of air, of twigs and air. He stepped back, then stood for a moment by Dotty, who handed him a padlock through the car window. "Hurry up!" she called after him. "Just put her in, goddamn it, then lock it!"

So he did; he stepped into the shack's black dampness, then squatted and eased her onto the dirt floor, feeling blindly with his hand for rocks or sticks that might hurt her. His fingers caught in the sticky thickness of a spider web as he leaned to kiss her.

"Poppy . . . ," she murmured, and he felt the air stir as she reached for him.

He stood up quickly and closed the door behind him.

"Lock it!" Dotty was calling. "Put the lock on!"

He slipped the padlock through the hasp.

"Lock it!" she called.

"Poppy?" came Canny's voice, small and muffled. "My head hurts. . . ."

"She's awake," he called to Dotty.

"I got a bad taste," Canny said.

"She don't feel good," he called. He stood with both hands still on the unfastened padlock.

"I'm gonna be sick," Canny groaned. "Poppy? Poppy, please help me. . . ."

"Lock it, goddamn you!"

His shoulders sagged as he stared down at the soft green moss that hemmed the bottom of the door.

"I can't get up . . . Poppy . . . oh. . . ."

When he opened the door she was on her knees, her hands groping blindly in front of her. Finger stripes of dirt streaked the side of her face.

"I don't feel so good," she said weakly, squinting up at him. "How come I'm here? What'd I do bad?"

"Jest rest," he whispered in her ear as he carried her to the car. "Jest rest. . . ."

"Put her back!" Dotty cried, opening her own door. "I said put her back, you stupid . . ."

It wasn't until he had laid Canny on the seat and backed out that he saw the gun Dotty pointed at him. "She's sick," he said. "She got scared."

"Get her out, you stupid bastard, and put her back." She gripped the gun with both hands.

He looked at the gun and he looked at her. "We'll take her with us. And then we'll call after," he said.

"We can't! If they see her, they'll grab us!"

"We can hide her," he said. "Like we done before—under a blanket or something."

"No! Now you listen . . ."

But he was already inside the car, starting it up.

"Aubie! Listen to me. It ain't like before. It's gonna be all over pretty soon."

She sat back crying a moment and then she drew back her hand and slapped the side of his head. Cursing, she pummeled him with her fists as he drove down the narrow road. Then with a gagging sound, she fell against him with her head on his shoulder. "We'll be dead . . . all of us . . . they'll shoot us . . . ," she sobbed.

He looked at her. "You shoot them little girls, Dot?"

Her head jerked and for a second she looked as if she were trying not to smile.

"He did," she said, rubbing her arm. "He went from one bed to the other. They were all sleeping. And then he started for Canny." Her voice had softened. "And that's when I got the gun. We were wrestling for it and he kept pushing me back—like this . . . ," she said, with the heel of her hand extended. "And all of a sudden, I heard it go off and he just whooshed down like something the air went out of. Pssssss," she made a whistling sound and her hand fell slowly. "Just like a dead balloon." Tears ran down her face, but she was smiling.

He kept driving. His hands were sweaty on the wheel. She was lying. She had killed that whole family. There was no doubt in his mind that she had killed them, one by one, and then she had set the house on fire. The horror of it rose in him, like a sickness in his chest, so that his pulse beat seemed to slacken and the air was thinner now and every breath drained him.

She sobbed and her voice caught and she shook her head and gasped a little, and he was afraid to look and find her laughing now. Her voice had that same cold, giddy tremble as that day when they had first met, when she pushed him into the river. Suddenly it occurred to him that she had tried to kill him that day. Maybe she did, he thought.

Maybe she did. Maybe he'd been dead all this time, ever since then. And this was a dead man's dream, where no one ever really got hurt or really got killed because he was still there, could see it now, could see it and hear it—it—himself, floating in that glistening pool, his head bent, his arms arched and weightless as wings, and, on his feet, the tar-encrusted metal plates that anchored him in place, safe from all that might happen.

By the time they found him, his skin was probably water-wrinkled and pure, pure white. They fished him out and buried him in clean new clothes, which was the mending Hyacinth had done that last morning, shortening the sleeves of the black suit and taking in the pants, her mouth braced with straight pins while she spoke of death to the two little boys. *What daddy? Which daddy? Yours acourse.* So that's why they never answered him. That's why they looked and saw straight through him—he was already gone; already in the dusty grave hole looking up at her with the boys on either side of her, dry-eyed and serious. There wasn't any sound, just the quiet, quiet stillness through which he could see their faces and his own, as blank and secretly exultant as theirs to be finally rid of the terrible burden that was Aubrey Wallace.

20

They drove along Main Street. It was still too early for the stores to be open. The only traffic was a gray van coming in the opposite direction. The light turned red and they both stopped.

"She sleeping?" Wallace asked, glancing over his shoulder.

"She better be," Dotty snapped. " 'Cause after we get the money, we're putting her back in the shed." She knelt and, from the floor in back, pulled up a dirty sheet, which she tossed over Canny.

Just as the light turned, Wallace realized that the man driving the van was staring at him. As he passed alongside, he could feel the man's eyes boring into his head. At the next set of lights, he turned right. There wasn't a car anywhere, not even any parked. There were no people, no dogs.

"Don't fuck this up," Dotty said. Her voice carried a thin urgency like prayer. "Please don't . . . just this one time . . . oh please. . . ."

"Can she breathe?" he asked, slowing at a stop sign.

Dotty shaded her eyes and pointed to the next intersection, where two churches stood on opposite corners, one of brown gritty stone and the other of white clapboards. The white church had a tall steeple with a gold-numbered clock in it.

"Go by the white one," she said, "and turn down the drive-way."

"Can she breathe?" he asked again. But Dotty still didn't answer.

He pulled into the driveway that horseshoed around the church, entering and exiting onto the same quiet, carless, peopleless street, where nothing moved, not a leaf or a bird or even a cloud in the hard blue sky.

"Park behind," she whispered. "There! Right there!" She pointed when they were directly behind the church, looking down over a hilly cemetery, hummocky and ridged with thin dark gravestones, some so old they sank in angles to the earth, like crooked, rotting teeth. "There's 'sposed to be a vault down there," she whispered, squinting down the hillside. "It says Henson over the door. But the door won't be locked. The money'll be inside in a duffel bag."

"I ain't going down," he whispered.

"I know that!" she said. "I'm just going over it, that's all." She looked around. "So quiet. I never been in such a quiet place." She rubbed her throat and coughed. "I can't even swallow. I'm so nervous, I can't swallow." She tucked the gun into the band of her skirt and bloused her shirt over it.

The stillness was strange. The world had stopped turning. When Dotty opened the door, its creak was like a sudden scream. "Shit . . . oh shit," she whispered, letting it hang open. Once out of the car, she looked back over both shoulders, and then she seemed to take a deep breath before stepping forward to the edge of the grassy hill. She skittered sideways between the gravestones, wary and startled as a night cat, jerking to a halt every few steps to look back frantically. She thinks I'll leave, he thought, and he wished he could.

She disappeared down the hill. In the back seat, Canny groaned. As Wallace turned to her, his eye caught a glimpse of bright glassy movement flashing in the sideview mirror. He froze, then saw it again. Up in the steeple, in a small louvered portal, just under the clock, stood a man in a pale summer suit, with binoculars to his eyes. He was looking straight down, in the direction Dotty had taken. Canny groaned again. The half-formed words of her drugged sleep sounded watery and distant under the sheet.

"Don't," Wallace whispered into the stillness that encased them like glass. "Jest stay still. Jest don't move."

In the mirror he saw the man lower the binoculars and bring what looked like a microphone to his mouth.

"C'mon . . . c'mon . . . ," he whispered.

She was coming back. She had to carry the duffel bag with both hands. She would take a step, then swing the bag before she took another step.

"Poppy? Poppy, my head hurts," Canny said. She batted away the sheet and sat up with her legs drawn to her chin. She swayed from side to side. "Where's Momma? She go someplace?"

"Shh." He glanced up and saw that the portal was empty. Probably the preacher, he assured himself. Probably goes up there couple times a day and looks things over.

Dotty came around to the open door and hauled the bag onto the seat. "A goddamn fortune!" she gasped. "What's she . . ." She looked from Canny to Wallace. "Get her down! Get her down, you asshole!" She jumped inside and slammed the door.

"Her head hurts," he said.

"Start it up!" she cried. Sweat ran down her face.

He started the car and drove around the side of the church. Dotty knelt on the seat, turning back to Canny. "Get down! Get down, Canny . . . cover up!"

"My head hurts. It . . . ," Canny was saying. There was a slap and Canny's quick, sharp cry. "Momma, don't . . . my head. . . ."

Dotty kept slapping her, telling her to lie down and cover up with the sheet.

"We're sitting ducks now!" she gasped. "If they're here, they seen her and they know we got her with us!"

"Nobody saw her," he lied.

"They got everything they want now," Dotty panted. "They'll shoot us, you goddamn little bitch. You want that? You want that?" Her hands flew, flailing and slapping Canny's covered head. Canny's thin wail filled the car.

"She's covered! It ain't her fault," he said, grabbing Dotty's arm as he drove onto the street. "She didn't know!"

"She knew!" Dotty said, still kneeling facing Canny. "She knew!"

"Course she didn't," he said. The thread was snapping, the air thinning. "She's jest a little girl. She don't know why we're here." From the corner of his eyes, he saw the glint of Dotty's upraised hand, which he jerked down next to him. She had been pointing the gun at Canny, who sobbed under the sheet.

"You gonna shoot her?" he asked, driving with his left hand while his right still pinned Dotty's forearm against his side. Her face was a welter of pain and confusion as she sagged down with her head bowed and her cheek against the seat back. With the gun still in her hand, she embraced the duffel bag with a harsh gagging sound.

She's going to shoot us, he thought. If not here, then on the road to the town forest, and if not there, then the shed, and even if she didn't then, even if they just kept driving, she'd do it sometime. First Canny and then him.

"We'll drop her off," he said quietly, turning right.

She looked up suddenly, turning toward the window. In the distance, there was the rhythmic sound of an approaching engine. It wasn't until it grew louder and nearer that he realized it was overhead.

"It's a helicopter!" Dotty said. "You think it's . . ." Her words were drowned out by the thunderous rack-rack-rack-rack that vibrated above them. The dull black blades whirled stripes of shadow and sunlight over the car and the road. Dotty squinted and turned her head, cringing with each gash of light, as if she'd been struck. Her mouth opened and closed, but he couldn't hear her. In the back, Canny lay motionless under the sheet.

Suddenly, the helicopter veered off with a jerk, as if by some invisible tether, and rose into the sky.

"It must be the cops," Dotty shouted, watching it disappear

beyond the treetops. "See! We got the money, so now they're looking for her! Stay down, Canny! Stay down under the sheet!" She leaned forward. "Keep going straight, Aubie! We'll get on the highway and then we'll just keep going. I gotta count it first! I gotta be sure we didn't get screwed. We can stop later and call." She was trying to unzip the bag. "Goddammit," she muttered, jerking the frozen zipper back and forth. It would only open an inch. She closed it and again tried to force it open. "Jesus Christ!" She opened the glove compartment and pawed frantically through papers and straws and road maps. She looked at Wallace. "Where's the can op . . . ?" Her eyes widened in disbelief and her mouth fell open as they turned the corner. "You little prick!" she moaned. "You stupid little prick. . . ." She shook her head and tears boiled out of her puffy, gashed eyes. "Where're you going? We're on her street!" She looked around wildly. "They'll kill us! You want that? You want us all dead, you stupid prick?" She raised the gun and, holding it with both hands, pointed it at his head.

"Don't stop, Aubie! Don't do it!" she cried as he slowed the car. She kept licking her split lips. She sat sideways now, facing him, a hissing, spitting turmoil of energy.

"Momma?" Canny called.

"Can you hear me?" Dotty screamed. "I said keep going!"

"Momma! What is it?" Canny wailed. "Tell me!"

"They're gonna shoot us and he doesn't give a shit!" she said to Canny, who flailed at the sheet to get it away from her. "You think they'll pick out you and me, you stupid prick?" Dotty asked him. "They'll shoot her too! We'll all be dead! Is that what you want?"

"Don't stop, Poppy!" Canny cried behind him. "Please don't, please don't," she whimpered over and over. Her breath ruffled the back of his neck like a warm breeze.

Ahead was the round, flaring porch of the Birds' house. Just like the old bandstand back home. Wouldn't they be proud of him there? Wouldn't they be happy? The band would all stand up in their crisp white suits and gold-braided hats and bow at the waist when they introduced him. . . .

This here's our long-lost friend . . . Hyacinth's long-lost husband and them two swell boys of his, Answan and Arnold's long-lost daddy, Aubrey Wallace, Hazlitt Kluggs would holler through the microphone so loud, the hills and mountains would echo it back all day and long into the heat of night like welcome thunder. *. . . Aubrey Aubrey Wallace Wallace Wallace.*

He almost smiled. Everything had become so clear and so simple that he was astonished at the ease of it all. Suddenly, as if a switch had just been pulled, all the right connections were being made. His brain knew what his eye saw and heard all that entered his ears, and more. So clear, so pure was his vision, that he could see through things. He could hear music, drums beating and trumpets blaring. Getting louder and closer. From far, far away emerged all the time he had lost, all the days and months he thought he had forgotten.

He felt lighter. His skin was clear and tight on his bones. He was a young man, a boy, a child. He and Canny were the best of friends. He would let her get there first, calling allee, allee, home free. . . .

Of all the connections and energies that flowed through him, the keenest, surest, most trustworthy one now was his heart. So if his eyes clouded, or his ears blocked, or his brain froze, it didn't matter. No sir! Now as he approached the big white house with the shiny black shutters and the bandstand flaring over the sidewalk, he knew exactly what to do.

"Don't you . . . ," she was screaming. She stretched her leg out to jam her foot down on the gas pedal. "Don't you do this . . . this is my last chance . . . ," she screamed, as they roared past the house.

Behind him, Canny was hysterical. "Please, Poppy!" she begged. "Do what she says, Poppy!" She put her arms around his throat and held him tightly, screaming, "They're coming after us! Look at them all!"

The only voice in the car now was Canny's, thin and harsh. "They're gonna shoot us, Poppy!" she kept saying.

There were police cars everywhere: three behind them, more pulling out of each driveway they passed. Ahead, at the tree-shaded intersection, two more cruisers with flashing lights crept forward.

With Dotty's foot hard on the accelerator, the car tore through the intersection in a storm of blinding dust. Out of nowhere had come the helicopter, swooping like a huge crow, flying so close to the car that the chop-chop-chop of its blades drowned out every sound.

The car skimmed over bumps and ruts and flew around curves, soundless and motorless, so effortlessly that there no longer seemed any need to steer over this tree-lined, snaking road.

He kept grabbing for the gun she had jammed into his ribs. Finally, his hand closed over hers and, as he squeezed, he saw her eyes widen, and then she threw back her head and screamed as they careened off the road and crashed through a dense wall of gnarled and ancient rhododendron that cracked and spit against the windshield. The car broke through a dappled stand of bushes and saplings, then came to the top of the wooded embankment, where it teetered briefly before its long sideward plunge of creaking, crunching, sagging, gasping metal into the muck of a yellow swamp-grass clearing below.

The car had stopped. Dotty was slumped forward with her cheek on the dashboard and the top of her head crammed against the shattered windshield. A thin bloody drool ran from her chin along the soft white curve of her throat.

"Canny?" he called softly, picking slips of paper from his face.

They were buried in these dollar-shaped pieces of newspaper that had burst from the duffel bag.

"Poppy!" answered Canny, as she struggled to pull herself up from the floor in back. Part of the front seat had torn loose, and it pinned her legs. "Momma's dead," she whispered, reaching over onto the seat for the gun. Only her eyes moved, from left to right at the policemen scrambling down the hillside. Their uniforms were different; some wore gray, others dark blue. Some wore ordinary clothes, plaid shirts, jeans. Some had on suits and ties. One carried a bullhorn and wore a tall, gray hat. They all carried rifles or hand guns.

The helicopter was returning. It brooded over the hilltop, its blades striking a softer clop-clop, a beat more of wings than of steel.

"They're gonna kill us too," cried Canny, looking wildly about. "They're gonna shoot us!"

"Canny," Wallace whispered, watching the policemen encircle the car.

"Get away!" Canny screeched, moving the gun from window to window. "You bastards! You goddamn pricks, you get the fuck away from us!"

"They ain't gonna hurt you, Canny," Wallace said.

Coming around the front of the car was a tall, thin, stoopshouldered man with sharp bony features and long, deep creases in his cheeks. His eyes were bloodshot and set deep with weariness. He was the only unarmed man. "Caroline?" the man called, his voice cracking as he stopped to look through the shattered windshield. He came to Dotty's side and, squinting, peered in at Canny.

Wallace knew at once who the man was and he was suddenly deeply ashamed for this wild-eyed, wild-haired creature who bit her lip as she raised the gun, pointing it at Louis Bird, just inches from his worn face.

"Canny," Wallace said, staring miserably over the wheel. "That's . . ."

"Get the fuck outta . . . ," she gasped, cringing as Bird leaned closer.

"Oh my God!" Bird cried in a thick, choked voice. "It's you, Caroline, my . . ."

It was then, then as he reached toward her in a gesture of such painful longing, then that Wallace's mouth filled with sickness, then that she squeezed the trigger with all four dirty, sweaty fingers, closing her eyes with the sudden jerking blast that threw her back against the seat, boneless and limp. And then, in that instant, as the bullet whizzed past Bird's head, the police, all thirty, or forty, or fifty of them instinctively raised their guns with both hands, their slitted eyes trained on the car, on the opening door, on the unshaven little man who darted out, a gun at his side.

"Stop!" one cried, crouching on powerful legs.

In a foot-dragging limp, Aubrey Wallace scrambled past them toward the embankment. In unison, they all turned and fired. At first his body jerked and quivered with each bullet's entry. Then it didn't hurt anymore. He could hear them whizzing into him, stuck, and biting hard, but the feeling was gone. He began to dive to earth. The plunge would take forever. His eyes were wide, wider than they had ever been, so wide, the whites seeped into the hard blue glare of the sky. He saw them take her, kicking and biting and swearing savagely.

Louis Bird ran alongside the policeman who carried her toward the embankment. Their feet made sucking sounds through the mud.

"It's going to be all right," Bird kept telling her. "It's going to be all right." He reached to touch her and she whacked away his hand.

"Bastard!" she wailed. "You killed him, you bastards!"

A siren screamed. An ambulance was coming. Above them, it screeched to a stop. Down the embankment ran two white-suited attendants. A man with a walkie-talkie to his ear called to them as they bent over Wallace. "Forget him! He's gone! Get her! Get her out of the car before she bleeds to death."

"Momma!" Canny wailed through the trees.

They were lifting Dotty from the car.

"Don't worry," someone said when she moaned. "You're okay. . . ."

"Jesus Christ!" said another. "Look at her face! Look at the job he did on her, the crazy son of a bitch!"

Another ambulance arrived. More attendants charged down

242

the hill, dust spitting from their heels. When they came to Wallace, they stopped.

"Poor bastard," one of them muttered. He lifted Wallace's wrist, then flung it down into the warm black ooze.

Aubrey Wallace was dead. Shot eleven times. Not a bullet had hit his heart. Not a one.

Epilogue

This is all so crazy. I been on four TV talk shows, and two magazines and a ton of newspapers want to interview me. All of a sudden I'm famous.

People keep asking me what's the truth; what's the real story and why he did it, why he took little Caroline Bird in the first place. And I tell them I don't know for sure. All I can do is guess. I think what happened was he was so simple, he didn't know much better, and he was so lonely, he just wanted love.

A lot of people say he's nothing but a vicious, money-hungry kidnapper, a killer. But that's not the way it was. Aubrey Wallace never meant to hurt a soul. Some people just got in his way, that's all. That's not to say I approve of what he did. Just that like everybody else, I'm trying to understand it.

Soon as I'm better, I'm heading out west. This guy read about me in the paper. His name's Brett Bracker and he said he could get me started in acting. He wants to be my agent. It's funny how things happen, isn't it? How a break like Brett Bracker could come out of such an awful tragedy—all those deaths, first my father and then the Hullers, all the ones he killed.

Aubrey used to watch me, I guess. Or that's what he said. I was just a kid then up in the mountains and what kid notices an old guy like him hanging around? I guess he just got it in his head one day that I was gonna go with him. Me and my Dad were out walking and up he comes behind us. And out of the blue, he smashes my Dad's skull in (with what, I'm still not sure) and then he tries to set him on fire. But that's when I took off and he chased me all over hell, for hours and hours, half the night, I guess. I don't know. So much of it's a blur now. All I know is he finally caught me and he tied me up to a tree and then the next day he came back and got me and dragged me into a truck and off he went. Like a bat out of hell, driving and driving, until we hit that little town, and we were low on gas and money, and I begged him to let me go, but he never said a word. He just got out of the truck and walked up on that big round porch and rang the bell and then he just opened the door and went in.

He was gone only a minute. My ankles and my hands were tied and I was squirming on the seat trying to get free when out he comes. Running, with this jar of dimes and the sweetest little baby girl in his arms. "Who's she?" I said. But he just set her on my lap and took off, and a few miles later, I asked him again and he said, "I dunno. She was making so much noise I had to pick her up."

"Leave her someplace," I said. "You can pin a note on her shirt and leave her off someplace."

"We will," he said, with that scared little voice he had. "We will," he'd say every time I said it. And I said it for miles and miles and days and months and then years. But he never did. We just kept on going and going. We lived everywhere, mostly down south, in different places, the kind of places people keep going to when the last place didn't work out. We lived in trailers and shacks and, once, even a tent; and that first summer, we lived mostly out of the car he'd sold the truck for.

He'd work a while one place and then the craziest little thing would scare him, like seeing the same little old lady on the sidewalk two days in a row, and then that'd be it—we'd have to take off to some new place.

People always ask me how come he never got caught. I tell them it wasn't because of any plan he had. In fact, I think it was just the opposite, that because he didn't have a plan somehow it all kept working out for him, like it was fate or something. Of course, in the Bird thing, at first they thought it was all planned by some kidnapper that wanted the ransom. So why would they ever be looking for poor Aubrey Wallace? His own family wasn't even looking for him.

I used to think he didn't talk to people because he was so shy. But then I began to see that nobody ever talked to him, that they'd pass him on the street and never even see him. It was almost like he was invisible in this weird way, almost like he even thought he was, or he wanted to be. That way nobody could hurt him. Nobody, I guess, but me.

People always ask how come I went along and never did anything. And all I can say is how half the time I was crazy with homesickness and the other half I guess I was just crazy. Scared all the time and crazy.

But I'm okay now. I feel like it's all been a dream, some good and some bad, and now it's all over, and I'm alive, and I'm going to live happily ever after. Finally.

FOR THE BEST IN PAPERBACKS, LOOK FOR THE

In every corner of the world, on every subject under the sun, Penguin represents quality and variety—the very best in publishing today.

For complete information about books available from Penguin—including Puffins, Penguin Classics, and Arkana—and how to order them, write to us at the appropriate address below. Please note that for copyright reasons the selection of books varies from country to country.

In the United Kingdom: Please write to *Dept. JC, Penguin Books Ltd, FREEPOST, West Drayton, Middlesex UB7 0BR.*

If you have any difficulty in obtaining a title, please send your order with the correct money, plus ten percent for postage and packaging, to *P.O. Box No. 11, West Drayton, Middlesex UB7 0BR*

In the United States: Please write to *Consumer Sales, Penguin USA, P.O. Box 999, Dept. 17109, Bergenfield, New Jersey 07621-0120.* VISA and MasterCard holders call 1-800-253-6476 to order all Penguin titles

In Canada: Please write to *Penguin Books Canada Ltd, 10 Alcorn Avenue, Suite 300, Toronto, Ontario M4V 3B2*

In Australia: Please write to *Penguin Books Australia Ltd, P.O. Box 257, Ringwood, Victoria 3134*

In New Zealand: Please write to *Penguin Books (NZ) Ltd, Private Bag 102902, North Shore Mail Centre, Auckland 10*

In India: Please write to *Penguin Books India Pvt Ltd, 706 Eros Apartments, 56 Nehru Place, New Delhi 110 019*

In the Netherlands: Please write to *Penguin Books Netherlands bv, Postbus 3507, NL-1001 AH Amsterdam*

In Germany: Please write to *Penguin Books Deutschland GmbH, Metzlerstrasse 26, 60594 Frankfurt am Main*

In Spain: Please write to *Penguin Books S.A., Bravo Murillo 19, 1° B, 28015 Madrid*

In Italy: Please write to *Penguin Italia s.r.l., Via Felice Casati 20, I-20124 Milano*

In France: Please write to *Penguin France S.A., 17 rue Lejeune, F-31000 Toulouse*

In Japan: Please write to *Penguin Books Japan, Ishikiribashi Building, 2–5–4, Suido, Bunkyo-ku, Tokyo 112*

In Greece: Please write to *Penguin Hellas Ltd, Dimocritou 3, GR-106 71 Athens*

In South Africa: Please write to *Longman Penguin Southern Africa (Pty) Ltd, Private Bag X08, Bertsham 2013*